New York Times and *USA Today* **Bestselling Author**

Diane Capri

"Full of thrills and tension, but smart and human, too. Kim Otto is a great, great character. I love her."
Lee Child, *#1 World Wide Bestselling Author of Jack Reacher Thrillers*

"[A] welcome surprise… [W]orks from the first page to 'The End'."
Larry King

"Swift pacing and ongoing suspense are always present… [L]ikable protagonist who uses her political connections for a good cause…Readers should eagerly anticipate the next [book]."
Top Pick, Romantic Times

"…offers tense legal drama with courtroom overtones, twisty plot, and loads of Florida atmosphere. Recommended."
Library Journal

"[A] fast-paced legal thriller…energetic prose…an appealing heroine…clever and capable supporting cast…[that will] keep readers waiting for the next [book]."
Publishers Weekly

"Expertise shines on every page."
Margaret Maron, Edgar, Anthony, Agatha and Macavity Award-Winning MWA Grand Master

JACK RABBIT

by DIANE CAPRI

Copyright © 2025 Diane Capri, LLC
All Rights Reserved

Excerpt from *Night School* © 2008 Lee Child

All rights reserved as permitted under the U.S. Copyright Act of 1976. No part of the publication may be reproduced, distributed, or transmitted in any form or by any means, or stored in a database or retrieval system, without the prior permission of the publisher. The only exception is brief quotation in printed reviews.

Published by: AugustBooks
http://www.AugustBooks.com

ISBN: 978-1-962769-93-8

Original cover design by: Cory Clubb

Jack Rabbit is a work of fiction. Names, characters, places, and incidents either are the product of the author's imagination or are used fictitiously, and any resemblance to actual persons, living or dead, business establishments, events, or locales is entirely coincidental.

Published in the United States of America.

Visit the author website:
http://www.DianeCapri.com

ALSO BY DIANE CAPRI

The Hunt for Jack Reacher Series

(in publication order with Lee Child source books in parentheses)
Don't Know Jack • (The Killing Floor)
Jack in a Box (*novella*)
Jack and Kill (*novella*)
Get Back Jack • (Bad Luck & Trouble)
Jack in the Green (*novella*)
Jack and Joe • (The Enemy)
Deep Cover Jack • (Persuader)
Jack the Reaper • (The Hard Way)
Black Jack • (Running Blind/The Visitor)
Ten Two Jack • (The Midnight Line)
Jack of Spades • (Past Tense)
Prepper Jack • (Die Trying)
Full Metal Jack • (The Affair)
Jack Frost • (61 Hours)
Jack of Hearts • (Worth Dying For)
Straight Jack • (A Wanted Man)
Jack Knife • (Never Go Back)
Lone Star Jack • (Echo Burning)
Bulletproof Jack • (Make Me)
Bet On Jack • (Nothing to Lose)
Jack on a Wire • (Tripwire)
Tracking Jack • (Gone Tomorrow)
Jack Rabbit • (Night School)
Shadow Jack • (Blue Moon)

The Michael Flint Series:
Blood Trails
Trace Evidence
Ground Truth
Hard Money
Dead Lock

The Jess Kimball Thrillers Series
Fatal Distraction
Fatal Demand
Fatal Error
Fatal Fall
Fatal Game
Fatal Bond
Fatal Enemy (*novella*)
Fatal Edge (*novella*)
Fatal Past (*novella*)
Fatal Dawn
Fatal Shot

The Hunt for Justice Series
Due Justice
Twisted Justice
Secret Justice
Wasted Justice
Raw Justice
Mistaken Justice (*novella*)
Cold Justice (*novella*)
False Justice (*novella*)
Fair Justice (*novella*)
True Justice (*novella*)
Night Justice

The Park Hotel Mysteries Series
Reservation with Death
Early Check Out
Room with a Clue
Late Arrival

Short Reads Collections
Hit the Road Jack
Justice Is Served
Fatal Action

CAST OF CHARACTERS

Kim Otto
Carlos Gaspar
Reggie Smithers
Frances Neagley
Marian Sinclair
Larry Knox
Brad Hooper
Paul Bennett
Charles Cooper
Lamont Finlay

and
Jack Reacher

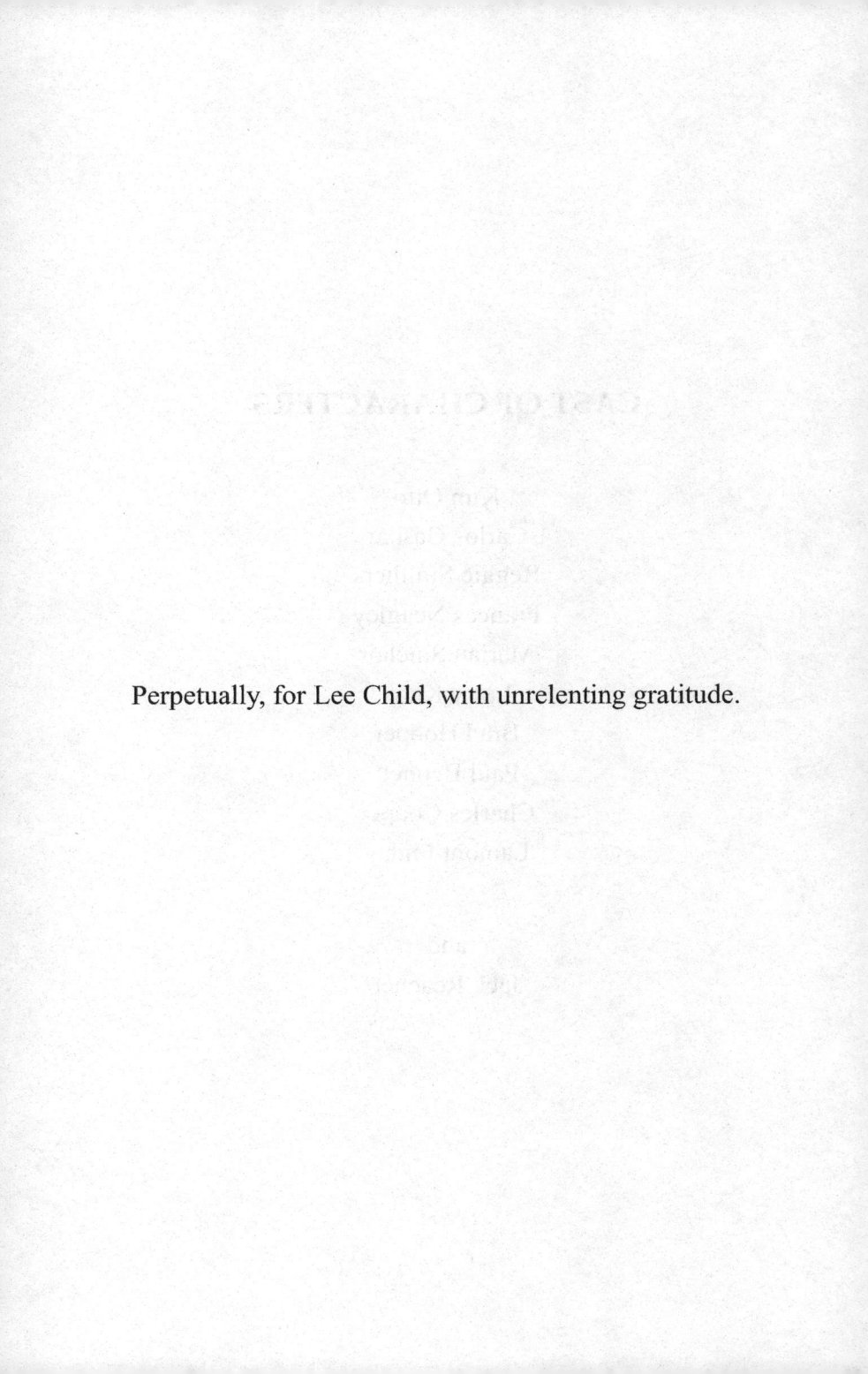

Perpetually, for Lee Child, with unrelenting gratitude.

JACK
RABBIT

NIGHT SCHOOL
By Lee Child

"I could say for people like me it's always the same gamble. Eggs get broken, the omelet gets made, and if it turns out tasty, then all is forgiven," Reacher said.

"And if it doesn't?" Sinclair asked.

"I'm always open to new experiences."

"What if it turns out good?"

"Then you won't turn me in and there won't be a trial. You'll get a glowing letter in your file, and I'll get another medal."

"Are you always this confident?"

"I used to be."

"What are you now?"

"Even more."

"Are you sleeping with Neagley?"

"No, I am not. That would be inappropriate."

CHAPTER 1

Tuesday, July 5
Washington, DC

DR. MARIAN SINCLAIR TOUCHED the gold NSA service pin on her lapel. The medal ceremony buzzed around her. The Director stood at the podium and recited Sinclair's career highlights including operations from Europe to Kabul, intelligence breakthroughs, terrorist cells disrupted, billions in American dollars recovered.

When he finally stopped talking, the audience applauded politely. Sinclair smiled without warmth. Everyone understood exactly what had already happened. The ceremony was pure theater.

Twenty minutes before, Director Phillips had pulled her into a side room filled with agency flags and official seals.

"The President wants fresh blood for the position, Sinclair. Early retirement is your only option." He had pushed an envelope across the table.

Sinclair had picked it up. Rage burned through her veins like molten lava. She'd been deputy director for more than a decade. First under Alfred Ratcliffe, a legend in the intelligence community. She'd been his right hand, serving with loyalty and dedication. Running operations while Ratcliffe handled Congress and mingled with the top Cabinet members as well as whoever happened to be sitting in the Oval Office at the time.

When Ratcliffe had retired, Sinclair expected to step up. Instead, they'd brought in Phillips from the outside.

"Fresh perspective needed," Ratcliffe had said, although they both knew it was bullshit.

She'd swallowed that betrayal. Stayed on as Phillips's deputy. Taught him the job. Covered his mistakes. Kept the agency running while he played politics and had affairs with the women who came through the agency like rotating players on a sports team that never wins.

Five more years of waiting, watching, building her case for taking the helm when Phillips moved on. Which he would. They always did.

And finally, Phillips was bumped upstairs. Sullivan's turn had arrived.

But that didn't happen.

They'd chosen Thomas Reid.

Sinclair's stomach churned as her anger mounted.

"The ceremony stays confidential." Phillips glanced at the door. "A final recognition."

Her fingers tightened on the envelope. Two decades of preparation. Every sacrifice, every operation, every piece of intelligence, all of it aimed toward this moment.

Her moment.

First denied after Ratcliffe retired and now denied again.

A woman might be forgiven for thinking this was the infamous patriarchy at work. But Sinclair had never bought into that nonsense.

She had been a member of the inner circle for a long time. She completely understood the real problem.

Simply put, Sinclair was better at the job than all of them.

Better than Ratcliffe. Better than Phillips. And sure as hell better than the new guy, Reid, who could barely find his ass with both hands.

But nobody seemed to care about the quality of the work. Promotions were never about the best woman for the job. There was always, always a hidden agenda.

The ceremony was almost done. Sinclair waited. The applause grew louder. Phillips approached with the medal. He leaned close as he pinned it.

"The cameras want a smile, Marian."

She met his eyes. "You never planned to choose me, did you? Just like they never planned to let me have Ratcliffe's job when they chose you instead."

Phillips gave her a nod and concluded the ceremony as if he were tying the whole thing up with a bow. Sinclair balled her fists behind her, itching to smash him in the face. The idea lifted her mouth in the first real smile of the afternoon.

At the reception, agents circled with rehearsed compliments. Their words bounced off her like bullets off armor. She nodded and smiled while fury pulsed beneath her skin.

All those years as deputy director.

Passed over twice. Two times too many.

On the way out, Sinclair gave each of her former colleagues a decisive nod while she stared directly into their cold, hard eyes.

Screw her over, would they?

Betray her to promote mediocre substitutes for political expediency? Okay. They could do that, obviously. They just did.

Failing to kill her when they'd had the chance was a classic mistake. She wouldn't go quietly into the night. Nope. Never happen. Not a chance.

The moment she could slip away unnoticed, she walked out and headed home.

Sinclair's Georgetown apartment felt foreign, as if she were trespassing on her own ambitions. She packed light. Two changes of clothes, her laptop, essential documents. The rest could burn.

Twenty-five years of diplomas and awards and ceremonial photos stared from the walls. Ratcliffe's retirement photo rested on her desk. Her mentor. Her friend. She'd thought.

She'd believed him when he said many times over the years, "You'll run this place better than I ever did."

Another lie.

Her secure phone buzzed. A text from Phillips. *Marian. Let's talk tomorrow. This transition doesn't need to be difficult.*

The man had a set of brass balls, she'd give him that.

She deleted the text without response.

The old Marian Sinclair would have answered. The good soldier. The team player. The woman who stayed loyal after the Ratcliffe betrayal.

That woman had died in the ceremony room today.

One of the agency's personnel files glowed on her screen. Thomas Reid.

Forty-eight. Yale grad. Ten years her junior. His record sparkled with successful NSA operations she had engineered while serving two directors who took all the credit.

"Your mentorship made this possible," Reid had said, glass raised in her honor.

Just like Phillips had thanked her when he took Ratcliffe's seat.

Reid's words had burned her throat like acid.

A second phone vibrated. The encrypted one. GPS coordinates appeared, followed by a time. Four a.m. She knew the location. A private airfield outside Baltimore.

Sinclair opened her wall safe. Inside a black passport, credit cards, and bank documents under another name. Insurance against this day.

Ratcliffe had taught her to prepare for every contingency. She'd learned well.

Her doorbell rang. She froze.

No one knew she lived here except the past and present directors. Security protocols demanded secrecy.

The bell rang again.

"Dr. Sinclair?" A man's voice. "Building maintenance. Water leak in the unit above you."

She moved silently to the door. Checked the camera feed. Two men in maintenance uniforms. They'd turned their faces away from the camera's view.

She scanned both men slowly. On the first look she noticed the truth.

The shoes were wrong. Both men were wearing combat boots. Not standard issue for the maintenance staff here.

She'd spent years designing agency response protocols. This was one she'd personally implemented. She understood the nuances.

The agency had moved fast. But she moved faster.

Sinclair killed the lights. The emergency exit waited in her bedroom.

They thought they knew her. They knew nothing.

She'd kept her best strategies secret as she'd watched lesser agents come and go over the years. Tips she'd picked up from more seasoned agents after a long, successful career. At the time, her secrecy had simply felt necessary. She didn't examine her motives too closely. Instead, she relied on instincts honed by years in the game.

Sinclair pressed a button to release the lock on the frame of the life-sized painting she'd bought in New Orleans long ago. Louis Armstrong holding his trumpet in the bayou with a quirky blue dog sitting nearby.

The lock released with a quiet click. Sinclair pushed the painting aside and slid open the bedroom window. A metallic crunch echoed from her front door.

The maintenance lie died fast.

They were breaking in.

Sinclair stepped out of the window and closed it again. She pressed the remote to return the Blue Dog to its place before she hurried along.

CHAPTER 2

Tuesday July 5
Washington, DC

THE FIRE ESCAPE RATTLED under her feet. She descended three floors swiftly. Her muscles easily remembered decades of field training and responded accordingly.

Above her, boots scraped metal. They'd followed her path.

She hustled faster.

The alley opened ahead. A security camera blinked red on the corner. She walked straight toward it. Let them track her. Give them a sense of purpose, she grinned.

Her Lexus was parked two blocks away. She left it there to keep them busy with weak surveillance that would yield nothing.

A cab rolled past. She raised her hand.

"Union Station," she told the driver.

His radio played soft jazz. She watched the mirror. No tail yet.

Phillips was using the tactical handbook she'd written herself years ago. The tactics were sound then and now.

Tactics were not the whole plan, though.

Phillips should have known that, too.

The station buzzed with late night travelers. She bought a ticket to New York with cash. Walked down the platform toward Track 4. Then she slipped into a maintenance door and out through the parking garage.

Her burner phone showed 11:40 p.m. Enough time until her appointment at the airfield.

Sinclair knew they'd watch every private plane within fifty miles. Phillips knew her methods because she'd trained him.

He wouldn't vary the protocols. That would take skills, talent, imagination. All of which Phillips had missed because he was standing behind the door when vital attributes were passed out.

A bus pulled into the station. *Baltimore* glowed on its display.

She boarded with the others in line and sat near the back. Old tricks worked best. The agency trained agents to look for complex plans. They forgot the simple ones Ratcliffe had taught her.

Her encrypted phone vibrated.

Another message. *They've activated ARGUS. Full surveillance net. Careful.*

Her stomach tightened. ARGUS. Her greatest achievement at the agency. A surveillance web that connected every traffic camera, every ATM, every storefront security system into one AI-driven network.

ARGUS was excellent and damned near infallible.

She'd designed its algorithms herself. She'd built-in access points and blind spots only she knew about.

Now ARGUS hunted her, but she wasn't worried. She knew what ARGUS would do and when.

ARGUS could not say the same about Sinclair.

The bus engine rumbled. Baltimore waited, ninety minutes away.

She closed her eyes but kept her body alert. The real work began at dawn.

Twenty years of secrets filled her memory. She knew where the bodies lay. Which deals bought which lies. How deep the corruption went. She'd watched it all from the deputy director's chair, serving too many who climbed over her to reach the top.

Phillips and his chosen ones would learn. Power didn't come from titles. It came from knowing the truth. And no one knew more truth than she.

The bus rolled north through Maryland darkness. Rain streaked the windows. Her encrypted phone lit up again. New coordinates. A closed gas station off I-95.

The bus wheezed to a stop outside Baltimore.

Sinclair counted four unmarked NSA vehicles in the parking lot. She smiled. Agency procedure was to cover the major transit points. Which meant they were following the standard playbook. The one she'd created.

She stayed in her seat. The bus continued north.

When the bus parked at a rest stop, she ducked into the toilet while a cluster of sleepy passengers went outside.

The tiny bathroom was a tight squeeze. Fortunately, she'd maintained her field fitness. She was taller than most, but no wider. Pride had kept her training even after they stuck her behind a desk.

Stretching to see through the narrow window above the toilet, she quickly spied the blue pickup truck waiting by the dumpsters.

She slipped out the back door of the bus. Hands shoved into her pockets, hood up to shield her features from prying eyes, she hustled to the truck. Keys were under the front tire, as promised. Her network of contacts had stayed reliable. Or maybe they hadn't heard she'd been kicked out the door yet.

The truck smelled of cigarettes and fast food. Perfect cover, although she almost gagged on the stench.

Sinclair fired up the engine and pulled away from the rest stop. She checked her watch. Two-fifteen a.m. The rain fell harder now, but the tires were good enough.

The agency would expect to intercept her at private airports. Looking for chartered planes and fake documents. Old protocols.

But she'd written those protocols, too. And she'd left herself backdoors.

The gas station sign glowed ahead. A single car sat by the darkened building. Right make and model. She pulled in and dimmed her bright lights.

A man stepped from the car. Tall, precise in his movements, wearing a tailored coat suggesting European refinement.

She recognized him easily.

Klaus Weber. Former Deutsche Bank executive. Seven years ago, she'd tracked a complex derivatives scheme that would have destabilized three currencies.

Instead of destroying him, she'd turned him. His financial network became her entre into the world of hidden money.

After knocking the rain from his coat, he slid into the passenger seat and closed the door.

"Your timing is exact," he said approvingly in German as he checked his watch. "Four minutes to spare."

She took the envelope he offered. "They're using ARGUS."

"As expected." Weber's eyes narrowed. "The blind spots you built into the system remain active?"

"Three hundred and twelve of them. Invisible unless you know where to look." Sinclair smiled. "The harbor cameras will show static at 5 a.m. Which will be interpreted as routine maintenance."

"Duration?"

"Seven minutes. Precisely."

Weber nodded.

She slipped a cargo manifest from the envelope. A container ship was leaving Baltimore harbor at dawn tomorrow. Destination Hamburg. The crossing would take two to four weeks. But she wasn't worried about that. NSA would board the ship in a couple of days to find her missing. Which would save him from pushing her overboard.

Phillips wanted her dead. Sinclair's plan might keep him satisfied long enough.

"Your cabin is prepared. No digital trace," Weber said with satisfaction.

It was a feint. Sinclair would not be on the ship. But the NSA would believe she'd left the country, which would give her a bit of room to move.

Sinclair studied the manifest. "The accounts?"

"The patterns confirm your analysis. Money moves in specific sequences. Always the same banks. Always the same timing." Weber spoke like he was dissecting a balance sheet. "The numbers tell a story. One that goes back to Ratcliffe's time."

The rain drummed on the truck's roof. Weber checked his phone.

"Search radius expanding. Time to move. Stay in touch. Let me know when you get to Hamburg. I'll keep my ear to the ground, just in case." He stepped out of the truck and blended into the scenery.

Sinclair flipped the windshield wipers on again and slipped the transmission into drive. Not a lot of wiggle room to waste.

Time to move.

First, she had to find Neagley and Reacher.

And after that, answers she'd hunted since she'd last seen them both. Years ago, she'd watched from the deputy director's chair, soaking up knowledge like a massive sponge.

The agency had taught her patience.

Now they'd learn what she could do with it.

CHAPTER 3

Friday, July 8
Sedona, Arizona

FBI SPECIAL AGENT KIM Otto squinted behind her aviators against the Arizona sun as she stepped out of the SUV and into the heat on the outskirts of Sedona. Her partner, FBI Special Agent Reggie Smithers, slid the transmission into park and followed her.

"Hell's welcome mat," Smithers muttered. He tugged at his collar where sweat darkened and dampened the fabric. "Cooper sends us to the most glamorous locations."

"The Boss has his reasons," Kim replied. She scanned the stretch before them. "Even if he never shares them."

She had learned over time that the boss, Charles Cooper, gave orders based on actual intel. This would be no different, even if they couldn't fathom it at the start.

Kim had seen enough of Reacher's preferences to know this was the sort of place that appealed to him. The lead was a long shot, but her gut said they were on the right track.

"Nine months Cooper has had you hunting Reacher and chasing your tail," Smithers stepped beside her. "You really think this time will be different?"

Kim's gaze fixed on the building ahead.

"Reacher leaves patterns if you know where to look," she replied. "Places like this that are off-grid, anonymous, forgettable to most. They're his comfort zone."

"You think he's inside now?" Smithers asked.

"Not likely," Kim replied.

The bar sat miles off the main road, tucked away like a secret known only to locals and travelers who missed the turn for Sedona off the road ten miles before. Planks framed the bar's exterior, bleached by years under the sun and sanded by unrelenting winds.

A neon sign above the door read *Dusty's Last Stop*. Two of the letters flickered or stayed dark, which made the sign more cryptic than inviting.

Dirt caked the front steps that creaked under each tread, as if every footfall stamped them into the bar's memory as well as carried them up to the entrance.

The idea was fanciful. But perhaps the guy they'd come to meet actually had intel on Reacher to offer.

"Our informant better be worth the trip," Smithers said. He checked his weapon with efficiency. "Cooper's patience is thin these days."

"Yours too, from the sound of it," Kim replied. The ghost of a smile touched her lips.

"Maybe I'd like a case that doesn't involve chasing shadows and dead ends for once," Smithers countered. "Or at least one that sends me to places with air-conditioning."

Kim gave him a grin. "Who knew you were so whiny?"

Smithers flashed a frown in return.

When she opened the door, sunlight cast a shadow across the room to the bar opposite the entrance. The surface of the planks showed scars and knots, no doubt each mark reminded people of some story.

Inside, the smell of beer, booze, leather, and sand clung to everything.

Photos lined the walls. They captured rodeo riders, prospectors, and old-timers who leaned around the bar and might still be alive now.

Bulbs cast a glow across stools and tables with worn and splintered edges. A mirror behind the bar reflected the bottles, most half-empty and coated in dust.

In the back, a jukebox wheezed out old rock hits. The music would have muffled the din of conversations, had there been any.

A few locals hunched over drinks. Kim figured they kept to themselves.

Her overall impression was this place hadn't seen renovation in decades and probably wouldn't any time soon. Which seemed to be the point for Dusty's Last Stop. It was worn and comfortable for the patrons who came here, and that's all it was.

Dusty's Last Stop didn't pretend to be anything otherwise and Kim appreciated that. Authenticity was a rare thing. Most people she'd come into contact with while hunting Reacher had something to prove and something to hide.

Smithers's gaze swept the room with the efficiency of a field agent.

"See him?" he asked quietly.

She spotted the contact. A man with a beard and an Army green baseball cap sat alone in the corner with his back to the wall. He was there to meet them.

Kim nodded once and tilted her head toward the corner. "Three o'clock. Green hat. He tries not to look nervous. Fails."

The man's gaze repeatedly flicked to the door and back, as if he weren't looking. He glanced up as they approached, but he didn't stand.

"I'll take point," Kim said. "He looks jumpy enough to bolt if we come on too strong."

"You're saying that I'm intimidating?" Smithers replied dryly, as if a man of his size showing up unannounced anywhere wouldn't be intimidating. Smithers knew that and often used it to his advantage. "Let's hope he's got something real that we can work with."

Kim slid into the seat across from the contact. "Thanks for coming, Edward."

She had no time to mess around. She had made that clear when they agreed to the meeting.

He was a survivalist. He lived alone in the desert. He wasn't interested in company or disclosure of his compound, he'd said.

Smithers leaned against the wall, arms crossed. He listened with one ear while he watched the room as Kim conducted the interview.

"People call me Ted," he replied. "You try to pin me down, I'll jump outta here quicker than you can say Jack Rabbit. You'll never see me again."

Dusty's Last Stop had been his choice of meeting spot. Now that they'd located him, Kim figured Dusty's was his usual watering hole.

His compound was probably nearby. Or at least, not across the state line or across the border into Mexico. Which would have presented other problems.

"Where did you see the man we're looking for?" Kim asked. Her voice stayed low.

The survivalist shifted in his seat. His fingers tapped a jittery rhythm on the table. "Passing through a few weeks back. Out in the canyons. He stayed one night. Slept in the shed. Didn't say much."

His name probably wasn't Ted and his story about Reacher seemed unlikely. But he behaved like a cunning animal, staying still, wary, nervous. He did look like he might bolt with the slightest provocation.

"Where exactly did you see him?" Kim leaned in, pressing him, watching his reactions.

"Like I said on the phone, I can show you. For a price." He worked his mouth as if he had a wad of chewing tobacco in his cheek. Which he probably did.

"We've come a long way. We're definitely interested. But you should have asked for the money before. We could have stopped at the bank," Kim replied, testing him. "As it is, I've only got about two hundred bucks in my pocket."

He opened his mouth to argue and then froze. His gaze locked on something behind her. Kim tensed, glancing over her shoulder.

A tall man stood at the entrance, rough-looking, his expression cold and hard. Kim saw the glint of metal in his hand.

Ted's face went pale.

"Too late," he whispered, just as the stranger raised a gun and fired before Ted had time to move.

The shot rang out, echoing loudly in the cramped space.

Ted's body jerked, then slumped forward, blood spreading across the table.

Shouts erupted as the patrons scattered, ducking behind tables and landing on the floor.

Kim moved for cover just before another shot cracked above her head. Glass shattered and bottles exploded behind the bar.

She pointed toward the far side of the room, signaling Smithers to flank the shooter.

Smithers was already moving. He was a big man, which made him an easy target. He slipped around the tables using whatever limited cover he could access along the way.

Kim stayed where she was. She drew her weapon and held it steady, tracking the shooter's every move.

"Drop the gun!" she shouted.

He backed toward the door, sweeping his pistol to train on her.

Then, he spun around swiftly and bolted out the door.

Kim took off after him, shoving past overturned chairs and spilling drinks as they passed the tables. Smithers was only half a step behind her.

They burst through the heavy door into the sunlight, blinking against the glare and the heat.

The gunman was already a hundred yards away, sprinting toward the red rock formations that stretched across the desert.

They raced after him, boots kicking up dust, weaving through scattered scrub and jagged rocks. The heat baked both the air and the ground, and every step was a struggle.

The gunman headed directly toward a narrow ridge where the rocks formed a natural path.

"Cut him off," Kim called, veering left, hoping to keep him from reaching higher ground.

Smithers pushed forward as they closed the gap.

The gunman threw a glance over his shoulder. Sweat dripped down his forehead.

He turned and fired blindly.

The bullet whizzed past Kim's ear, close enough that she imagined she felt the heat.

She had a clear shot. She could have taken him down.

But she wanted him alive.

Hard to interrogate a dead man without a competent psychic. She'd neglected to bring one along.

Kim kept moving and tried again. "Stop running!"

The man ignored her, throwing himself up the ridge. His hands scrambled for grip on the rough surface of the rocks.

Smithers's long stride reached him first, grabbing his ankle, pulling hard.

The gunman kicked backward.

His boot connected with Smither's shoulder, almost knocking him off balance.

Kim was petite but fast.

She grabbed the gunman's arm and twisted it hard, up and back.

The gun fell from his grip, clattering against the rocks. He snarled, fighting with wild strength, fists swinging as he tried to break free.

She'd pinned him against a boulder and forced him to face her.

"Who are you? Why did you shoot that guy back at Dusty's?" Kim demanded, as she jerked his arm up.

He bared his teeth, defiance flashing in his eyes as he tried to shove her aside. "Get the hell away from me."

The rumble of an engine cut through the noise. Kim's gaze shot to the distance.

An unmarked SUV barreled over the desert speeding straight toward them sending a fresh wave of adrenaline through her.

"We need to go," Smithers said, his voice tense. "Bring him along."

"Dream on, man," The gunman laughed, twisting his head toward the approaching vehicle. "They won't let you leave here alive."

Kim tightened her grip and jerked his arm up higher. He yelped with pain.

She grabbed a quick look at the approaching threat.

No time. They couldn't take the shooter back to their SUV. They'd never get him secured before they faced whoever was coming.

She met Smithers's gaze.

Kim released the gunman and shoved him back against the rocks just as the SUV skidded to a stop, doors flying open.

A hail of gunfire cracked through the air from inside the SUV, forcing Kim and Smithers to drop behind the rocks for cover.

The gunman took off sprinting toward the dusty SUV. He dove inside as the vehicle spun around, speeding away in a blinding cloud of red dust.

Kim lifted her head and watched the SUV disappear over the ridge.

"Looks like our shooter is the real Jack Rabbit," Smithers murmured, dusting red dirt off his hands. "Another lead vanished with nothing to show for it."

They'd lost their witness and the man who'd killed him.

The boss would not be happy.

Kim wasn't all that thrilled, either.

"Now what?" Smithers asked as he walked up to stare after the SUV's dusty trail.

CHAPTER 4

Friday, July 8
Chicago, Illinois

THE SHARP THUNK OF her sturdy boot heels echoed through the narrow alley as Frances Neagley closed in on her target. Inside the alley, dim light concealed both the man and his pursuer.

Neagley was feeling the July heat, but she kept going. His body gleamed with sweat as he ducked between dumpsters, too.

"You'll never catch me!" the lanky thief called out, his voice bouncing off the alley's brick walls as he dashed between inadequate hiding places.

He glanced back and met her gaze, his eyes wide with panic, as if he were shocked to see her continuing to follow him.

She gave him a grin when he realized she was gaining ground.

The antique pocket watch chain dangled from his fist. It was the one piece of evidence linking him definitively to the gallery heist. The lanky dude wasn't the first hapless thief to try stealing the gallery's valuables. But this would be the last time for him. Three strikes and he was done.

Neagley's long-time client owned the gallery over on State Street. The gallery had paid Neagley a monthly retainer for years, simply to handle ambitious thieves like this one.

Once she caught him with the watch still in his grubby hands, he'd go to prison for the rest of his life. His actions pushed him way past every limit the law allowed. There would be serious prison time in his future.

Without warning, he veered right. His sneakers skidded on a disgustingly stinky puddle covering the pavement as he bolted toward the elevated train platform.

Metal stairs clanged under his feet as he dashed upward, taking two steps at a time until he reached The L, the elevated train that served as a part of Chicago's mass transit system.

Neagley leapt onto the fourth stair and grabbed his jacket before he could reach the top, yanking him backward.

He spun, throwing a wild punch that she blocked with ease. He was a thief, not a street fighter. Obviously.

Too bad for him.

Because Neagley was great at street fighting. She'd been doing it her entire life. Long before she'd joined the Army and served with Jack Reacher.

She slammed his wrist down hard against the steel railing. Not hard enough, it turned out, since she didn't break anything.

He grunted but twisted free, scrambling up the last few steps until he was out of reach again.

The train roared past on the opposite track, whipping a great gust of wind through the elevated station. Commuters pressed themselves against the walls, phones raised, recording Neagley's confrontation with the thief.

Swell. That's all we need.

Video splashed around online would make the late night news if she was unlucky.

"The watch," Neagley said when she caught up with him, palm out, breathing controlled, her voice deadly calm. "Or I take it from you. Which, I promise, you will not like."

He laughed but the sound was tinged with desperation. "You're not scaring me."

"Proves how stupid you are," she stepped forward. "Hand it over."

He lunged toward her as if to knock her out of the way.

She sidestepped, catching his arm and twisting it high behind his back.

The watch slipped from his grasp. Its gold case caught the light as it bounced across the elevated platform.

While she was distracted, he shifted his weight suddenly, breaking her hold, and dashed away. He chased after the watch and grabbed it up again.

"Really? We're doing this again?" Neagley muttered as he wove through the scattered commuters.

He sprinted toward the maintenance gap in the safety railing.

Metal flashed in his hand.

A knife this time.

"That's not going to help you," she said, closing the distance between them.

Knife fights were not her first choice, but knives were not all that much bother, either.

Many had tried before this guy, but Neagley had never been cut by a perp with a knife. Not once.

This lowlife wouldn't ruin her record.

"Watch me," he snarled, slashing wide again and again.

She easily dodged left, then right, letting him wear himself out with hard downward arcs and heavy exertion.

He got lucky once.

The knife caught her sleeve, but her expression never changed.

She waited calmly for her moment.

He was breathing heavily and his slashing slowed as he seemed to tire.

Exactly as she'd expected.

A knife gets heavy after a while.

With one swift move, she grabbed his wrist, twisted until he released the knife. She kicked it aside.

"Enough," she said, advancing on him. "Let it go. You're done."

He backed up until he stood too close to the edge of the platform.

Neagley saw the fear flash in his eyes as she moved toward him, hand out with her palm up.

"The watch," she said so quietly that he leaned in to hear. "Last chance."

Instead of answering, he looked over his shoulder at the long drop to the pavement below. The sidewalk was crowded with people and vehicles of all sorts filled the streets. He'd land on them. Would they break his fall? Or would he break all his bones instead?

He stared too long.

Those moments of distraction were all she needed.

Two quick steps.

She grabbed the watch from his hand.

Then she planted one palm squarely in the center of his chest and shoved. Hard.

He was already off balance before she pushed him.

He stumbled and tried to right himself.

He failed.

Neagley made no move to catch him or to prevent his fall.

His arms windmilled and he toppled backward.

For a split second, his gaze met hers, a flash of panic in his eyes. Then gravity grabbed him and sucked him down into the empty space below.

He screamed all the way to the ground.

First his body and then his screams were stolen by the wind.

His screaming stopped abruptly, immediately after he splatted on the pavement.

Neagley walked to the edge, glancing down for a brief moment. He lay crumpled on the street below, motionless. A crowd of horrified onlookers began to circle his mangled body. Sirens sounded in the distance, drawing closer.

She turned to blend into the crowd, just another face disappearing into the city.

Sirens grew louder as Neagley slipped the antique watch into her pocket and strode across the platform to the exit.

She'd call a couple of friends at the precinct and give her statement later. No reason to spend the rest of her day sitting in the back of a squad unit.

As she hustled down the stairs to the street below, her phone buzzed. She answered without checking the number.

"Neagley," she said, moving through the dispersing crowd.

"Hello, Neagley." The voice on the other end was one she hadn't heard for many years. "It's Marian Sinclair."

Blast from the past. Neagley's excellent memory supplied accurate images of an intense experience in Hamburg, Germany, when Sinclair was almost as high up in the government as any woman could go back in the day.

"How can I help you?" Neagley replied.

Because no one called her simply to shoot the breeze.

Especially not women like Marian Sinclair.

Never had.

Never would.

Neagley didn't have girlfriends. No gossipy chats over wine or lattes. No lingering lunches or happy hours or clubbing nights in the city. Girlfriends had never been on Neagley's radar. A fact she'd long ago learned to appreciate.

"I understand you own your own investigations firm now," Sinclair said. "I'd like to hire you."

"For what?" Neagley said, still walking.

"I'd prefer to explain that in person. I'm at the Drake Hotel. Twenty minutes," Sinclair said, as if she still had the right to give Neagley orders. Which she definitely did not. "And bring Reacher with you."

Reacher? Neagley froze mid-step and her hand tightened around the watch in her pocket.

What could she say in response?

She hadn't seen Reacher recently. And she hadn't been able to contact him at will for more than fifteen years. Not since the 110th Special Investigators were disbanded before Reacher left the Army.

She could find him again.

If she wanted to.

Which she didn't.

Reacher didn't want to be accessible, simple as that. Neagley understood and respected his choice.

Which meant she couldn't find him unless she worked on the problem strategically. Even then, the odds were less than fifty percent that she'd succeed.

Neagley hated losing. She avoided losing whenever possible. If she got in it, whatever it was, she played to win. Every time.

So if she wanted to find Reacher, she could.

She'd done it before.

She could do it again.

Eventually.

But she absolutely couldn't find Reacher and take him to meet with Sinclair on twenty minutes notice.

Even if she'd wanted to.

Which, at the moment, she did not.

She wouldn't make excuses, either.

Never complain, never explain.

That had been her motto for most of her life. She saw no reason to change it now.

A moment later, she realized no reply to Sinclair's demand was necessary.

The line was already dead.

A moment later, she received Sinclair's text. Meeting location: Millennium Park.

CHAPTER 5

Friday, July 8
Chicago, Illinois

THE BLINDING SUMMER SUNLIGHT'S reflection pierced Neagley's dark glasses as she looked out over Millennium Park.

Her gaze fixed on the brightly polished curve of "The Bean." The sculpture's shiny surface was inspired by liquid mercury, designed to reflect the Chicago skyline and provide a sort of gateway to the city. Or so she had been told.

Today the park was alive with the usual blend of tourists and locals. After a few sweeps, she spied her contact. Neagley's focus honed on Marian Sinclair's orbit. She stood fifty feet away, glancing at her watch, lips pressed thin.

The thing was, Neagley didn't fully trust her. Sinclair had a strong strategic reason for everything she did, and a simple meet-up in a public place like this wasn't one of her usual moves.

But whatever Sinclair had in mind was important enough for her to reach out in person. That alone made Neagley more cautious.

If Sinclair had planned a trap of some sort, Neagley didn't see it.

One glance confirmed there were no additional operatives in the immediate area.

But modern surveillance being what it was, Sinclair could have positioned her backup in a dozen different clandestine locations.

Neagley shrugged. Nothing she could do about Sinclair's methods.

Continually scanning from behind her sunglasses, Neagley sauntered across the park to the bench where Sinclair was waiting.

Sinclair checked the area again before she nodded, "Thanks for coming."

"You said it was urgent," Neagley replied, her tone steady. "Do tell."

Sinclair took a breath and lowered her voice. "I have a job for you. It's sensitive. We need an operative who knows how to handle herself."

Neagley raised an eyebrow. "I'm not interested in getting pulled into your NSA games."

Sinclair gave her a stern look and replied firmly. "It's about Hamburg."

Hamburg? After all this time?

The assignment had been classified and only a small handful of top brass were aware of it. Sinclair ran the successful operation for the NSA. Together, Reacher and Neagley and a select few others, had saved the world.

Literally.

Medals and commendations and back slapping all around had resulted.

But Hamburg was a long time ago. After Neagley and Reacher had finished with the 110th but were still in the Army.

Back then, Neagley followed orders because she had no choice.

Reacher had followed orders, too. In his own way. When he felt like it.

A slight grin briefly crossed her lips.

Neagley controlled the grin and waited for Sinclair to make her point.

Sinclair leaned in. "You remember the map, I'm sure."

Neagley's curiosity sharpened. "Horace Wiley's treasure map?"

"Yes."

"I remember it well enough," Neagley said, calling up the image in her memory.

A large-scale map. Fine lines. A lot of detail. Folded and unfolded many times. Ragged, creased, dirty from years of use.

One specific area on the map had been touched repeatedly with grimy fingers, making it easy to locate and remember the precise spot.

There were plenty of more accurate technologies than Wiley's old-school paper map, even back then. Which they had assumed was an indication that Wiley wasn't a very sophisticated guy.

Yet he'd managed to pull off the crime of the century. Which had been a major blow to the likes of the NSA, CIA, FBI, and more.

Turned out all that sophistication at the very top echelons of the government pyramid couldn't thwart an Army grunt from achieving his private mission.

Army wins. Again. Neagley coughed to cover her desire to grin like a fool.

"There was more to the situation than we realized at the time," Sinclair said. "When Wiley ordered a portion of his millions transferred, he activated a set of instructions he had established with the bank in advance."

"Yeah, I remember. He sent some of the money to buy a ranch in Argentina," Neagley confirmed. "The deal was done, and we couldn't undo it."

"Exactly." Sinclair nodded for emphasis. "There are things we missed. Money we never found. Details we couldn't unwind back then."

"And you want to try again."

Sinclair nodded again. "Something like that."

Neagley recalled discussions with Reacher about the money Wiley collected in exchange for delivering certain contraband. He'd been paid millions. Some of it was neither located nor repatriated.

Reacher hadn't liked the result. He didn't approve of loose ends. Said it felt like the job wasn't finished.

Neagley didn't approve of loose ends, either. "And you're saying there's new intel on this?"

"Before I left NSA, I confirmed that Wiley's map is sitting in an archive, gathering dust." Sinclair didn't answer the question, but her gaze was steady. "I want us to retrieve it."

Neagley stayed silent, her expression unreadable. *What would Reacher do?*

"I'll cover all expenses and pay you a flat fee," Sinclair said, probably thinking she was sweetening the deal. "Just help me get the map."

"And then what?"

Sinclair shrugged. "Depends on what we learn in the process."

Neagley cocked her head and kept her tone neutral. "You could hire anyone for a retrieval job. Why not use the NSA? They report to you. You have the right to boss them around. Tasks like that are exactly what you pay them for."

Sinclair's eyes narrowed. She cleared her throat before she replied. "I need someone I can trust. And someone who doesn't mind bending a few rules."

Neagley looked away, pretending to be unimpressed, but she was thinking fast.

She definitely didn't need the hassle of chasing a dead man's scattered dreams across international borders.

But there was something almost desperate in Sinclair's tone.

And that was both unusual and an opportunity.

In Neagley's line of work, being on the right side of the NSA was more useful than being on the wrong side.

Plus, the unfinished business thing was still hanging out there.

It was a lot of money. Millions. *Hard to turn your back on that.*

"I'll take my flat fee up front. Before we start," Neagley said, her tone calm. "And fifty percent of whatever we recover, after expenses."

Sinclair's lips tightened. She paused for at least a full minute.

Neagley waited, giving Sinclair plenty of time to decide. She wasn't desperate for cash, and she wasn't that fond of Sinclair, either.

She'd named her price. Sinclair could pay it, or not. Neagley would be fine either way.

Hell, if she wanted the money badly enough, Neagley could find it on her own. Sinclair, apparently, could not. Otherwise, she wouldn't be asking.

"Fair enough." Sinclair finally nodded, but she obviously didn't like the deal.

Neagley didn't care whether she liked it or not.

"One more thing," Neagley said, giving Sinclair a knowing look. "If you're thinking the money went missing because Reacher took it, he's not your guy."

"No?"

"I was with him the whole time in Hamburg, except for the time he spent with you," Neagley said flatly. "He doesn't have the map or the money. No reason why he would."

Sinclair had spent her entire career listening to lies and threats without flinching. She said nothing.

Neagley said, "If Reacher had stolen it, what makes you think he'll give it up now without a fight?"

Sinclair's jaw tightened. "Reacher has nothing to do with this."

Neagley didn't blink. "You're sure about that?"

"Look, Reacher was there in Hamburg. He may have seen things we missed," Sinclair replied, her tone clipped. "But he's not the goal. He's a possible asset, a means to an end. Nothing more."

"If you want to find him, that's your problem," Neagley held her gaze, unflinching. "I'll help you get the map. But any hint that you or anybody else is turning this thing into a manhunt for Reacher, and I'm gone."

Sinclair didn't argue. A flash of frustration crossed her face before she nodded. "Fine. We focus on the map. No Reacher."

Neagley extended her hand. "Then we have a deal."

Sinclair hesitated for a split second, then offered a hard, firm grip. "See you in Boston tonight."

"Boston?"

"That's where we'll start," Sinclair said.

"Why?"

"Wiley told his banker to start the process, we learned back then. We now believe that process included hidden directives that could lead us to the missing thirty million dollars," Sinclair said. "We want another look at that map. We think it could contain details we missed."

"And this map is in Boston now?" Neagley asked.

"The intel we have right now says it's archived there. We may not find it. But Boston is a good place to start." Sinclair stood, turned, and moved away with quick, deliberate steps. "I'll send the details. We'll discuss things further once you're up to speed."

"See you in Boston," Neagley said as Sinclair walked away.

Neagley watched her slip through the crowd, weaving with an urgency she hadn't shown during their conversation.

Boston. Reacher. Wiley. And thirty million dollars floating around in Brazil. A lot to chew over.

Neagley pushed through the crowd, rounded the corner, and spotted Sinclair up ahead, moving faster now, head down.

Which was when Neagley saw that Sinclair was being followed.

CHAPTER 6

Friday, July 8
Chicago, Illinois

TWO MEN, DRESSED IN dark jackets, were moving through the crowd behind Sinclair. Solid spycraft, Neagley noticed. They stayed just far enough from Sinclair to go unnoticed. Pace steady. Eyes firmly fixed on the prey.

As Sinclair reached the edge of the park, the two men moved to close the distance.

Neagley didn't hesitate. She quickened her pace, her focus never leaving the men. As Sinclair passed a narrow alley, one of them veered off, slipping into her blind spot. The other stayed behind, closing in.

Neagley kept steady. She crossed the street, coming up beside the man in the alley just as he stepped forward, reaching out toward Sinclair.

Without a word, Neagley grabbed his arm, twisting it behind his back with a quick, brutal jerk and lifted his feet slightly off the ground just for show. The man grunted in surprise as he struggled against her iron grip.

"Walk away," she said, low and cold, as she set him down again. "Now."

She saw the realization flash across his face. He'd been seen, identified, and neutralized.

The second man noticed the commotion and stopped moving. His gaze darted from Neagley to Sinclair. For a brief second, he seemed to consider his options. Decision made, he walked briskly back toward the crowd.

"You're done here." Neagley let go of the first man and shoved him forward.

He straightened, rubbing his wrist, his eyes narrow and calculating. But he didn't argue. He, too, disappeared into the crowd.

Neagley watched them until they were gone. Sinclair was standing a few feet away as if she'd been watching the show.

"Friends of yours?" Neagley asked drily as she approached.

Sinclair's face was pale and tense. "No. I didn't see them at all."

"You're being followed and you didn't even know it." Neagley looked her over. "That's the kind of training NSA dishes out these days? What would you have done about those two if you'd been on your own?"

"You've already dealt with them. Let's just stick to the plan," Sinclair replied.

Neagley didn't like the feeling crawling up her spine. "Send me the details. We'll go from there."

Sinclair nodded before she hurried away.

Neagley didn't trust Sinclair and now she had reason to doubt her competence. But the job was set. Neagley had given her word.

She wondered again what Sinclair was really after and what it had to do with their time in Hamburg. A time when Neagley and Reacher had cut a lot of corners. Which was always Reacher's way. He focused on results rather than rules of engagement.

Even as they were doing the job in Hamburg, Neagley had expected blowback. For years, she'd been half expecting retribution from Wiley's contacts.

All of which meant that the situation should be resolved, once and for all.

The fastest way to clarify things was to stick as close to Sinclair as possible. Hell, close supervision disguised as cooperation might be the only way. Sinclair's skills might be slipping, but even at less than one hundred percent capacity, Sinclair was better than most.

Neagley slipped her hands into her pockets, glancing around to make sure the two men hadn't doubled back. For now they seemed to be gone.

She figured they'd return. Sooner or later. She gave Sinclair a long lead and then followed.

All she could do for now was stay alert until she had a few more answers.

She scanned the crowd while she watched Sinclair retreating into the distance. Sinclair moved fast, head down, keeping close to the edges of the park, blending in.

But Neagley caught it anyway. Sinclair was rattled.

Neagley felt a surge of annoyance. She'd had enough cloak and dagger for one day.

Up ahead, Sinclair had stopped at the corner, waiting for the light to change. Her body language was all wrong. Rigid, coiled, like she was expecting someone to jump her.

Neagley felt more than a twinge of irritation. Sinclair wanted her help and insisted on meeting in person. But she was acting like she couldn't handle her own shadow.

Neagley was walking into this thing, whatever it was, with too many open questions and no solid answers. Which was not okay. Not even remotely.

She closed the distance until she was only a few paces behind Sinclair. Neagley moved quickly, weaving through and around all obstacles until she was almost on Sinclair's heels.

Sinclair turned slightly as if she'd noticed Neagley, who grabbed her arm and steered her toward a narrow alleyway out of sight from the street. Sinclair pulled back, eyes wide, but Neagley held firm.

"What are you doing?" Sinclair said with plenty of both annoyance and alarm.

"Making sure we don't have more company." Neagley released her grip, positioning herself to keep watch on the alley entrance. "Those guys, are they yours?"

Sinclair's expression hardened. "No. They're not mine."

"Then who are they?" Neagley crossed her arms, waiting. "Because they were locked on you from the moment we met. And don't tell me you didn't notice. You're not that careless. Or clueless."

Sinclair's mouth tightened into a grim line. "Probably local security contractors. I don't know them."

"Local security contractors? In Millennium Park, trailing an NSA deputy? Come on, Sinclair, try a little harder." Neagley's tone was as sharply edged as a steel blade. "If you want me to participate in your mission, whatever it is, I need answers. Real ones."

Sinclair's gaze shifted and she clenched her jaw. She was silent for a beat, gaze fixed on some point over Neagley's shoulder. Neagley could tell she was calculating, weighing how much to reveal.

Neagley said nothing. She'd said all she meant to say until Sinclair conceded. But she wouldn't wait forever, either.

"They could be related to my current situation with the agency," Sinclair said sharply. "That's all you need to know."

Neagley took a slow breath as she shook her head slowly. "You're making this about Wiley's map to get me involved, but really, you need me to watch your back while you handle whatever mess you're mixed up in."

Sinclair flashed with irritation. "You're wrong."

"Prove it. Tell me the whole story." Neagley held her gaze, refusing to back down.

Sinclair didn't move for a long moment, as if her face was actually set in stone. Until she exhaled with, perhaps, a hint of resignation.

"Look, I've made some decisions. Decisions that certain people in certain places don't like. It's not safe to discuss specifics here," Sinclair said. "You were there. In Hamburg. You know the map and Wiley's money are very real. You know that's not a lie."

"And the people watching you?" Neagley pressed.

"They're not supposed to be there. But it doesn't change the job. If you're in, we're in this together. If not—" Sinclair shrugged. "You can walk away. I won't hold it against you."

Neagley's instincts screamed at her to do exactly that. Walk away, let Sinclair handle her own baggage.

But too much curiosity gnawed at her. Too many questions that wouldn't go away.

And Reacher? Neagley wouldn't let him get blindsided, either.

Neagley said, "What's the play, here? Because I'm not interested in stumbling blind."

Sinclair had regained her cold professionalism. "We fly to Boston separately. We'll arrive a day early, assess the situation, and finalize a plan. You'll have full access to anything you need. On my dime."

"And if we're tailed in Boston?"

Sinclair's lips curved in a slight, humorless smile. "If they're watching me there, we'll make sure they're watching the wrong thing."

Neagley considered the plan. Sinclair was tense, but she wasn't lying. Or at least she wasn't lying about the parts Neagley cared about.

"Fine," Neagley said. "For now."

Sinclair's expression returned to an unreadable mask. "Understood."

"See you tonight in Boston." Neagley gave a decisive nod and turned to leave the alley.

Before she stepped out, she felt a familiar prickle on the back of her neck. The early warning that she was being watched.

She spun around, scanning the rooftops, the alleys, the clusters of people nearby.

No sign of the men from earlier. No immediate threat.

She'd learned to thrive within the risks with her line of work. This felt different.

What the hell was Marian Sinclair up to?

Neagley looked back to see that Sinclair had already blended into the crowd again. She had simply disappeared among the tourists and locals. The woman was good—a solid operative with well honed skills. Neagley gave her silent respect for those skills.

But Sinclair was also manipulative, evasive, and driven by motives that probably didn't align with Neagley's. Her decision to stick with Sinclair wasn't about trust. It was about curiosity, the kind that stuck with her like a burr, refusing to let go.

And, admittedly, it was about Reacher. She'd been Reacher's strong right arm for a short but intense period of time long ago.

Loyalty was baked into Neagley's DNA. Loyalty up, loyalty down. That was the Army way.

Reacher's way.

It was Neagley's way, too.

One last look around the park and then she headed in the opposite direction.

Boston. Not long to prepare.

CHAPTER 7

Friday, July 8
Sedona, Arizona

"WHATEVER WE'RE DOING HERE next, let's do it fast and find some air-conditioning." Smithers swiped sweat from his brow and squinted one last look at the dust behind the speeding SUV. "It's hotter than the hinges of Hell out here."

"We need to find Ted's home base," Kim replied as she snagged her phone from her pocket. While she agreed that the beating sun was oppressive, the dry air had already sucked the perspiration off her body. "He was planning to lead us to his place to show us proof of Reacher's visit. His crib can't be far from here. I'll climb up that hill to take a look. Get the drone and bring it. We'll have more range."

Smithers hustled to the SUV to retrieve the portable drone Kim had stashed with her travel bag. She unfolded the drone's arms and propellers before she paired its signal with her phone and set it to record the video feed, just in case.

A few seconds later the drone was in the air.

The drone whirred softly overhead, its bird's-eye view slicing through the underbrush like a hawk scanning for prey. The slightest movement on the ground would be more than enough to capture the drone's view and be captured on the video.

Otto's eyes narrowed as she scanned the footage display as the device hummed to life, rising above them. Kim watched the screen intently, directing it across the barren landscape. The camera revealed each detail of the harsh terrain. Scattered rocks, twisted vegetation, and deep shadows revealed isolated fragments of the scene.

After a few moments, Kim raised her gaze from the screen to the terrain for better geolocation. She motioned to Smithers, who was crouched near the shooter's last location as if he'd discovered something.

"Look here," Kim said after a few minutes of searching, pointing to the screen. "A cabin just beyond that ridge."

Smithers straightened and joined her to view the images on the screen. He brushed dirt from his hands and focused on the emerging structure as Kim circled the drone's camera around Ted's place.

The one-room cabin had seen better days. Weathered wood and chipped paint reflected years of neglect tainted by ominous silence.

Ted had lived alone. Kim didn't expect to find anyone else foolish enough to hole up here in the suffocating sun. How Ted had survived out here was yet another mystery.

As the drone's eye zoomed in on the cabin, strange shapes caught Kim's attention. She tapped the screen to enlarge the view while the drone hovered steadily in place.

"Are those fresh footprints?"

Smithers leaned closer, intensely studying the shape on the screen. "Probably Ted's."

Smithers started off toward the abandoned structure as Kim replied, "Let's find out."

She pushed the home button on the remote for the drone and waited for it to land near her feet. She left it where it could be easily retrieved later and followed Smithers.

Quickly, they slipped into the brush, keeping low and quiet.

She didn't expect to find Reacher here, but Ted could have enemies or even a small posse lurking nearby. Which might be okay, if they were friendly. Not a risk Kim wanted to take in the moment.

As they approached the decrepit cabin, she felt a slight breeze tug at her jacket, a whisper of something lingering just beyond the trees. The cabin, not much more than a lean-to, stood there like a specter, cloaked in shadows, door slightly ajar.

Kim motioned for Smithers to stop.

"On three," she breathed when she caught up with her heart drumming in her ears. They exchanged a quick nod. "One… two… three."

They rushed forward and pushed through the door.

It creaked loudly on rusty hinges, the screech reverberating like a warning.

Inside, the air was stale, thick with the smell of neglect. Kim scanned the small space, and her gaze fell on a table littered with scraps of paper. A scrawl of illegible notes mixed with hastily drawn maps.

And two coffee mugs, both partially filled with black coffee, both stone cold.

"Looks like he was keeping something here," Smithers said, moving toward the table.

"And he had a visitor," Kim nodded.

But before she could say more, a flicker of movement outside caught her eye. She turned sharply, adrenaline surging through her as she squinted through the grimy window.

A shadow darted past the edge of the clearing, too quick to identify.

"Did you see that?" she asked urgently, tensing.

Smithers nodded, gaze darting toward the door, muscles coiled like springs ready to explode.

"First rule of the hunt," he said, voice low. "Don't assume it's safe. That could be our shooter or something worse."

Kim guessed that Ted had been running from the man who killed him, possibly to protect whatever he'd been hiding. Now it seemed that danger hung in the air like a festering wound.

When the shadow failed to present itself as an imminent threat, she said, "Let's check the rest of the place quickly, while we have the chance."

She shifted her focus back to the table. The papers included hastily sketched maps but also bore unfamiliar symbols. A pattern she'd need time to decipher.

She riffled through the notes and snapped a few photos before instinctively grabbing the largest piece and sliding it beneath her jacket.

Smithers moved toward the back of the cabin, floorboards creaking ominously with every step. "If Ted has been hoarding secrets, maybe he left something behind."

Kim continued her quick search of the small room. Glossy photos coated in dust found their way into her fingertips.

She slid quickly through images of Ted wearing military fatigues, with an unfamiliar group, all similarly clad.

The setting was a desert, probably somewhere in the Middle East, Kim guessed. Iraq, Afghanistan, Saudi Arabia, maybe. Forbidding mountains surrounded the group. She flipped the photo over. Nothing scribbled on the back.

Smithers rejoined her, glancing down at the photos. He frowned at the unkempt Ted, renegade hair, and defiance gleaming in his eyes.

Kim tapped one photo. "Ted might have been involved with this group. Maybe this was his unit."

Smithers nodded. "Or a special operations mission of some sort."

A loud crash sounded outside, shattering the quiet.

"What the hell was that?" Kim's gaze darted toward the door. "We need to move."

She felt the urgency pulse through her veins as she tucked the photos into her pocket. "Let's find another way out. Last thing we need is more dead witnesses."

They crept through the small cabin.

"Back room?" Kim suggested, leading the way while Smithers followed along a brief, narrow hallway with a closed door at the other end.

They crouched, placing each footstep deliberately and silently as they approached the door.

Kim reached for the doorknob, hesitating only a moment before she gave it a gentle turn.

The door swung open, revealing a dimly lit room. Emptiness echoed against the rickety walls, but Kim sensed something dangerous still lingering that had been tucked away under the weight of dust and neglect.

Suddenly, a loud voice shattered the silence from just outside. "I know you're in there!"

CHAPTER 8

Friday, July 8
Sedona, Arizona

"OUT THE BACK?" SMITHERS urged. "Or take them on in here?"

"Outside. More room to maneuver," Kim said as she slipped into the darkened room, moving quickly toward the far wall where a small, dingy window cast a barely discernable light.

"Go," Kim insisted, pushing Smithers ahead.

Smithers slid through the narrow window one leg at a time, boots scraping against the frame as he dropped down the hillside onto the hard-packed dirt. His size made the escape awkward and he landed with a grunt as his body hit the ground.

Kim crouched at the sill, gun in hand, keeping her eyes on the doorway across the cabin.

"Clear?" she whispered, stealing a quick look to confirm that Smithers was still okay.

He met her glance while crouching against the rough wall of the cabin. "Looks clear. Come on. We need to go."

Kim holstered her pistol and hoisted herself through the window. The tight fit forced her to twist awkwardly, and her boots scraped against the wood. As she dropped down beside Smithers, the sound of approaching footsteps from the front of the cabin reached her ears.

"They're close," she muttered. "Move."

Smithers nodded, and they hustled toward a cluster of boulders a few yards away, staying low.

They'd barely covered half the distance when something snapped beneath Smithers's boot. A metallic twang followed and the next second, he was yanked off his feet faster than he could react.

A hidden snare caught his ankle and jerked him upward, leaving him dangling with the top of his head four feet off the ground.

"Dammit!" Smithers hissed, flailing as the wire dug into his ankle above his boot.

Kim spun, her pistol already in hand.

"Keep quiet," she whispered sharply.

"Easy for you to say," Smithers grunted. "Get me down before one of these dudes starts swinging at me like a piñata."

A voice interrupted him. "You're not going anywhere, man. Relax."

Kim turned sharply with her pistol raised.

Two men emerged from the shadows near the cabin's back corner. Both were lean and dressed in dark, dusty clothes. The one who'd spoken carried a rifle, barrel pointed at Kim's chest. The other had a handgun held loose but ready.

"Drop it," the man with the rifle said, his voice icy calm.

Kim didn't move. She assessed the angles, the weapons, the distance for an opening. No luck. She had no clear shot and Smithers was still dangling like bait.

"I said drop it," the man repeated. He stepped closer, rifle steady. "Last chance."

Otto's grip on the pistol tightened.

Smithers glared at the two men, arms crossed over his chest despite his ridiculous position. His expression said *don't even think about it.*

She was about to act when a sharp crack split the air.

The rifleman's head jerked violently to the side.

Red mist sprayed everywhere as he crumpled to the ground.

"What the hell?" The second gunman froze, his pistol half-raised, eyes darting wildly, seeking the threat.

Another shot rang out dropping him, too, with a neat hole punched through his chest. His weapon clattered to the dirt.

Kim pivoted, scanning to locate the sniper.

The bullets had come from somewhere beyond the cabin, but she couldn't see the shooter. She crouched low, Glock sweeping the horizon as her pulse hammered in her ears.

"Who's there?" she called, keeping her voice steady.

No response.

"Otto," Smithers muttered, still dangling in the relentless sun. "I'm not enjoying the view from here. Get me down."

"Soon as I can," Kim replied, her focus never leaving the shadows.

The sniper had demonstrated incredible precision.

One shot, one kill.

Twice.

No hesitation between shots.

Not an amateur, for sure.

Minutes passed when the only sound was the faint rustle of desert wind.

Kim waited, every muscle tense, but no one stepped out of the shadows. No movement from the ridge, either.

After a while, she concluded that he was long gone. No point in continuing to look.

She turned her attention to Smithers. "Hold still."

She located wire cutters in a nearby shed and severed the wire snare cutting off the circulation in his ankle.

Smithers dropped to the ground with a grunt and rolled to one side. He rubbed his ankle, wincing, before standing to test his weight-bearing capacity. He didn't fall, which was a good sign.

"Did you see him?" Smithers asked, looking around as he brushed red dust off his pants.

"No," she said, scanning the ridge beyond the cabin. "But she saw us."

"She?" Smithers asked, raising both eyebrows in question.

"We shouldn't limit our scope to men only," Kim shrugged. "You could have made both those shots. So could I."

Smithers nudged the first body with his boot. "Any idea who these guys are?"

"No." Kim knelt beside the second body, quickly searching his pockets.

She pulled out a weathered notebook, flipping through the pages. Most of the notes were written in some sort of shorthand she didn't recognize.

She held it up. "This might tell us something."

Smithers frowned. "You think these two were working with whoever killed Ted?"

"Maybe," Kim glanced back toward the shadows one last time. "But the better question is who took these two gunmen out? Helluva shot. Trained military snipers could have done it. But why would they?"

Smithers shrugged, adjusting his holster. "Why would a military trained sniper be out here? And why would he kill these two to keep us alive?"

Kim shook her head slowly as she scanned the terrain between Ted's place and the sniper's probable position. "Ted said Reacher had been here but moved on. What if he didn't? Move on, I mean. It's not like he's got to get back to a day job, after all."

"I don't know, but I'm not comfortable sticking around here to give him a chance for more target practice," Smither's replied sourly.

"Not to worry. If Reacher wanted to kill us, we'd be dead already," Kim said. "I'll check things out while you bring the SUV around."

Without waiting for his reply, Kim headed toward the ridge where the sniper had most likely positioned himself. It was the spot she'd have chosen, based on the angles and the terrain, as well as the results he'd achieved.

Smithers didn't argue. He obviously felt the sniper was long gone. Which he probably was.

Kim didn't want to focus too much on how and why the sniper had been waiting there. Or who or what, exactly, he was hunting. And, most importantly, why?

She found the fanciful notion that Reacher was the sniper strangely comforting. Reacher could easily have killed her. Smithers, too. But he didn't. Which made sense, in an odd way.

Kim had come to the tentative conclusion that she had nothing to fear from Reacher. It was a foolhardy belief based on nothing, really.

But she couldn't shake the desire to believe Reacher meant her no harm.

Not today, anyway.

The silence felt heavy, like she was still being watched as she trudged ahead, in full view of what she assumed was the sniper's nest. She almost expected him to shoot again, but he didn't. Which made her a bit bolder.

When she reached the ridge, she climbed steadily up the shallow incline and over.

Nothing happened.

No shots.

No shouts.

No cloud of dust in the distance, even.

From what she believed was the sniper's location, she looked back to the dead bodies. Two fatal shots could as easily have been four. He could have killed her and Smithers, too.

Why didn't he?

"Or she," Kim murmured.

She slid down the backside of the ridge and landed on her feet. She pulled her pistol and crouched behind a boulder, just in case he had changed his position. Or his intentions.

She peered into the hazy heat. She swiveled her head and scanned a full 360 degrees. Saw nothing threatening.

No shooter. No active sniper. No guns or supplies, or anything else noteworthy.

Kim came out from the boulder's cover and walked the dusty desert floor, searching for anything that seemed out of place. She heard Smithers pulling up in the SUV over on the dirt road. He shut the engine off and walked toward her.

"Find anything?" he asked as he approached.

At that moment, she reached what she'd calculated as the sniper's position. Which was when she spied an open cardboard box resting in the shadows.

The box was battered and stained, as if it had spent most of its life exposed to Arizona's harsh sunlight.

"Not sure what that is," Kim said to Smithers as she proceeded cautiously toward it, still feeling the weight of the shooter's presence.

The survivalist had seemed paranoid. Which meant the box could be some sort of booby trap he'd deployed. An IED, perhaps, given his military background.

Or something worse.

Kim crouched near the box, scanning it for tripwires, pressure plates, anything that could be a trap. The battered cardboard seemed harmless enough.

Smithers stopped a few feet away. "Looks old."

Kim reached into her pocket, pulled out a pen, and used the tip to flip open the top flap. The inside was empty. No explosives. No supplies. Just dust and sun-bleached cardboard.

But something was stuck to the bottom. A small rectangle, partially hidden in the crease where the box met the dirt. She used a surgical glove to pluck it free and turn it over in her fingers.

A business card.

She brushed off the grit, reading the text. *Kessler Protective Services.*

A private security firm.

Boston address.

She flipped it over.

One word hastily printed in heavy black ink. *Neagley.*

Kim stared at the name. What were the odds?

Ted had said Reacher was through here.

Then a sniper saves her life.

Then she finds a business card with Neagley's name written on the back.

Kim stared at the card, the inked name standing out against the white background. Neagley.

She turned the card over again. Kessler Protective Services. Boston.

Smithers stepped closer, frowning. "Neagley? As in Frances Neagley?"

Kim nodded. "Has to be. Reacher's only got one Neagley."

Smithers glanced around the empty landscape. "So how the hell did her name end up out here?"

Kim ran her thumb along the edge of the card. "That's the question."

Smithers crossed his arms. "You think Reacher left this?"

Kim considered it. If Reacher left a trail, he wanted her to follow. He was precise, deliberate. If the card was deliberately left like this, the communication could be from him.

But that didn't mean the whole situation wasn't a setup.

"Possibly," she said. "He knows we're looking for him. If he wanted me to find this, he made sure I would."

"So he could shoot you?"

"If he'd wanted to kill me, I'd have been dead a good long while now," Kim replied flatly.

Smithers sighed and then gestured at the box. "Or someone else planted it. Could be a trap. Lead you into something."

Kim studied the missive again. The card was wrinkled and dirty, but the black ink on the back was fresher. The card's edges weren't worn, and it showed no obvious weather damage, suggesting it hadn't been sitting out there long.

"It's a business card. Not a text message, not an email or even a voicemail. That's old-school messaging, Reacher style." She pulled an evidence bag from her pocket and slipped the card inside.

Smithers exhaled. "And Neagley?"

Kim pocketed the evidence. "No idea why her name's written on the back, but there's a way to find out."

"You could call her," Smithers nodded. "Or call the boss. Cooper can find her easily enough."

"Or we could go to Boston and talk to her in person." Kim dragged her gaze from the sniper's nest and pulled out her phone. "There's nothing more to do here."

"Cooper won't like it if we bug out without calling this in first," Smithers reminded her.

"True," Kim shrugged. "Not the first time I've done something Cooper didn't like."

She spent the next ten minutes capturing the entire scene on video as she walked back to the SUV. After she uploaded the video to her secure server, she climbed into the passenger seat beside Smithers.

"Boston it is," he said with a weak grin.

"Back to Dusty's first."

"Why?"

"I've got a few questions." Kim placed her alligator clamp onto the seatbelt at the retractor as Smithers started the SUV and flipped on the air-conditioning full blast. "And I want to take another look at Ted's body."

Smithers said nothing more as he pulled the SUV onto the dusty road.

CHAPTER 9

Friday, July 8
Sedona, Arizona

THE DOOR TO DUSTY'S Last Stop creaked when Kim pushed it open and stepped inside, her gaze locking immediately on Ted's slumped body near the pool table. The body had not been moved. He lay surrounded by a drying pool of blood.

Smithers followed, gaze darting to every shadowed corner of the room, alert to anything they might've missed before.

Behind the bar, Dusty stood like a statue, one hand resting on the counter, the other clutching a glass of whiskey he hadn't sipped. His face was pale after the unexpected violence that had invaded his quiet bar.

"Dusty," Kim said, sharp but measured.

"Figured you'd come back," he muttered, nodding toward the door and then returning his stare to the glass. "Sheriff's on his way. Takes a while to get here from the county seat."

"Good," Kim replied, pulling her phone from her pocket and approaching Ted's body. She snapped several photos first, then gloved up to search his pockets.

He carried no wallet and no keys. No phone, either. She found a wad of folded bills, mostly fives and tens, in one pocket and a pair of sunglasses in another. Nothing else.

She photographed it all and then returned his possessions. She snapped photos of his boots, including the soles.

Kim chose the application on her phone that allowed her to collect fingerprints, which she did swiftly, realizing the sheriff would arrive soon. She snapped images of his face from several angles.

She swabbed his cheek for DNA and pocketed the swab, she sent the data to her secure server and dropped the phone into her pocket. A moment later, heavy boots thudded on the porch, and the door swung open again.

The man's broad shoulders filled the doorway. His sharp gaze landed first on the body, then Otto and Smithers. He walked over and quickly processed the situation.

"Sheriff José Garcia," he said, handing his business card to Kim. "You are?"

"FBI Special Agent Kim Otto. My partner is Reggie Smithers," she replied, nodding in Smithers's direction.

"FBI?" he asked. "Why is the FBI interested in this homicide?"

"We were here when it happened," Smithers replied.

"Sheriff Garcia," Dusty interrupted, his voice cracking slightly. "Took you long enough."

The sheriff's gaze shifted to Dusty. "Coroner's on the way. Forensic team heading out to Ted's property, too. Let's all talk this through."

Garcia gestured to the barstools, then pulled out one for himself. Otto and Smithers exchanged a look before taking their seats, neither fully at ease. Dusty stayed where he was, rooted behind the bar like he needed the counter to hold him up.

"This wasn't a random murder," Garcia said, leaning forward on his elbows. "So either someone wanted something from Ted, or they wanted him gone. Which was it?"

"Good question. We didn't have much of a chance to talk before the shooter came in." Otto kept her tone neutral. "Shooter killed Ted and ran out. We followed, but we lost him. Just got back."

"Why were you focused on Ted?" Garcia asked. "He kept to himself. Never traveled. Law abiding citizen as far as I know. What's your interest?"

"Ted had intel on a guy we're trying to find," Kim replied. "Jack Reacher. Ted said he'd been through here recently."

Garcia raised an eyebrow. "Reacher? Name doesn't ring a bell."

"Big guy," Smithers added. "Military background. Drifter. Doesn't stay in one place long."

"Doesn't sound familiar," Garcia said, rubbing his jaw. "But if Ted said he was here, I won't argue. Any idea why Reacher was here or how Ted knew him?"

"Like I said, we didn't have enough time to ask," Kim shook her head. "Ted didn't go into detail. Just said Reacher stayed at his place a couple of nights and then moved on. Didn't leave much behind."

The sheriff sat back, frowning as he mulled things over. "Maybe Ted got caught up in something he didn't see coming. You think the guy who shot him was Reacher? Or someone looking for Reacher?"

"Either is possible," Kim said. "Any other strangers in town?"

"Not that I've heard," Garcia replied. "But I'll ask around. Folks don't miss much, although there's nothing much happening, you know? Pretty quiet around here usually."

Smithers leaned forward. "You mentioned you've sent forensics out to Ted's property. What do you expect to find there?"

Garcia shrugged. "Standard procedure. But I don't expect much. Ted wasn't the kind to leave secrets lying around. Lived simply, kept to himself. If he was hiding something, he wouldn't have kept it on his property. Too obvious."

Kim and Smithers had found nothing hidden at Ted's place. But his connection to Reacher, however fleeting, could have put him in the crosshairs.

"Sheriff," Kim said, meeting his gaze directly, "we'll need to know what you find at Ted's property. Records, belongings, anything."

Garcia's eyes narrowed slightly. "That's the deal, then. I'll share what I find, but you keep me in the loop on your investigation. Federal badge or not, this is my town."

"Fair enough," Kim replied.

The sheriff stood, towering over the table. "You'll know when I know. But if this Reacher guy's mixed up in this, you'd better find him fast. A man like Ted doesn't get killed for no reason. Reacher could be next."

Kim figured Reacher could take care of himself, but she didn't say so. "We're working on it."

The coroner's team came in at that point. Sheriff Garcia became fully occupied.

"Let's go," Kim said. Smithers nodded and followed her out onto the wooden porch.

Kim paused, scanning the quiet street. Dusty's bar was aptly named. It felt like the last outpost on the edge of nowhere.

Smithers stepped up beside her. "You think Reacher's still around here?"

"No," Kim said, shaking her head. "But whatever happened with Reacher could have put Ted in the line of fire. We need to figure out why."

Smithers nodded with a tight expression. "And fast."

Kim adjusted her sunglasses, looking toward the horizon.

Reacher's trail was growing colder by the second.

Again.

CHAPTER 10

Friday, July 8
Phoenix, Arizona

KIM HAD TRACED THE shooter's vehicle to a Phoenix rental lot that had seen better days. She stepped out of the SUV onto sun-bleached pavement spiderwebbed with cracks. A few weeds had struggled through, reaching for the sunlight and wilting almost instantly once they found it.

A tired sign creaked overhead. *Valley Rentals. No Credit Cards? No Problem!*

Beneath the sign, the bullet hole in the office window confirmed this was not where the rich and famous of Phoenix brought their business. Even the local drug dealers wouldn't use this place. Which was okay. Kim wasn't here for local small-time crime.

"Curious for mercenaries to rent a car," Smithers muttered, coming up behind her. His dark sunglasses reflected the blistering sunlight, but the tension in his jaw revealed his unease.

Kim replied, "It's intentional. Who pays attention to a sketchy place like this?"

Inside, the office reeked of stale coffee and cheap air freshener. A fan whirred in the corner, struggling against the desert heat and losing the battle.

The clerk had a face like a dried-up riverbed. Wrinkled, cracked, and disinterested. She barely looked up from her paperback.

"Let me guess, can't find your key drop?" The woman's voice was hoarse, impatient, and used to dealing with tourists too cheap to spring for the pricier airport rentals.

Kim flipped her badge open just long enough to make her point but not so long that the woman could read the details. "We need to talk about a black SUV rented from here."

The clerk's eyes darted to the closed badge wallet and then to Kim's face. Something flickered there. Recognition? Suspicion? Hard to tell.

Her demeanor shifted, more guarded now. "Lots of SUVs come through here."

Smithers leaned in closer, and his shadow swallowed the counter. Whether he exploited it or not, his overwhelming presence had a way of making people talk. "The one we're interested in had bulletproof glass, special tread tires. You know the type. Not exactly standard in a place where no credit cards are no problem."

The clerk swallowed hard. "Yeah, well, maybe I remember something like that. What's it to you?"

"The SUV is now a federal crime scene." Kim pushed forward. "There's nothing legally confidential about your rental agreement. Hand it over and let us do our jobs. Or we can come back with a warrant. Your choice."

The clerk's lips pressed thin. Her fingers tapped the counter nervously. Kim waited, unflinching, as if she had infinite patience and unlimited time.

Finally the woman muttered a curse, ducked under the counter, and emerged a moment later with a battered file folder. Lack of humidity had made the edges curl.

"This the one you're looking for?" She slapped the folder down, as though that might make the act of handing it over somehow less incriminating.

Kim opened the folder, scanning the individual pages to spot inconsistencies. The contract was paper-thin with very few details. A generic corporate name, prepaid card, and almost illegible signature. *Horace Wiley*.

Smithers peered over Kim's shoulder to read. "Every heard of this guy?"

"Horace Wiley," Kim repeated. The name wasn't ringing any immediate bells, but it had to mean something. In her experience, almost nothing was random. "Did he leave anything behind?"

"Whatever he left, it's not here, I swear." The clerk raised her hands defensively. "We clean out the cars after every return. Just junk usually. Fast food wrappers, empty water bottles, crap like that."

"He say anything strange? Act nervous? Pay extra attention to what he was driving or where he was going?"

"Not nervous, exactly." The woman shifted uncomfortably. "But he was cold. You know, the type that doesn't smile or chit-chat. Just handed the money over, signed the paperwork, and left. I didn't ask questions. Didn't want to."

Kim exchanged a glance with Smithers. They'd get no more out of her, but that didn't mean the lead was a dead end.

"Let us know if he comes back," Kim said, snapping the folder shut. She handed over her card. The woman took it reluctantly, her eyes flickering between them before she slid the card under the counter.

"What about the other guy?" the clerk asked as she examined Kim's card.

Kim raised her eyebrows. "What other guy?"

The clerk shrugged. "Didn't say much. But he gave off a creepy vibe."

"How so?" Smithers pressed her.

She shrugged again. "Quiet. Menacing. Felt like he was waiting for an excuse."

"To do what?" Kim asked.

"Dunno. Start trouble or rob the place or something." The phone rang and she jumped on it like a drowning woman grabbing a life ring.

Back outside, Kim shoved sunglasses onto her face and opened the file again, reviewing the details. While most of it felt like a dead end, one thing stood out. The vehicle's GPS.

"This SUV had tracking enabled by a company we know," she said. "The service is required to cooperate with law enforcement."

Smithers leaned against the car, wiping sweat from his neck. "Did we just catch our break?"

"We don't have time to assume otherwise," Kim said. She grabbed her phone and dialed the special number for the GPS service security office. "If the tracker is still active, we might figure out where Wiley went."

Smithers crossed his arms, scanning the lot like trouble might step out from behind one of the rusted sedans. "You think he's working alone with a small crew?"

Kim shook her head, the phone ringing in her ear. "Not likely. Guy rents a fortified vehicle under what's likely to be a fake identity and disappears into the desert? No. He was either planning something or already in the middle of it when he rented the SUV."

Before Smithers could respond, someone picked up Kim's call.

"GeoTrack Solutions, how can I assist you today?" a courteous yet disinterested voice said.

"FBI Special Agent Kim Otto," she said smoothly and offered her security access number.

"Certainly. What do you need?"

"Real-time location data for a vehicle linked to a federal investigation," Kim replied. "Black SUV." She read the Arizona license plate number.

"Please hold while I pull up authorization for your request."

Kim clenched her jaw as the tinny hold music kicked in. She hated waiting for anything, much less bureaucracy. Smithers kicked at a loose piece of asphalt, sharp and impatient.

The operator came back on the line.

"Ma'am, I show that the vehicle's GPS remains enabled. Last ping was two hours ago." There was a pause as the sound of typing filled the silence. "Location was just outside of Black Canyon City. Want me to send you the coordinates?"

"Text them to this number." Kim rattled off her cell number. "And mark this vehicle for priority tracking. If it moves again, I need to know immediately."

The reply was brisk. "Coordinates sent. Anything else?"

"Not at this time." Kim ended the call while checking for the notification.

The coordinates blinked onto her screen. A spot in the middle of nowhere, surrounded by nothing but desert.

Smithers tilted his head, studying the phone over her shoulder. "Black Canyon City. Not much out there besides rocks and rattlesnakes."

"You know the area?"

"Some. Desert's always been a good place to get rid of things," Smithers said grimly. "Which could mean Wiley never intended to leave anything behind."

Kim frowned, juggling possibilities as she stepped back into the rental sedan. "Either he dumped something, picked something up, or both. But if he wanted to vanish, why keep the tracker enabled? It doesn't add up."

Smithers slid into the passenger seat, pulling the door shut with deliberate force. "Unless he wanted someone to follow him. Could be bait."

"Could be sloppy," Kim countered, as Smithers turned the ignition. The engine rumbled to life. "Either way, we'll find out soon enough."

CHAPTER 11

Friday, July 8
Phoenix, Arizona

THE DRIVE OUT OF Phoenix was suffocatingly hot, the AC struggling against the sun's unrelenting barrage. Kim preferred silence when she was thinking, but Smithers didn't seem to care.

"You ever stop and think how we're balancing two investigations that might be connected but are technically worlds apart?" His voice was casual, but his question wasn't.

"Are you saying we're stretched too thin, Agent Smithers?" She kept her tone neutral.

"No, I'm saying maybe we're being pulled in a direction someone wants us to go." He gestured vaguely out the window.

Kim replied, "Someone wants us moving, no doubt about it. But the question is toward or away from what?"

The road ahead began to curve, stretching mean and lonely into the horizon. The landscape was unforgiving, the type of place where secrets never stayed buried, though plenty had tried. Kim stared ahead, her fingers drumming against her thigh.

"Wiley was very careful," she said finally. "The fake ID, the vehicle upgrades, the choice of this place. There's a plan in the chaos."

Smithers looked skeptical but didn't argue.

As they approached the coordinates, the desert flattened into an eerie expanse of cracked earth and skeletal shrubs, void of any visible landmarks. The GPS chirped its mechanical voice, announcing their arrival, though there was nothing but oppressive heat waves rippling off the ground. Smithers slowed the car to a crawl, eyes sharp, scanning the perimeter.

"Two hours ago," Smithers muttered, leaning forward. "Whatever he dropped off or picked up might already be gone."

"Or it might not." Kim pointed and he steered off the dirt road, tires crunching over brittle rocks until the vehicle came to a stop. Smithers killed the engine, the sudden silence heavy with the weight of the desert's emptiness.

The two agents got out and Kim squinted into the distance. The horizon shimmered like a mirage.

Smithers unlocked the trunk and retrieved a pair of binoculars. Scanning the area, he muttered, "No structures. No vehicles. No sign this spot matters to anyone."

But Kim's gut told her otherwise. She crouched, running her hand over the ground and rubbing the sandy residue between her fingers. It had been freshly disturbed.

"Look closer," she said, her voice low, contained, pointing at faint, overlapping impressions in the dirt. "See these tracks? The SUV didn't stick around. But someone else came later."

Smithers crouched beside her, examining the disturbed earth. "Tire treads. At least two vehicles. Heavy, like off-roaders."

"And they weren't stopping here for sightseeing." Kim rose, brushing the dust from her hands and reaching for the pistol at her side. Her keen sense of danger whispered that they were already being watched. "Let's fan out. Check for anything buried or left behind. Look for disturbances in the terrain."

Smithers nodded, moving off to the left and sweeping the area in tight, deliberate arcs. Kim moved to the right, her hand still resting lightly on the gun as she scanned for anything that didn't belong.

Every muscle in her body was taut, ready to spring at the first sign of trouble.

After a few minutes, Smithers's voice carried across the empty plain. "Over here."

Kim turned quickly. The soles of her boots kicked up fine dust as she approached Smithers, who was crouched near what looked like freshly disturbed dirt.

He had already pulled on a pair of gloves and was using a folding pocket knife to scrape away at the dry earth.

Kim dropped to one knee beside him, studying the patterns on the ground. Someone had deliberately covered something up.

"Looks like a shallow grave," Smithers muttered, his voice even but laced with caution. "But not for a body. Too small."

Kim didn't need him to clarify. Even experienced operatives made mistakes when hiding evidence.

The disturbed soil was compacted down, but not enough to blend perfectly. She gloved up and used her hands to clear away the loose dirt. Heat burned through the thin latex, but she ignored it, focused on the task at hand.

After a few painstaking minutes, something began to take shape beneath the dust. She found an object wrapped tightly in dark burlap. Smithers gently yanked it free, his motions slow and deliberate, like the whole thing might detonate if handled too roughly.

Kim instinctively widened her stance and shifted her weight, weapon in hand now as her eyes scanned the horizon for any sign of movement.

Smithers laid the bundle out on the ground, unraveling the fabric.

Inside was a metallic box, no bigger than a shoebox, with no discernible markings except a small, carved emblem Kim had seen before.

"Lone Wolf Security," Smithers murmured, frowning. He looked at Kim and tightened his grip on the box like he'd found unstable uranium, and he didn't want to drop it. "It's them."

Kim felt her pulse quicken. Lone Wolf Security was infamous. A private contractor group often linked to shadowy deals and deniable operations that skirted both national and international laws.

She'd never faced Lone Wolf before, but she'd heard plenty about the outfit, none of it good.

Her thoughts snapped back to the black SUV, the most likely fake credentials, and some guy named Wiley. Lone Wolf probably didn't leave anything to chance, but by the looks of it, this box wasn't meant to be found.

"Open it," Kim said, still wary.

Smithers hesitated. "Could be booby-trapped. These guys don't mess around."

"Which is why we're careful," Kim countered, already unclipping her small field toolkit from her belt.

She holstered her weapon and knelt beside the box. Kept her hands steady as she examined the latch. It was a basic mechanism. No visible wires or signs of tampering. Which didn't mean it was safe.

She ran through possibilities. Motion triggers, pressure plates, chemical reactions. "It's not buried deep enough for a long-term stay. Someone expected to come back for this."

"Meaning?" Smithers prompted, his voice low.

"Meaning we're either early, or we've just upset his timetable." Kim didn't like either option.

She pulled a slim probe from her kit, running it carefully around the edges of the latch. Tiny scratches near the seam caught her attention. Faint, but noticeable if you knew what to look for. Someone had opened the latch recently.

"Give me your phone." Kim held out her hand without looking up.

Smithers passed it over. "What are you thinking?"

"First, I'm recording this for evidence. Second, if it blows, you'll want this footage."

"You're such an optimist," Smithers said dryly, stepping back a few paces.

Kim tilted the phone's camera toward the box, her hands steady as she angled it to capture the emblem and the surrounding terrain. If something went wrong here, higher-ups would need as much context as possible.

With the camera recording, she turned her attention back to the box. "Latch first. Slow and steady."

The metal was hot to the touch, the smell of baked dust intensifying as she eased the latch upward millimeter by millimeter. Each click felt amplified by the desert's oppressive quiet. Sweat trickled down her temple, but she ignored it.

With a faint click the latch gave way.

Smithers tensed visibly with his body angled like he was ready to dive for cover.

Kim waited for the subtle hiss of gas, a mechanical whir, or the snap of a spring. But nothing happened.

She exhaled slowly and lifted the lid, revealing the contents inside.

CHAPTER 12

Friday, July 8
Black Canyon City, Arizona

STILL CROUCHING, KIM CALLED to her partner.

Smithers crossed the gap quickly, his shadow falling over the box.

Inside, neatly arranged in foam padding, were two items.

A slim, sealed envelope.

And a stack of high-capacity memory drives.

"Not what I was expecting," Smithers admitted, his forehead creased as he eyed the contents.

Kim reached for the envelope first, with cautious but deliberate gloved fingers.

The envelope was devoid of markings except for a faint indent where the Lone Wolf Security emblem had been embossed in the corner. Slowly, she pried it open, revealing a single sheet of folded copy paper.

The handwriting was clean, bold, and to the point.

Phoenix drop successful. Coordinates attached secure payload. Wiley relocated south.

Beneath that, a second set of coordinates.

"Wiley's already on the move," Kim felt her stomach knot as she handed the paper to Smithers. "And 'remain stationary'? Sounds like someone else is supposed to still be here."

Smithers scanned the note and nodded grimly. "Or watching right now from a remote location."

Her eyes flicked back to the barren vista surrounding them. It was too quiet, too still. As if the landscape itself was holding its breath. Every instinct screamed that enemy eyes were on them.

And then there was the second coordinate set. Another breadcrumb leading them where, exactly?

Kim nodded toward the box. Smithers returned the note and she closed everything securely inside. "Whatever's on these drives might tell us who Wiley is, who he's meeting, and what they're trading."

For all Kim knew, they could be loaded with volatile encryption or even self-wiping mechanisms.

Lone Wolf no doubt had access to technology like that. It made the stakes higher and the answers even further out of reach.

"Chain of custody stays tight on this," she said. "Until we have a better idea what we're dealing with."

They stood up at the same time, hyper-aware of the exposed position they found themselves in. The outcroppings of distant rocks and hills could hide a sniper or an army.

Then a faint hum reached Kim's ears.

She stiffened, tilting her head toward the sound. Smithers caught the movement and froze too, his hand drifting toward his sidearm.

"Drone?" he asked quietly, his voice nearly swallowed by the surrounding heat haze.

Kim squinted against the glare of the sun. The hum was faint but growing. Rapid, mechanical, and definitely getting closer.

Her gut twisted. Lone Wolf wouldn't leave loose threads. Odds were, Wiley wasn't acting alone.

"If it's a drone, it's not here to deliver mail," she muttered, slamming the metal box shut and cradling it under her arm. "We're leaving. Now."

Smithers didn't need to be asked twice. He pivoted back toward the sedan, breaking into a light jog but keeping low, his gaze shifting restlessly from the horizon to the open sky. Kim was right behind him, her weapon drawn now, the box still secure under her arm.

The hum grew louder, sharper. It wasn't a drone. At least, not the small, commercial kind. It sounded bigger. Heavier.

"Vehicle," Smithers rasped, confirming her thoughts. His gaze hadn't stopped scanning the horizon.

Kim skidded to a stop and turned. Dust rose in the distance. A broad plume from the direction they'd come. The road ahead remained clear, but the one behind them was no longer deserted. Her breath quickened as she calculated their odds.

"Single vehicle," Smithers noted, squinting into the binoculars he'd swung back up. "Pickup truck. Fast. Could be locals."

"Could be Lone Wolf back to solve their problems," Kim countered, her tone sharp. She moved quickly now, making decisions based not on what if, but on what next. "If they're hostile, we can't risk a confrontation in the open. We need terrain and cover."

Smithers nodded, discarding any counterarguments, and matched Kim's pace to the sedan.

They jumped in and the engine rumbled to life under Smithers's steady hand. He reversed fast, whipping the wheel to angle them off-road, toward a shallow rise to the west. A winding canyon stretched out just beyond it. Not much protection, but it would have to do.

The dust plume grew closer. The sound of the truck's engine was distinctly low and guttural. Unrelenting. Lone Wolf operatives were professionals, not amateurs. For all Kim knew, the box in her hand was bait as well as evidence.

"Hold on," Smithers said, slamming the pedal down.

The SUV wasn't built for off-roading, but it leapt forward with a reluctant groan, kicking up dust and gravel as it veered toward the canyon. The ride was jarring, every bump and dip an assault on the suspension. No choice. Staying in the open was suicide.

Smithers kept twisting in his seat, eyes locked on the truck gaining ground behind them. "Whoever they are, they're not here to talk."

Kim bit back a retort as Smithers focused on navigating the uneven terrain.

Adrenaline surged through her as the canyon walls grew nearer, offering at least some hope of breaking their pursuers' sightline. But hope wouldn't be enough if that truck carried more than just manpower.

Smithers suddenly snapped his pistol free from its holster. "Rifle barrel on the passenger side. They're armed."

"Of course they're armed," Kim muttered, her knuckles white on the arm rest. Ahead, they were almost at the canyon. If they could make it inside, they'd have a chance.

But if the truck closed the distance first, it wouldn't matter.

The rising dust cloud ahead made visibility poor. An ambush could easily unfold.

Kim gritted her teeth, glancing at the GPS still mounted to the dash. The second set of coordinates sent a prickle of unease down her spine.

"You see any other vehicles tailing us?" she asked, swiveling to look back.

Smithers shook his head. "Just the one. But Lone Wolf doesn't usually operate in singles, does it?"

Which meant Lone Wolf had backup coming. Hell, reinforcements might already be here.

The SUV lurched violently as Smithers braked hard at the edge of the canyon. The drop was steep enough to make him hesitate.

Kim was already out, moving fast to assess the slope as the truck came into full view behind them. A black Ford F-350, grille gleaming with menace through the dust streaks marking its hood.

"We can't outgun that," Kim called over the roar of the pursuing engine. "Best chance is making them think we're ghosts."

Smithers killed the engine. The sudden silence was jarring in the chaos. "You mean vanish without a trace?"

"Got a better idea?" Smithers shot her a look, one hand gripping his weapon tightly as he scanned their surroundings. "Because we're fresh out of welcoming committees, and running uphill isn't exactly part of my workout routine."

Kim didn't respond. Instead, she hoisted the memory drives. Her sharp gaze darted to the canyon wall ahead, already mapping escape routes.

Running blindly wasn't an option. Against a truck like that with Lone Wolf likely calling the shots. They had to be smart. Tactical.

"Into the canyon," she ordered, her voice steady but urgent. "If we hug the shadow side, we can lose visual contact long enough to—"

Her voice cut off as the unmistakable crack of a rifle shot split the air, followed immediately by the sharp ping of a bullet ricocheting off the hood of the sedan.

"Go!" she barked, diving low and sprinting for cover.

Smithers followed without hesitation, boots kicking up a storm of dust.

CHAPTER 13

Friday, July 8
Black Canyon City, Arizona

THE CRUNCHING ROAR OF the truck's tires was closer now, pursuit tightening around them like a noose. Kim slid in behind a jagged boulder, chest heaving. She motioned sharply for Smithers to take position to her left.

"They've got the high ground," he shouted through the din, hunkering down and glancing toward the canyon opening. "If they post up there, we're sitting ducks."

Kim risked a glance back. The truck skidded to a stop about fifty yards out, sending a plume of desert dust spiraling upward.

Two men spilled out of the vehicle, both armed. The glint of a rifle's scope caught the sunlight. She ducked instinctively.

"They're not moving in yet," she said, pressing her back against the rock. "They're sizing us up. Cowards."

"They're stalling," Smithers corrected. "Waiting for reinforcements. S.O.P. for Lone Wolf type organizations. Suppress, surveil, and smother."

"Not today," Kim snapped, pulling her weapon close. "We cover ground until we lose them in the terrain. It's too hot to circle back to our SUV. Keep sharp. Operatives get sloppy when they think their targets are desperate."

Smithers nodded grimly, adjusting his grip on the Glock. "So what are we working with here, Agent Otto? Boulders and bad odds?"

"Bad odds," Kim confirmed, her voice cold as steel. "But that's their problem, not ours."

The two agents moved quickly, low and quiet, slipping deeper into the canyon's jagged shadows. The oppressive heat was a constant reminder of the Arizona desert's unforgiving nature. Kim had no time to think about that. Her focus was on the sound of boots crunching gravel. Too far back to see yet, but closing in.

The mercenaries weren't subtle, and they weren't in a rush. Confident, then. Mistake number one.

Kim gestured silently to Smithers, directing him toward an outcropping of rocks to the right. He nodded and broke off, surprisingly nimble as he moved.

Kim perched herself behind the base of a jagged boulder that jutted out like a knife from the canyon's wall. The rough surface pressed against her back as she crouched.

Situational awareness was everything now, and every sound was amplified. The scuff of boots, the hum of desert animals, the faint rattle of her own breathing.

She tightened her grip on the pistol. Timing was critical.

A voice carried through the haze of heat and dust, low but distinct. Male. Texan drawl. "You sure it's them? Or are we chasin' ghosts?"

Another voice responded, calmer, tinged with an unmistakable cruelty that Kim instinctively marked as the leader. "It's them. And they've already got the payload. Boss wants 'em brought in. Clean."

Kim's stomach twisted. She whispered in a harsh, low tone. "Smithers, you catch that?"

Another gunshot rang out, louder this time. The sound bounced off the canyon walls in sharp, disorienting echoes.

A chunk of the boulder near her head exploded into shards of dust and rock. Lone Wolf, if that's who they were, was probing now, trying to flush them out. It was classic predator behavior. Corner the prey, force them into the open, and strike with intent to kill.

Smithers's voice again, low and tense. "Two shooters confirmed. One on foot, circling left. Other's staying back, covering with the rifle. I don't see a clear route out."

Kim gritted her teeth. They were pinned, no doubt about it, but pinned didn't mean defeated.

"We don't need a clear path," she murmured, scanning the terrain in front of her. The canyon snaked off to the right, but it narrowed sharply before opening up again. It was a risk, but the tight gap could be their only advantage.

"They're too comfortable." Her tone was sharp with urgency. "The rifle's a crutch. They think they've locked us down. Let's make them adjust."

"Got it. Flanking?"

"Not yet. I've got an idea. Cover me."

There was no hesitation in his reply. "Copy that."

Kim crouched lower, steadying herself with one hand on the rough surface of the boulder. She glanced down at the metallic box tucked against her side.

They wanted it, and bad, which meant it held more answers than Kim was willing to lose.

But right now, it was also a distraction. A shiny lure to dangle in front of the operatives.

Decision made, Kim switched the box to her left hand. Her breath came steady as she counted down silently in her head.

Three… two… one.

She darted from cover, keeping her profile low, and dashed toward the narrow stretch of canyon ahead.

The instant she moved, the crack of a rifle round reached her ears again, followed by a puff of dust just behind her feet.

She threw herself left, sliding behind another outcropping, her gun already raised and sweeping for targets.

"Movement left!" one of the mercenaries shouted. The Texan voice. "She's on the run!"

Perfect. Let them think that.

CHAPTER 14

Friday, July 8
Black Canyon City, Arizona

ANOTHER RIFLE SHOT SLAMMED into rock mere inches above Kim's position, spraying stone chips over her head and powdering her face with dirt. The tangy metallic taste in the back of her throat intensified her determination.

The rifleman was methodical, his pacing controlled, each shot calculated to box her into smaller and smaller hiding places. But he wasn't hunting.

He wasn't looking to kill. Not immediately. If he were, she'd be dead. He was that good.

A long game, then.

She listened carefully and timed her motion with the distractingly loud crunch of a tumbling rock dislodged by the Texan's heavy boots echoing somewhere to her left. Dust spun slowly in the dry air.

Kim whipped around to better cover under the shade of another rock cluster.

Hunched low now, Kim focused forward. The rifleman was the biggest threat.

"Steady," she whispered.

To her left, a gravelly scuffle echoed as if on cue. The Texan's heavy tread was deliberate. Slow, quiet, predatory steps closing in for the kill.

He was savoring what he believed to be inevitable.

The next sound Kim heard was deafening in the quiet canyon.

Smithers had fired off a controlled shot. "Got him."

The Texan's reaction was immediate. A sharp yelp cut off mid-syllable as his body crumpled onto loose gravel just feet from where Kim had been crouching.

She nodded approval of Smithers's timing but didn't waste a second to revel in it. The rifleman had doubtlessly heard the takedown. He was an operative. He'd adapt his strategy quickly.

A moment later, as expected, the rifle fire stopped.

The absence of gunfire was almost louder than the shots themselves. Kim stayed pressed against the rock, body low, her gun steady in her hands.

The rhythmic click of the rifleman adjusting position echoed faintly in the canyon. Boots shifting loose gravel sounded loud in the silence.

He was clever, she'd give him that much. But clever would never be enough.

Standard military and law enforcement tactics. Which meant Kim had learned and lived them, too.

Smithers said, "Rifleman's repositioning. Looks like he's falling back. Not sure if it's a retreat or regroup."

"Neither," Kim muttered, her pulse steady. "He's stalling. Reinforcements are coming. We can't give them a chance to regroup. Follow my lead."

She edged around the boulder, angling her body for maximum cover as she scanned the shadows up ahead. The rifleman was pulling back toward a more defensible perch. The gamble suggested he wasn't certain of the numbers.

His uncertainty presented her with a chance.

With catlike silence, Kim edged along the canyon wall, balancing the general weight of the metallic box tucked at her side.

She had studied the canyon's twists and breaks. The rifleman's position would force him toward a narrow bottleneck for elevation and a clear sight line.

She would get there first.

Kim motioned silently to Smithers to sweep left, clear as he went.

Smithers nodded in acknowledgment and moved. For a man his size, it was uncanny how he melted into the environment.

Kim's respect for Smithers's fieldwork remained constant. His precision made her feel like every risk they took was grounded in tactical precision, not blind guesses. Even when the feeling was unfounded.

She moved swiftly now, hugging the shadowed edge of the canyon until she saw the narrow pass ahead. The rifleman would be setting up just beyond that choke point if her analysis was correct.

Operatives played the terrain like a chessboard. But Kim thrived in chaos where the rules were unfixed.

The metallic box pressed against her ribs as she crouched. She leaned her back against the canyon wall just outside the bottleneck.

From here, she could hear him. The faint shuffle of boots on gravel. A metallic scrape as the bolt action on his rifle chambered another round.

His moves were careful, deliberate. They defined him as a soldier.

Before he had a chance to settle into position, Kim darted into the bottleneck, weapon raised.

The rifleman had no time to react before she fired.

One, two, three controlled shots aimed center-mass.

His body jerked back when two bullets landed. The third ricocheted off the rock behind him.

He dropped his rifle as his legs gave out and he fell hard against the wall of the canyon.

She advanced quickly, pistol still trained on him as he bled against the rock. His breathing was labored, but he glared at her with icy defiance.

"Who's pulling your strings?" Kim demanded, her voice cutting through the tense silence.

He didn't answer. His jaw clenched like he was weighing whether to respond or die silent.

Kim had seen the type before. The kind who lived in the service and never spoke unless they believed they had leverage.

She pushed the pistol closer, expression flat.

The man spat blood, a defiant smile curling his lips. "You think taking me down changes anything? You're already in it. Deeper than you know."

"Let me guess," Kim replied evenly. "You're untouchable, right? That the message? Because from where I'm standing, you're as vulnerable as anyone else spilling blood in this canyon."

His laugh gurgled, faint but derisive. "Not vulnerable. Replaceable. Whatever you think you've got," his gaze flicked briefly to the metallic box at her side. "It's not worth the trouble coming your way."

Kim noted the flicker of panic he couldn't quite mask. It was subtle, buried under layers of bravado, but it was there.

He had been trained to face death without flinching, but the knowledge that he'd failed his mission gnawed at him.

"You're right," she said coldly as she leaned in. "You are replaceable. But the intel in this box? If Lone Wolf doesn't want me to have it, they'll send better replacements than you."

His smirk faltered, just for a second. As if he hadn't expected her to know about Lone Wolf. But he didn't deny it.

Smithers emerged from the shadows behind her. "What's the play, Otto? Reinforcements are five minutes out, at most. We can't sit here playing twenty questions."

Kim straightened, stepping back from the downed mercenary but not lowering her weapon. She watched as his breathing grew shallower, his life draining with every drop of blood soaking into the dry canyon floor.

Whatever answers he might have had wouldn't be coming.

"Leave him," she said, her voice flat. "He's done."

The rifleman's smile faltered for real this time. There was betrayal in his eyes. Maybe not directed at her, but at whatever cause he'd given his life to. In his final moments, the realization must have crawled up his throat that his employer didn't care one ounce about him.

Smithers didn't hesitate. He swiped the rifle off the ground, checked the chamber, and slung it over his shoulder. "What about the box?"

"We keep moving," Kim said, holding the box tighter as she stepped over the mercenary's body.

Behind them, the faint echo of more engines carried on the wind. Reinforcements were closing in. Kim didn't plan to be there when they arrived.

CHAPTER 15

Friday, July 8
Black Canyon City, Arizona

KIM AND SMITHERS RETREATED deeper into the canyon, moving quickly. The terrain grew rougher as the canyon narrowed and twisted until the sunlight barely filtered through. The engines faded for a moment, muted by the bends in the rock, but Kim didn't relax.

Lone Wolf's reinforcements were professionals. While the twisting canyon offered cover, she was well aware that they were funneling themselves into the perfect trap.

Her gaze darted to Smithers, whose steady, deliberate movements mirrored her own urgency. Against the odds, she could feel adrenaline sharpening her instincts.

"We won't shake them," Smithers grunted between breaths, crunching over loose gravel. He glanced back once before focusing ahead. "And if they're smart, they'll split up and box us in."

"They won't risk spreading themselves thin until they visually confirm us," Kim said, shifting the weight of the metallic box under her arm. "Their lead vehicle is running blind. When they realize they've lost sight, they'll regroup. That gives us a couple of minutes."

"Minutes to do what? Stage a two-person ambush?"

"To disappear." Kim's gaze flickered up toward the ridges of the canyon. The jagged walls cast heavy shadows, the kind perfect for concealing movement. She stopped abruptly, raising a hand to signal Smithers to halt.

"We're climbing." Kim was already scanning for the clearest route.

Smithers followed her line of sight, then cursed under his breath. "You've got to be kidding me. In this heat?"

"Think of it as cardio," Kim quipped, though not even a flicker of a smile touched her lips. "We need to get out of the canyon before they catch sight of us again and lock down our position."

Smithers didn't argue further. He adjusted his grip on the slung rifle and followed her toward a rough incline of jagged rocks jutting out from the canyon wall like makeshift steps.

Kim led the way as her boots sought narrow footholds. The heat was relentless, each breath searing her lungs, but every step higher gave them an edge.

Halfway up, Smithers paused to glance back. "They'll see the dust trail from the vehicle soon. You really think they'll lose interest if we're out of sight?"

"They're predictable," Kim responded without looking back, her voice calm despite the burn in her muscles. "These guys are trained to secure objectives, not chase ghosts. If we vanish, they'll revert to fallback tactics and sweep the area instead of pushing blindly into potential traps."

"So you're betting they value their own skins more than they value finding us," Smithers finished as he hauled himself up after her.

"Exactly," Kim said, reaching for the next handhold. Her grip was firm despite the sweat slicking her gloves. "Lone Wolf churns through operatives, but their protocols are well known. They don't overextend unless the mission's critical."

"And that box?" Smithers glanced at the metal case. "Critical or not? We could leave it here, since they're coming fast for it. They might stop once they retrieve it."

Kim didn't answer immediately. She reached a small outcrop and crouched, scanning the approach below.

The dusty trail created by pursuing vehicles was unmistakable, kicking up dirt like a beacon against the canyon floor. Had to be at least two more trucks, and they weren't holding back.

"They want it bad enough to scare off anyone else poking around." Kim's gaze narrowed, tracking the patterns. "But not bad enough to lose half their team in the process. This box, and whatever is in it, is a distraction. Not Lone Wolf's endgame."

"Assuming this is a Lone Wolf operation, which is just a guess at this point," Smithers pulled himself up beside her, breathing heavily but controlled. "A distraction for what?"

"That's what we need to find out," Kim said, crouching low and pointing toward the ridge ahead. "If we crest that ridge, we'll double back. The terrain's rough enough to buy us breathing room, but only if we move now."

Smithers set his jaw, nodded, and fell in behind her as they pressed on.

The canyon's harsh ridges tore at their gloves and boots. Relentless heat blistered the exposed skin of their necks.

Kim didn't slow down. If they could shake their tail, they could focus on what had drawn Wiley south, and what connection it had to Reacher.

Fifteen agonizing minutes later, they crested the ridge. Kim dropped to her stomach, breathing hard but keeping her profile low against the jagged rocks.

She edged slightly forward and scanned through the binoculars. The canyon below was eerily silent, but the plume of dust from the trucks had stopped. Parked vehicles now sat still as ants against the rocky expanse.

Smithers crawled up beside her. The rifle slung across his back shifted slightly as he looked through the binoculars.

"They're regrouping," he murmured, eyes narrowing. "Looks like they've realized we're not where they thought we'd be."

The operatives had dismounted and were moving around their vehicles. Some of them were scanning the nearby terrain, rifles sweeping across rocky crevices. Others were conferring in tight clusters. No frantic movements. No signs of panic. These weren't men who spooked easily.

"They'll split up soon," Kim said, voice low. "A small team will scout ahead while the rest form a perimeter. They're cautious, but the clock's ticking. Reinforcements or not, they only have so much time before pushing further gets too risky."

Smithers adjusted the focus on his binoculars. "So what's the move? Keep running?"

"No," Kim said firmly. "We've bought some space. Now we figure out what they're protecting."

She unhooked the metallic box from under her arm and laid it on the ground between them. The Lone Wolf Security symbol etched into its surface was unmistakable. A snarling wolf's head encased in a shield.

Lone Wolf didn't take small jobs. The contents of the drives inside the box had to be big enough to warrant the risk of operatives hunting them down across the Arizona desert.

Kim glanced sideways at Smithers. "Let's find a place to examine the contents of those drives."

"And maybe grab a cold water somewhere?" Smithers countered as if his throat were parched. Which it probably was.

"They'll eventually catch us if we hang around here too long," Kim admitted. "Or worse, we'll lead them straight to wherever this path intersects with Reacher's."

"You think they're hunting Reacher?" Smithers asked.

She pressed her gloved fingers against her temple, pushing back against the exhaustion clawing at her concentration. Every decision felt like a tightrope walk. One misstep and she'd fall to her death.

CHAPTER 16

Friday, July 8
Phoenix, Arizona

KIM AND SMITHERS REACHED the outskirts of another nowhere town, the kind with a single gas station, a liquor store, and a handful of dusty motels that all looked the same. Smithers rolled the SUV into the parking lot of the least conspicuous option. No cameras, no nosy front desk clerk, a cash-only policy and a blinking neon vacancy sign that buzzed in the silence.

Smithers killed the engine. Neither of them moved for a beat. The last few hours had been a nonstop sprint.

Kim pressed her fingers to her temple, pushing back the exhaustion clawing at the edges of her focus. "We need to see what's on the drives we found in that box."

Smithers exhaled, stretching his neck. "And figure out who the hell Wiley is and how he's connected to all of this."

They grabbed the laptop and the metallic box that held the external drives and headed inside. The motel room smelled like stale cigarettes and bad decisions, but it had electricity to keep the air-conditioning humming. And privacy. Good enough.

Kim placed her laptop onto the scratched desk and opened it.

She glanced at Smithers. "Let's get to work."

Kim's fingers moved fast as she booted up the secure network. The motel was the kind of place no one looked twice at. Faded curtains, a flickering neon vacancy sign, and a vending machine with nothing but expired candy bars.

But the motel sat in the open where Kim had clear access to satellites and right now, that was all they needed.

Smithers locked the door, double-checking the latch before pulling the curtains together using the plastic handle attached to the curtain rod. He dropped the box onto the desk beside her laptop, then turned his attention to the old photographs they had recovered.

"You really think this is gonna work?" he asked.

Kim didn't answer. She used her secure hot spot to launch the facial recognition software linked to government databases.

It was a long shot, but government databases were extensive these days due to the proliferation of social media and decades of digitized headshots, capturing crowds, and the ever-burgeoning government employment sectors.

There were hordes of government workers who did nothing but stare at screens and manipulate data.

Smithers flipped through the photos, stopping on one that had drawn Kim's attention earlier. Black-and-white, slightly grainy. A group of men standing together, all in military fatigues, expressions blank but alert.

"How about we start with this one?" One man near the center caught Kim's eye. Something about his posture and the way he carried himself suggested he was the man in charge.

She pulled the photo from Smithers's hand and positioned it under the portable scanner, watching as the software isolated each face, analyzing features, matching them against thousands of records.

The program ran its database for a while as the screen flashed rapidly through a sequence of possible matches before narrowing in on one. Finally, a name appeared at the top.

Bradley Hooper.

Kim sat back and clicked on the profile. She read the data aloud for Smithers's benefit. "Former US Army. Special Operations. Honorably discharged after thirteen years. Terminal at major. Last known employment, private military contractor. Current status unknown."

Smithers leaned in for a closer look at the headshot. "Hooper. You know him?"

Kim shook her head. "No. But Reacher might. The dates of his military service intersected with Reacher's."

"That was a years ago. Thousands of soldiers have passed through military service since then," Smithers frowned, crossing his arms. "Besides Hooper's a long way from active duty now."

Kim clicked through the file, scanning records, deployments, after-action reports. "He was in Hamburg at one point. That's a hell of a coincidence."

Smithers exhaled sharply. "Hamburg? When Reacher was there?"

"Looks that way, although there's not a lot of data on whatever they were doing at the time." Kim leaned forward to narrow the search. "If he was career military, there's got to be more intel on the guy somewhere."

A few keystrokes later, she hit an unexpected roadblock. After Hamburg, Hooper's files were redacted. Missing files, blacked out pages, and not enough pages for a paper-producing machine like the Army.

Smithers nodded. "Somebody scrubbed his records."

"Just like Reacher's Army files," Kim replied. "Which means he's been involved in something classified. Or something dirty. Either then or now."

"Both, most likely. Leopards don't change their spots." Smithers pointed to the screen. "Scroll down."

Hooper had left the Army but hadn't vanished. He'd re-emerged with a different employer.

German Intelligence.

Smithers let out a low whistle. "That's not nothing."

"No," Kim said. "It's not."

Smithers rubbed his jaw. "If Hooper's connected to Wiley, we need to find him before Lone Wolf, or whoever is running this operation, does."

Kim's gaze was locked on the screen. "Or before he finds us."

Outside, a truck rumbled past on the highway. Headlights flashed against the crack between the motel's curtains before disappearing into the night.

Kim didn't move. She didn't blink.

Smithers wandered outside and came back with two bottles of water. "Sorry. Best I could do if you wanted something without bugs in it."

She winced, swigged the water, and continued searching for another hour before she gave up and closed the laptop. She'd tried to open the encrypted drives and hit another wall.

"No luck?" Smithers asked.

Kim shook her head. "If Hooper's still active, even in the shadows, we'll need higher level help finding him."

Smithers raised both eyebrows. "Where do we start?"

Kim rummaged in her bag and pulled out a new burner phone. It was one of three she carried, each cycled out regularly, never preloaded. She'd memorized the contacts that mattered.

She sat cross-legged on the motel bed, back against the headboard, the phone balanced in her palm. She powered on, opened a secure messaging app buried behind layers of encryption, and typed a message.

The recipient was listed under a simple alias: Orion.

She kept it short. No names. No unnecessary details. Just enough.

Smithers paced near the door, arms crossed. Every few moments, he parted the curtains and scanned the parking lot like he expected trouble.

"You sure your guy's still good?" Smithers asked after a while.

"I gave him twelve minutes," she said as she hit send. Then she waited.

Smithers leaned against the desk with his arms crossed. "If he doesn't bite?"

"He will," Kim said.

Orion was one of the best data scrapers she'd ever worked with. He'd left the agency after a disagreement about oversight after he'd redacted too many files for too many people who wanted things buried.

Now, he worked privately, pulling data from places where official channels didn't.

Orion wouldn't answer an open-ended question. He wouldn't respond to guesswork. But if he had something? He'd say just enough to keep them both out of serious hot water.

Seconds stretched. The motel room was silent except for the occasional rumble of a truck outside.

The phone buzzed once.

Kim picked it up and read the message. "Hooper's not currently listed in the system. But someone asked the same questions two days ago."

"Yeah? Why?"

"Dunno." Kim shrugged. "Hooper's headed to Copley Square. German Embassy."

Smithers's jaw tightened. "Someone else is already looking for the guy?"

"Boston," she said scanning the message again as she requested transport.

Smithers stopped pacing. "What's happening there?"

The rest of Orion's text was cryptic. She read it aloud. "Hooper's an operator. Well connected. Dangerous. Watch your six."

"What the hell does that mean?" Smithers scowled. "And what does any of it have to do with our dead survivalist? Or Reacher?"

Kim shut off the phone and pocketed it. "Let's go find out."

Smithers grabbed his bag, holstered his weapon, and double-checked the locks on the door. Kim adjusted her jacket, slipping the burner into an inside pocket, and collected her stuff.

Five minutes later, they were on the road.

CHAPTER 17

Friday, July 8
Boston, Massachusetts

MARIAN SINCLAIR KILLED THE rental car's engine, settling into surveillance position across from Copley Place. Rain hammered the windshield, transforming the Boston streets into mirror-black rivers. Steam rose from nearby grates, swirling through the amber glow of streetlamps.

She watched the main entrance, noting how the German Consulate blended seamlessly into the upscale shopping complex. No fortifications. No obvious security presence. Just another corporate suite hiding behind glass and steel.

Frances Neagley drained the last of her coffee, the paper cup crackling in her grip. Her eyes never left the revolving doors, tracking each person who passed through. More than a decade of military experience had honed her ability to spot threats, analyze patterns, catalogue details.

Right now, her instincts screamed danger. Which was okay. Neagley didn't shrink from conflict. She reveled in it. Which was one reason Sinclair had chosen her.

"German Consulate General," Sinclair said, her voice low. "Suite 500." She drummed her fingers against the steering wheel, the rhythm matching the wipers' steady beat.

Neagley shifted in her seat, the leather creaking beneath her. "Access points?"

"Main entrance through the mall." Sinclair gestured toward the glass doors. "Central elevators lead to the Sky Lobby. Transfer there for the consulate floor."

Neagley nodded.

Sinclair's jaw tightened. "Standard office security awaits. Check-in desk. Badges. Metal detectors."

"Complications." Neagley's tone carried the weight of experience.

"Less than you'd think." Sinclair leaned forward, studying the building's flow. "Security concentrates inside. No external patrols. No roving guards."

They watched as people moved through the entrance. Business suits mixed with designer shopping bags. Not one person glanced toward the consulate directory.

Sinclair's phone cast blue light across her face as she pulled up encrypted files. "Tomorrow night is the reception. German officials hosting American defense contractors. Intelligence officers mingling with champagne glasses."

"Higher stakes," Neagley said. "More variables."

"More cover." Sinclair's lips curved. "We disappear in the crowd."

"Maybe. Before you got fired," Neagley replied. "But not now. Anyone recognizes you, our cover is blown."

The phone screen reflected in Sinclair's eyes as she scrolled. "We're not on the official guest list under our real names. Anybody asks, we're Kessler Protective Services. Small German firm, just establishing US presence. So they figure we've been vetted by Kessler, even if we haven't. Perfect cover."

"Credentials?" Neagley's question carried an edge.

"Waiting at check-in." Sinclair met her gaze. "Quality work. They'll scan clean."

Neagley didn't press. Some questions were better left unasked. Some facts were better unknown.

"Floor plans next." Sinclair's finger traced their route. "Reception fills the main space. You work the room, watch the guards, clock their patterns."

"While you?"

Sinclair zoomed into the blueprint's details. "Archives section. Restricted access, but nothing impossible. Card readers. Basic cameras. Not cutting edge security."

Rain drummed harder as Neagley studied the layout. "You've got a method?"

The small case in Sinclair's lap clicked open. Metal glinted inside. Precision tools for precision work. "What is it the tech nerds say? Move fast and break things."

"Yeah, well we're not sitting safely behind a keyboard shooting fake bullets at simulated evil dudes. We're facing the real thing." Lightning flashed, illuminating Neagley's face. "Fifteen minutes. That's your window. After that, I come in."

"Sweet of you." Sinclair's tone stayed light.

Thunder rolled as Neagley turned. "I don't joke about extraction."

Their eyes met. Agreement passed between them, forged through a deep understanding of shared risk.

"Copy that," Sinclair said.

The storm intensified, rain sheeting down the windows.

Tomorrow they'd walk those polished halls, badges displayed, playing their parts.

And somewhere in that building, locked away in the archives, they'd find Wiley's map. Again.

Lightning struck twice more, closer now. Neagley's hand moved to her concealed holster.

"Someone's watching us," she said.

Sinclair didn't turn her head. "Where?"

"Black SUV. Third spot down." Neagley's voice remained steady. "Driver's been there twenty minutes. Engine running."

Sinclair checked her side mirror. The SUV sat motionless, its windows tinted dark against the storm. Water cascaded down its surfaces, but no steam rose from the hood.

"Engine's not running," Sinclair said. "Hasn't been for hours."

Neagley watched a man emerge from the SUV's passenger side. Tall. Military bearing in his stride. Collar turned up against the rain.

Sinclair's hand slid toward the ignition. "We need to move."

"Wait." Neagley gripped her arm.

The man walked past their car without breaking stride, heading straight for Copley Place's entrance. As he passed under the streetlights, Sinclair caught the glint of a diplomatic pin on his lapel.

"German intelligence," Neagley said. "Had to be watching the consulate, not us."

"Possibly." Sinclair watched him disappear through the revolving doors.

"You want to abort?"

"No. But we need to know who he is." Sinclair pulled out her phone, fingers flying over the screen. She pulled up a database, encrypted and unofficial. As if she'd never met the man, she said, "Got him. Klaus Weber. BND officer, diplomatic cover."

"Which means he'll be at tomorrow's reception."

"Yes." Sinclair zoomed in on his credentials. "And he works in the archives section, among others."

Thunder cracked overhead. Neagley checked her watch. "Dawn in five hours. If we're still doing this, we need to prep."

Sinclair stared at Weber's photo, memorizing every detail. "The map's worth the risk."

"You sure about that?" Neagley's eyes narrowed.

"One thousand percent." Sinclair closed the file with the final word.

Sinclair's certainty hung in the air between them as another lightning bolt split the sky. Tomorrow night's reception would celebrate the new research partnerships. A perfect blend of academia, industry, and diplomacy that would fill the consulate with hundreds of mostly civilian guests.

"Guest list?" Neagley asked, keeping her eyes on the building.

"MIT professors, defense contractor executives, German military research leads." Sinclair scrolled through her phone. "They're announcing three new facilities. Aerospace testing in Bedford, materials research in Cambridge, and some kind of quantum computing lab they're keeping quiet about."

The rain intensified. Drums of water hammered the roof. Sinclair adjusted the rearview mirror, scanning the parking lot out of habit. The surveillance position had given them what they needed. A clear view of security patterns, entry points, and general flow of traffic through the building.

"Fifteen minutes," Neagley repeated her earlier warning. "That's all you get in the archives. Any longer raises risk beyond our comfort levels."

"I'll be quick." Sinclair patted the case of tools in her lap. "Card reader won't take more than two minutes to bypass. Another three to handle the cameras. That leaves ten to locate the map and extract."

A sharp tap on the passenger window made both women freeze. Through the rain-blurred glass, Sinclair saw a uniform and flashlight, police badge visible on his chest.

"Ladies," he said, his other hand moving toward his hip, "I'm going to need you to step out of the vehicle."

Sinclair felt Neagley tense beside her. In the mirror, she caught the slight shift of the officer's weight. He was preparing to draw his sidearm. Not a real cop. Not even close.

"Of course, Officer," Sinclair said, using her calmest voice. Her left hand crept toward the transmission while her right stayed visible on the steering wheel. "Just let me grab my—"

She gunned the engine.

At the same instant, Neagley's arm whipped up, smacking the flashlight away. The beam cartwheeled into the darkness as the man stumbled back. Rain pelted through the open window as Sinclair threw the car into drive.

The crack of a gunshot competed with thunder. The vehicle's rear window exploded inward, sending glass shards across the backseat. Sinclair swerved, tires fighting for grip on the wet pavement.

Another shot punched through the trunk.

"Police scanner," Neagley barked, pulling her own weapon. "Now!"

Sinclair thumbed the radio to life as she took a hard right, nearly hydroplaning. Static crackled, then cleared.

No reports of suspicious vehicles, no officers dispatched to Copley Place.

"Behind us," Neagley said sharply. "Black sedan, no lights."

Sinclair checked her mirrors. The sedan was gaining, suggesting a professional behind the wheel. "Who the hell are these guys?"

"Less talking, more driving." Neagley turned in her seat, tracking their pursuer through the rain-streaked back window. "And maybe consider canceling tomorrow night."

"No." Sinclair cut through an alley, scraping paint off their right side. "The reception's our only shot at the map. After that, security doubles to safeguard the research facility personnel after the announcements."

"And you know so much about all of this protocol because?" Neagley asked.

"I created the protocols and put them in place," Sinclair replied.

Neagley grunted. "Figures."

The sedan followed them into the alley. Sinclair heard the growl of its engine over the storm.

"You know what this means," Neagley's delivery was deadly calm. "Someone else has plans for that reception."

"Yeah." Sinclair's hands tightened on the wheel as they burst out of the alley onto a wider street. "Question is, who?"

The sedan's headlights suddenly flooded their vehicle with light. In the rearview mirror, Sinclair caught a glimpse of their pursuer for the first time.

A slight grin lifted her mouth at the corner.

Two agents she recognized. She took a sharp left at the next corner, squealing the wheels across the wet pavement.

"What the hell?" Neagley asked.

"Those guys are NSA. They'll know me if they get a good look."

"Yeah, so we'd better make sure that doesn't happen," Neagley snapped.

CHAPTER 18

Saturday, July 9
Boston, Massachusetts

KIM OTTO HAD SPENT every minute of the long flight from Phoenix working while Smithers slept. Kim wouldn't even consider sleeping on a plane. Her first priority was to stay alive, which required her full attention.

She didn't fear flying. She feared all of the other things. So many ways for the flight to go sideways. From initial manufacturing to maintenance, flight crew training, weather, and on and on. Too many possible screwups to list.

No matter how good they were, they couldn't be perfect all the time. Humans were fallible and made mistakes. Fighting that truth was as useless as hand-wrestling a tornado. No way to get a good grip on it, for starters.

Kim knew jetting around in a steel tube at warp speeds was a particularly foolhardy way to travel. No one could persuade her otherwise, even before jihadists began using passenger planes as missiles.

Yes, she knew all of the risks and simply did it anyway.

Because air travel was the only way she could do her job.

When there's only one choice, it's the right choice.

Was she brave? Or foolhardy?

The question was irrelevant. She didn't have time to indulge her healthy distrust of aeronautics today.

Her laptop screen glowed in the dim cabin light as she read quickly through a collection of reports and background files. She needed reliable facts, and there were precious few to be found in the materials she could access.

She glanced around the first-class cabin. Businessmen, a couple of college kids heading east, a woman reading a crime novel by Lee Child tapping her thumb against the hardcover.

Smithers opened one eye and checked his watch. "What's the play when we land?"

Kim didn't look up. "Straight to the hotel. Drop bags. Change."

Smithers nodded. "Then?"

"Hooper."

Smithers let out a breath and closed his eyes again.

Kim had dug up everything she could find on Bradley Hooper. Army, spent years in Germany, now a contractor floating between German intelligence and possibly the paramilitary group called Lone Wolf.

Inside the Lone Wolf operation, if he was connected, Hooper would be a mercenary who sold discretion and enforcement across borders. His history connected at various times with people in Reacher's orbit both inside the Army and out. At one point, he was attached to the 110th Special Investigators, the group Reacher started and led for a few years before he moved on.

Kim had called in a favor to confirm Hooper's whereabouts. He'd be attending tomorrow night's diplomatic event at the German consulate in Boston. Which was where she intended to confront him.

The knowledge came with a new concern. Nothing too obvious, but here and there, she'd noticed certain records seemed to have been disturbed. Erased or tampered with, possibly. As if someone else had been researching the same files. Recently.

Who? Why?

Smithers stretched his legs out, the limited legroom making it pointless. He waved the flight attendant down and asked for coffee. "Think he'll talk?"

Kim closed the laptop and leaned back to rest her eyes. "One way or another."

Smithers smirked. "Subtle."

"The Reacher Way. Whatever works," she shrugged.

The flight landed just before dawn at Boston's Logan Airport. Kim's knowledge of aviation history included too many tragic crashes at Logan. At takeoff, on landing, and other air disasters here made Kim particularly uneasy. Her fingers clawed both armrests as she braced for landing.

To his credit, Smithers didn't ask questions about her foibles. Her views on air traffic safety were already well ingrained before their brief partnership began. He'd told her several times that her fears were unfounded. She remained adamant and he let it go.

When their plane landed smoothly on touchdown and rolled into an easy taxi toward the gate, Smithers said, "See? Nothing to worry about. Just like I said."

Kim ignored him and began to breathe normally again. They collected their bags and headed out through the jetway into the terminal.

A black SUV waited at the curb, pre-arranged. The ride into the city was silent except for Smithers occasionally checking his phone, and Kim working again. Her head was already inside the consulate, picturing angles, exits, contingencies.

By the time they reached the hotel, the city was waking up. Coffee shops filling with caffeine addicts and morning joggers moving in packs.

Smithers exhaled as he stepped out of the SUV. "Long night."

Kim didn't break stride toward the lobby.

They had several hours until the event. Enough time to catch a nap, clean up, and get in position. They checked in, planned to meet up later, and went to their rooms.

Later, the Boston air had a bite, dry and sharp, cutting through the alleyways between Beacon Hill's brick facades.

Kim and Smithers stood across from the German consulate, watching arrivals shuffle through the security checkpoint. The event inside tonight was a diplomatic mixer—ambassadors, corporate executives, intelligence types. A safe zone for spies to swap information under the cover of cocktails and small talk.

Smithers adjusted his tie, scanning the crowd. "You sure Hooper's going to show?"

Kim kept her gaze on the entrance. "He's on the list. He's got a reputation for being careful, but this is a soft target for him. Low risk."

They had tracked Hooper from the moment his name surfaced. He was a shadow figure with just enough visibility to make him real, but not enough to pin down.

Did he have a bead on Reacher?

A black sedan pulled up and a driver in uniform stepped out to open the rear door. A man exited, tall and lean. Short-cropped hair, steel-gray at the temples. No hesitation in his steps.

"Hooper," Kim said, nodding in his direction.

Smithers clicked his tongue. "Guy looks like he could vanish in a crowd."

Kim nodded. "That's why we're not giving him the chance."

Hooper approached the checkpoint and flashed his identification. Security waved him through. Kim and Smithers followed a few paces behind, waiting for their turn.

They carried credentials that would hold up under a casual glance.

Inside, the room was a mix of German and American officials. Murmured conversations floated under the clink of glasses.

Hooper had already moved toward the bar, standing alone, his posture relaxed but deliberate. Kim motioned to Smithers.

"I'll go first. Watch his hands."

She walked up beside Hooper, signaling the bartender. "Whiskey. Neat."

Hooper didn't glance her way, but his grip on his glass shifted slightly. He knew he was being approached. Kim leaned on the counter, eyes forward.

"You spent time with some of the same people I'm looking for," she said.

Now, he turned. Just his head. His expression stayed neutral. "Do I know you?"

"No," Kim said. "But I know you. And I know you don't talk unless there's a reason."

Hooper took a sip of his drink. "You got a reason?"

Kim nodded. "Jack Reacher."

Hooper set his glass down. "Never heard of him."

Smithers stepped up on the other side. "That's funny. Because we've got a whole file that says otherwise."

Hooper exhaled, like a man realizing he'd just been boxed in. He gave Kim a long look, then turned to Smithers. "You ATF? CIA?"

"Close enough," Smithers said.

Hooper glanced around the room like a cornered wildcat. No obvious exits. Security at the doors. His shoulders tensed slightly, but his voice stayed even. "I don't know where Reacher is."

Kim tilted her head. "Not what I asked."

Hooper studied her. He wasn't rattled. He was thinking. Calculating. Kim let the silence hang. The first to break the silence lost. Hooper knew that too.

Finally, he set his glass down and straightened. "You don't want to have this conversation here."

Kim shrugged. "Then let's walk."

Hooper nodded once, grabbed his drink, and downed the rest. "No time at the moment."

He nodded to a group of passing guests and walked away. Nothing Kim and Smithers could do without causing a scene and putting a spotlight on the situation.

Hooper blended into the crowd as if he belonged there.

"Come on," Kim said. "We'll choose a better time and place to deal with Hooper."

"I can hardly wait," Smithers deadpanned.

CHAPTER 19

Saturday, July 9
Boston, Massachusetts

THE ROOM IN THE German Consulate buzzed with polite laughter, murmured conversations, and the occasional clink of glasses. Neagley studied the room and the guests, mentally assessing threats and challenges.

Sinclair had slipped away moments ago. Her departure was smooth and seemed to go unnoticed. Neagley had been paying attention, but she didn't let her gaze linger anywhere long enough to cause concern.

The archive room was Sinclair's target tonight. Neagley's job was to make sure nothing derailed the mission. Or at least nothing they couldn't recover from.

She sipped her sparkling water, her gaze drifting casually across the room and resting on a familiar face. One she hadn't seen in more than fifteen years. Not since Hamburg.

Bradley Hooper. He was easy to spot when you knew what to look for.

He moved like a man who didn't need to prove anything, confident without being arrogant. He wasn't the kind to draw unnecessary attention, but Neagley was certain he'd already clocked every exit, every security guard, and every potential threat in the room.

That's what made him dangerous. Quiet precision. Calm awareness. Skills developed by the US military and Reacher, when he commanded the 110th Special Investigators Unit, the best trainers in the world.

Neagley didn't know Hooper well, but she'd known his boss very well before he died. Orozco had been one of the best Reacher had ever trained. He'd be appalled to see how Hooper turned out.

He was moving directly toward her.

Neagley didn't flinch. She'd seen him coming from the moment he stepped into the room, but she didn't betray a single hint of recognition. Instead, she let him approach, body language neutral, expression calm.

When Hooper finally stopped in front of her, a faint smile played at the corners of his mouth.

"Frances Neagley," he said, his voice low and smooth, tinged with genuine surprise. "Of all the gin joints in all the world where I might have expected to run into you, this wasn't one of them."

Her stoic expression gave away nothing. "Hooper. Long time, no see. Small world."

He chuckled softly. Almost disarming. Almost. "World tends to get smaller in rooms like this, doesn't it?"

Neagley shrugged, taking another sip of her drink. "Something like that."

Hooper leaned against the nearest cocktail table. His posture was casual but the gaze was sharp and missed nothing. "I have to admit, you don't strike me as the diplomatic mixer type."

"That makes two of us," she said evenly. "But you know how it is. The work takes us to strange places."

"Does it ever," he agreed. His tone was light, but his gaze probed like he had X-ray vision. "So, what brings you here? Business? Pleasure? Or something in between?"

Neagley gave him a small, tight smile. "You know me. I like to keep things simple."

Hooper tilted his head, studying her. "Simple. Sure. That's one word for your brand of activity."

Neagley shrugged. "Live well or die. Pretty simple code."

They both let the silence hang for a moment, the noise of the room fading into the background. Neagley knew what he was doing. Gauging her, trying to figure out why she was really here.

She'd seen him play this game before, including back in Hamburg. He was good at it, but so was she.

"I heard a couple of FBI agents are sniffing around," Hooper said, almost casually. "Asking questions about an old friend of ours."

Neagley raised an eyebrow. "That so?"

He nodded, his expression carefully neutral. "Word is they're looking for Reacher."

The name hung between them.

Neagley didn't react, didn't give him the satisfaction of seeing even the smallest flicker of emotion cross her face. She set her glass down on the table to leave her hands free.

She knew who the two agents were. Knew what they were doing. But she revealed nothing to Hooper.

"And what does any of that have to do with you?" Neagley's radar went up, as it always did when Reacher was mentioned. She had Reacher's back and he had hers. Simple as that.

Hooper shrugged, the motion slow and deliberate. "Nothing, as far as I can tell. But you know how these things go. People start asking questions, and eventually, those questions lead to people like me. And you."

"Funny," Neagley said drily. "I don't remember inviting you into my business."

He smirked. "Come on, Neagley. You know how this works. They're looking for Reacher. They're going to come knocking on a lot of doors. Yours, mine, a few others you haven't thought about yet."

She didn't respond right away. Instead, she let the silence stretch, watching him carefully. Hooper was playing at something, but she couldn't tell what yet. He'd dropped Reacher's name for a reason.

"Why don't you just tell me what you really want, and we can skip the small talk?" Neagley suggested.

Hooper chuckled again, but this time there was something colder beneath the surface. "What I want, Neagley, is to stay out of whatever mess you've stepped into. We worked together once, for a short time a long time ago. Reacher was in the thick of it then, too."

"So?"

"The situation worked out okay for the good guys in the end. It was not an experience either of us want to repeat," Hooper said bluntly. "But since I know you, I'm sure you're not going to stand down. Consider this a friendly warning."

"A warning?" she echoed, her voice flat as she gave him a level, steely gaze. "About what?"

"About who you can trust," he said seriously. "These two FBI agents. Otto and Smithers. You don't know them. You don't know what they're really after. You don't know who's pulling their strings. And if Reacher's involved, we can be damned sure it's not simply routine curiosity about our old friends."

Neagley's eyes narrowed. "And you know all of this because?"

"We've both been in this game long enough. We can tell when the pieces don't add up," Hooper said. "And right now, Neagley, they don't. Not for you, not for me, and definitely not for Reacher. You're going to get hurt here if you don't stand down."

"It's touching to know how worried you are about us all," Neagley replied flatly.

Before she could say more, a faint buzz of static crackled in her earpiece, followed by Sinclair's voice, cool and composed. "We've got a problem."

Neagley didn't react but shifted gears instantly.

"Which is?" she murmured, keeping her eyes on Hooper while counting on the loud buzz in the room to conceal her words.

"Consulate security's moving," Sinclair said. "Someone's tipped them off. I need an exit. Now."

Neagley grimaced. She glanced at Hooper, who continued watching her with an unreadable expression.

"Looks like we're both out of time," he said, straightening. "Good luck, Neagley. You're going to need it."

He turned and walked away, disappearing into the crowd before she could stop him.

Neagley didn't waste time watching him go. She tapped her earpiece. "On my way. Hold tight."

She slipped through the crowd, her movements smooth and unhurried, as if she were, indeed, a guest. Hooper's words lingered. But Sinclair was the priority.

Whatever game Hooper was playing, she'd figure it out later. Assuming they all lived that long.

CHAPTER 20

Saturday, July 9
Boston, Massachusetts

THE ARCHIVE ROOM SMELLED of aged paper and stale air.

Sinclair moved quickly and precisely though the stacks to the filing cabinets until she reached the one she'd identified. Hooper had been here with her, but he was called away. Which was okay. She'd rather not have him breathing down her neck.

Gloved hands scanned through the file drawers under the dim glow of the desk lamp she'd switched on. The German Consulate had spared no expense on security, but Sinclair knew how to bypass the systems. She'd designed some of the best.

The map was there, exactly where she'd been told it would be.

Yellowed edges confirmed its age, and the faint ink markings across the surface were just as she remembered.

But something else caught her attention. She leaned closer, narrowing her eyes.

The markings on the map weren't coordinates or notes, as she'd believed. They were faint but deliberate symbols. She reviewed them in context for a few seconds before she realized what she was seeing.

Instructions.

Steps.

Could the markings explain Horace Wiley's "process?" Could retrieving the map possibly be this easy?

Sinclair fished a small digital camera from her pocket and began snapping photos. Wiley's actions back then had been cryptic, but logical and based in historical facts. But these symbols were something she hadn't noticed before.

A faint buzz in her earpiece made her pause.

"Heads up," Neagley's low voice said.

Sinclair froze. "Yeah?"

"Two FBI agents are closing in."

Damn it. Sinclair resisted the urge to curse out loud.

"Who are they and why are they here?" she murmured, stuffing the map into her pocket. She returned the empty folder to its proper location and slid the drawer shut with a soft click.

"They're on the move," Neagley's voice came through the earpiece. "You've got maybe two minutes."

Sinclair took a breath. Calm under pressure was her specialty. "I'm leaving now. Meet me by the east exit."

"Copy that," Neagley replied.

Sinclair turned off the desk lamp and pocketed the camera. She adjusted her blazer, making sure it concealed the small pouch she'd sewn inside to carry documents. She stepped toward the door, heels silent on the carpeted floor, and cracked it open just enough to peer into the corridor.

The hallway was clear, but it wouldn't stay that way for long.

She slipped out, closing the door behind her, and started down the hall at a brisk but not hurried pace.

She could easily blend into crowds when she needed to.

The consulate's event was still in full swing. The buzz of conversation and clinking of glasses filtering down the corridor covered whatever muffled noises she made.

She turned the corner toward the east wing when something moved ahead.

Sinclair stopped, pressing herself into the shadows along the wall. Voices she didn't recognize carried to her position.

"Otto, did you see her go this way?" the male agent asked.

"Definitely," Otto replied. "Seems she's trying to stay ahead of us."

Sinclair's jaw tightened. She hadn't expected them to be this close, this fast. What did they want?

She scanned her surroundings. The hallway led to the main event space if she doubled back. The east exit was closer, but Otto and the male agent were between her and the door.

She needed a distraction.

Sinclair reached into her pocket and pulled out a small metal device no larger than a lipstick tube. A gift from an old contact in Berlin. She twisted the cap, activating the timed trigger, and rolled it down the hall toward the opposite corridor.

She counted silently. Three... two... one.

A sharp, piercing alarm blared from the device, echoing through the halls.

Sinclair didn't wait to see the reaction. She slipped into an adjoining side passage, moving swiftly toward the east exit.

Behind her, she heard Otto's voice. "What the hell is that, Smithers?"

"Some kind of alarm," Smithers replied.

"It's a decoy. She's close. Go left, I'll check the right."

Sinclair smiled grimly. Otto was sharp. Too sharp.

Sinclair turned another corner and spotted Neagley waiting near the east exit, posture tense.

"Took you long enough," Neagley said under her breath.

"Had to leave a parting gift," Sinclair replied on her way out.

They pushed through the exit and into the night air. The salty cool breeze off the Atlantic Ocean was biting against Sinclair's skin.

The alley was dark and narrow. Neagley had already scoped it out. She led them toward a black sedan parked discreetly near the back gate.

"You get the map?" Neagley asked as they approached the car.

Sinclair nodded. "And Wiley left something behind. Something we missed before."

Neagley opened her mouth to respond, but her head snapped to the side, eyes narrowing. "We've got company."

Sinclair followed her gaze. A man stepped out of the shadows, blocking the path to the car.

Bradley Hooper.

"Ladies," he said, his tone cool and calm. "Going somewhere?"

Neagley's stance shifted, her body tensing like a coiled spring. "Not in the mood, Hooper. Move."

Hooper's smile didn't waver. "You've got something that doesn't belong to you."

Sinclair stepped forward, assuming the cloak of commanding officer she'd worn for decades. "This isn't your fight, Hooper. Walk away."

"Can't do that," he said, his gaze flicking to Neagley. "Not when you're dragging old friends into your mess."

Before Neagley could respond, the sound of footsteps echoed from behind them.

Sinclair turned to see Otto and Smithers emerging from the shadows, weapons drawn.

"Hands where I can see them," Otto ordered, her voice steady and unyielding.

Sinclair had the map, but now she and Neagley were trapped between Hooper and the FBI agents.

No clean exit.

She glanced at Neagley, who gave her a barely perceptible nod. As always, Neagley was prepared to fight their way out.

Sinclair's fingers twitched toward her jacket pocket where she kept a carefully concealed weapon as she calculated angles, timing, probabilities.

"Last chance," Otto said, stepping closer.

Sinclair met her steely expression. "You're making a mistake."

Otto didn't flinch. "Funny. I was about to say the same thing to you."

And then everything exploded.

Sinclair moved first.

In the split second before Otto could react, Sinclair flicked her wrist and sent a burst of pepper spray from a concealed canister directly into Hooper's eyes.

He stumbled back with a guttural shout, hands snapping to his face.

Neagley, already in motion, spun on her heel toward Otto and Smithers, her movements fluid and deliberate.

"Move!" Sinclair barked, her voice sharp and commanding as she dove toward the sedan.

Neagley didn't hesitate. She launched herself forward into a roll, coming up low and fast just as Otto's gun tracked toward her. Neagley kicked out, catching Otto's wrist and sending the weapon skittering to the pavement.

"What the hell's wrong with you, Neagley?" Otto cursed but didn't lose her footing.

Neagley didn't stand aside. Nor did she make any excuses.

Otto pivoted to deliver a sharp elbow aimed at Neagley's head. Neagley ducked, countering with a jab to Otto's ribs that knocked the agent back a step.

Sinclair yanked the sedan's door open and slid inside. The map was secure, tucked against her side, but none of it mattered if they didn't get out of here now. She fumbled for the ignition, her pulse hammering in her ears.

Smithers moved to flank Neagley, weapon still trained on her. "Stop! Hands up! Don't make this worse!"

Neagley's eyes narrowed. "It's already worse."

Sinclair pushed the electronic start, and the engine roared to life with a growl that reverberated through the narrow alley. She slammed the vehicle into reverse. Tires screeched as the vehicle lurched backward, forcing Otto and Smithers to scatter.

Hooper was still reeling from the pepper spray. He staggered aside with a never-ending string of curses. Sinclair had no time to deal with him now. Hooper was on his own.

"Neagley! Now!" Sinclair shouted.

Neagley didn't need to be told again. She darted toward the car.

Otto lunged to grab her, but Neagley twisted out of reach, delivering a quick backhand that sent Otto stumbling, unhurt but outraged.

Neagley reached the sedan's open door and dove inside, slamming it shut behind her.

"Go, go, go!" Neagley snapped.

Sinclair didn't wait. She threw the car into gear, the tires screaming as the sedan shot forward down the alley.

Behind them, Otto and Smithers scrambled to recover. Smithers raised his weapon to fire.

Sinclair swerved hard, the car skimming the edge of a dumpster just as a shot cracked through the night. The rear windshield shattered, glass spraying across the backseat.

"Dammit," Sinclair hissed, her hands steady on the wheel as she gunned the car down the narrow alley and into the open street.

"Hooper's managed to disappear. They'll have backup on us in minutes," Neagley twisted in her seat to look back. "We need a route."

"I've got it," Sinclair replied, her voice clipped. She'd memorized the layout before the mission, anticipating contingencies. "Hang on."

She veered right. The car fishtailed as she tore through a red light. Horns blared and headlights flashed as drivers slammed on their brakes to avoid the speeding sedan.

Sinclair barely registered the chaos as she navigated the streets of Boston.

Neagley leaned forward to scan behind them using the rearview mirror. "Hooper's not going to let this go. He'll regroup. And Otto and Smithers will be back. Soon."

Sinclair cut in. "We'll deal with them all later. Right now, we need to disappear."

"You've got somewhere in mind?" Neagley asked, her tone skeptical.

Sinclair's jaw tightened. "I always do."

CHAPTER 21

Saturday, July 9
Boston, Massachusetts

SINCLAIR DROVE FAST, ONE hand on the wheel, the other patted her pocket to confirm the folded map rested inside, snug against her thigh. The car smelled of sweat and adrenaline while the city lights blurred in the rain-streaked windshield. The wipers slapped in a steady rhythm, clearing her view of empty streets. Boston was quiet at this hour. The kind of quiet that made her uneasy.

Neagley sat in the passenger seat staring straight ahead. Neither of them had spoken since they'd escaped the German consulate after the operation went sideways.

Otto and Smithers had been too close. Too aggressive. Sinclair hadn't expected the FBI presence at the consulate, let alone running interference. The confrontation had been messy. Too many variables out of her control. She hated that.

Neagley had saved them both, getting them out before the FBI locked the place down. She was worth her weight in gold.

Sinclair checked the rearview mirror again. No one behind them. No headlights stretching through the dark.

Which didn't mean they were not being tracked.

FBI agents were nothing if not methodical. If Otto and Smithers had any way to follow, they would.

A green highway sign loomed ahead. Logan International Airport.

She should take the next exit. Buy a ticket somewhere far away. Leave this whole mess behind.

Instead, she took the ramp toward the industrial district and turned off onto a side road, pulling into a narrow alley behind a row of old brownstones. She cut the engine. The silence pressed in immediately.

"What now?" Neagley exhaled her frustration. First sound she'd made in twenty minutes.

Sinclair didn't answer. She grabbed her duffel from the backseat, shouldered it, and pushed the door open. Neagley followed without comment.

They climbed the stairs quickly while moving in silence. The third-floor apartment was a safe house rented under a false identity. Sinclair had prepped this one and several others months ago. Just in case.

Inside, she locked the door, dropped her bag onto the table. She spread the map out flat, straightening the edges and the creases it had acquired after years of being folded small enough to fit into Wiley's pockets. She weighed the edges down and stared at the map's details.

Neagley shrugged out of her jacket, tossed it over a chair, and leaned against the wall. She didn't ask questions. She watched, waiting. For what?

Sinclair wasn't in the mood for an interrogation. She tuned Neagley out, focused on the paper in front of her.

It was the same map she'd seen back in Hamburg. She was sure because she had reviewed the photos countless times over the past few months.

But something was different here.

She ran her fingertips along the edges and across the margins to study the newly discovered symbols, handwritten long ago. Faint, small, precise markings she had seen before but never paid attention to.

She should have.

The map had been seized and archived by German intelligence. It had been sitting in storage for more than a decade. No one had touched it. That meant the markings had been there since the beginning. How had she missed them?

She grabbed her field notebook. Flipped through the pages, scanning the old intel from the Hamburg operation.

She found what she was looking for. Wiley's financial reports, asset seizure records, data on his offshore accounts.

Next, she cross-referenced the symbols.

They weren't coordinates.

Not military codes.

Her vision blurred and she blinked to clear it, which was when she realized they were banking numbers.

Back in Hamburg, she hadn't been looking for financial data. She had been tracking Wiley to piece his arms network together. The money had seemed secondary at the time. The nukes he was selling were priority one.

Now, she saw the pattern.

Wiley's offshore accounts had been tied to a Hamburg-based bank.

When she searched the databases, she found that bank had been shut down in the early 2000s. Its assets were liquidated or absorbed into other financial institutions.

But not erased.

She ran several more quick searches until she found it.

The records had been transferred. The institution that had taken over Wiley's assets years ago now operated under a new name.

In Miami.

Sinclair leaned back, exhaling slowly.

The map had been the key all along. Not to the ranch itself, but to the money.

The process.

Wiley hadn't simply been hiding assets.

He had also set up a way to retrieve them and to create more, long after his death.

Sinclair closed the laptop and picked up her phone.

Booked a flight.

Didn't tell Neagley.

A chair scraped against the floor behind her.

Sinclair didn't turn. "You're too quiet. I thought you left."

Neagley stood in the doorway, arms crossed. "I could have. It's dangerous for you to zone out like that, you know."

Sinclair slid the map into her bag. "Why are you still here?"

Neagley didn't answer.

Sinclair zipped the duffel, feeling the weight of it in her hands. Neagley was watching her movements, tracking every detail.

"You're going somewhere," Neagley said.

Sinclair slung the bag over her shoulder. "You're good."

"You didn't answer the question."

Sinclair headed for the door. "You didn't ask one."

Neagley's mouth twitched, but she didn't smile.

"Miami's hot this time of year," Neagley said.

Sinclair's fingers tightened around the strap. She kept her expression neutral. Didn't react.

Neagley held her gaze.

Sinclair opened the door.

Neagley let her pass but spoke once more before she left. "Be careful."

Sinclair didn't stop. Didn't look back.

She had a flight to catch. She slung the bag over her shoulder and hustled down the fire escape to the alley below where a car was waiting.

Half an hour later, she moved through Logan's TSA security checkpoint without hesitation. No checked bags. No wasted motion.

She boarded. Found her seat.

Pulled out her burner phone. Sent a single-word message.

Moving.

Turned it off.

Across the terminal, an exceptionally fit woman in a gray T-shirt blended into the morning crowd. Neagley.

When the plane lifted off for Miami, Sinclair wasn't alone.

Whether Neagley knew Sinclair had noticed was another issue.

CHAPTER 22

Sunday, July 10
Boston, Massachusetts

KIM'S REFLECTION GHOSTED AGAINST the surveillance footage as she leaned closer to the laptop screen. Her fingertips left smudges on the cheap particleboard desk. The ancient wall-mounted AC unit rattled, and the sour mix of burnt coffee and rain-soaked carpet filled the out-of-the-way motel room.

She ignored it all, focused on her mission.

Smithers shifted on the sagging mattress. He winced as he rotated his shoulder. The bruising from the consulate firefight showed purple.

Kim clicked her fingers through the footage. She focused on the moments before things erupted. Every frame held potential answers. What happened inside that building to light the fuse?

She tapped the spacebar and slowed the feed.

A woman emerged from the consulate. Security lights caught her fashionably styled and streaked blonde hair. Kim recognized her military bearing. Her spine stood straight as a ruler.

Kim froze her finger over the keyboard.

Smithers leaned in. The coffee scented his breath. "Who is that?"

"Dr. Marian Sinclair." Kim spoke the name like a key turning in a lock.

"The NSA Deputy Director?" Tension edged Smithers's voice.

Kim kept her eyes on the screen. "She stood one step below Director before she left last week."

"She got promoted? Or she quit? What?"

"Well, some say she was pushed out. Rumor is that she was absolutely livid about it," Kim said.

"I can imagine. Worked her entire career for that final promotion and then she gets kicked aside? Men have killed for less." Smithers's reflection frowned in the laptop's glow as he leaned in to stare at the rows of names. "I don't see her on the guest list."

Kim advanced the footage. She clenched her jaw. "No. She was not there officially. If you only had the guest list to prove it, she wasn't there at all."

"Right."

A second person stepped behind Sinclair. Dark clothes absorbed the light around the tight, compact frame as she moved with a predator's grace.

"Neagley," Kim breathed.

Smithers straightened. "Frances Neagley? One of Reacher's 110th Special Investigators?"

"Yep." Kim nodded. "The one and only."

Neagley had served as an Army MP before she moved to private security. She'd turned violence into an art form. But that wasn't the only reason Neagley was dangerous.

"Still connected to Reacher?" Smithers spoke with an edge.

"Yes."

"What about Hooper?"

Kim shook her head. She scanned the frame. "Possibly. We can check how or when he could have been connected to them. He's younger, but he could have been a soldier before Reacher was discharged. Right at the tail end of Reacher's service."

Smithers pointed at the frozen image. "Then why does Neagley shadow Sinclair here?"

The question filled the stale air. Kim shook her head as she advanced the footage.

Sinclair and Neagley turned from the main exit. They walked toward the building's flank, away from the crowd.

Kim pushed the feed forward some more.

A third person stepped into the frame.

Tall. Boxy. But unlike Reacher, he didn't resemble a defensive lineman. He did walk with the same casual confidence. As if he commanded the actual ground beneath his feet as well as the sky above and everything in between.

Which he probably did. That kind of guy wasn't easily led. Or supervised.

When his face turned toward the camera, Kim frowned.

"Hooper," Smithers muttered. The name dropped like lead.

Kim bunched her jaw muscles. They had followed Hooper to Boston thinking they had anticipated his next move. Instead, they'd caught him meeting Sinclair and Neagley.

"I see no coincidence here," Smithers said in a low voice.

"No. They planned this."

Kim watched Sinclair and Neagley walk together to the rear lot. They hopped into a sedan and whisked themselves into darkness.

A few frames later, Hooper walked through the main doors. He disappeared into the crowd. Then he vanished from view.

Kim leaned back. Her chair creaked.

"What do we do next?" Smithers asked in the dark room.

Kim snapped the laptop shut. "Let's figure out what happened inside that building."

She stood and stretched, her muscles tight from hours hunched over the laptop. The rain tapped against the window, a constant reminder of the Boston weather she'd quickly grown to hate. She grabbed her phone and the keycard from the desk.

"Where are you going?" Smithers asked.

"The consulate. I need to talk to someone who was working security."

"At this hour?"

Kim checked her watch. "Marcus Chen works the shift. He owes me a favor from that mess in Singapore."

Smithers pushed himself off the bed. "I'm coming with you."

"No." Kim's voice was firm. "Your shoulder needs rest, and I need you to do something else. Pull everything you can find on Sinclair after she left the NSA. There won't be much since she's been gone less than a week. Focus on the six months before and whatever we have after her departure. Someone pushed her out. I want to know who and why."

"And Neagley?"

"Leave her for now. She's a ghost when she wants to be. I'm almost sure she's no threat to either of us. But Sinclair is another story." Kim slipped on her jacket. "Someone as high-profile as Sinclair leaves a trail, even when she tries to hide it."

"What about Hooper?"

"That's what I'm going to find out." Kim pulled her weapon from the holster and checked it. "If Chen was on duty last night, he saw Hooper inside. Maybe even caught some of the conversations. He's more likely to open up to me if I'm alone."

"Be careful," Smithers said. "If they coordinated that exit, they planned the shooting too."

Kim nodded. "Keep your phone on. If I'm not back in two hours, come after me."

"I'll call in the cavalry." Smithers grinned, but his eyes remained serious. "Try not to get shot."

Kim's hand rested on the door handle. "One more thing. Check if Sinclair had any connection to the 110th while she was at the NSA. It's not a coincidence that Neagley's involved here. It suggests they've had prior dealings."

"Copy that," Smithers replied with a single nod for emphasis.

Kim stepped into the hallway where the fluorescent lights hummed noisily overhead. The pieces were there. Sinclair's forced retirement, Neagley's presence, Hooper's involvement.

She just had to figure out how they fit together.

And why someone thought it was worth killing to keep them apart.

And how Reacher fit into it all. Because Kim was absolutely certain Reacher was involved.

CHAPTER 23

Saturday, July 9
Boston, Massachusetts

KIM PULLED INTO A parking lot behind a rundown coffee shop in South Boston. The rain had let up, leaving everything slick and gray. She scanned the area. No sign of a tail, either.

Inside, the place was quiet. Dim lighting, cracked vinyl booths, a counter lined with battered stools. Marcus Chen sat in the back, shoulders hunched, fingers tapping against a ceramic mug.

Kim slid into the seat across from him. "Appreciate you coming on such short notice."

Chen barely looked up. "I don't owe you a favor, Otto."

She ignored that. "We were inside the consulate last night. Walked out and directly into trouble. I need to know what happened before that."

Chen sighed, rubbed a hand over his face. He looked like a man who hadn't slept. "I don't know what you think I can tell you."

Kim leaned in. "Who did Sinclair meet inside?"

Chen's fingers tightened around the mug. "You already know she was there?"

"We saw her leave. I need to know what she was doing before that."

Chen hesitated. "She didn't come through the checkpoint. Her diplomatic clearance was revoked when she left NSA. Which means she was not listed as a US operative on the official guest list and therefore, we did no prearrival security check."

"Who authorized her?"

"Good question," he said. "Someone high up. I don't have access to those names."

Otto nodded. That tracked. Sinclair had operated at the highest levels of intelligence. If the Germans let her in quietly, she had something they wanted. Or they owed her. Which was probably the case.

"Who was she with?"

Chen exhaled. "Guy named Brad Hooper. Military contractor."

Kim's stomach churned. Guessing was one thing. Confirmation was another. Hooper and Sinclair. Together.

"What did they do once they were inside the consulate?" Kim asked.

Chen cleared his throat. "They accessed a restricted archive room. No cameras inside. But they weren't in there long."

"What were they looking for?"

Chen shook his head. "I don't know. But when she walked out, she looked pleased with herself."

Kim sat back. Sinclair wasn't merely gathering intel. She had a mission. And Hooper was part of it. Neagley, too, most likely.

"Thanks." She finished her water and stood. "If you remember anything else, call me."

Chen scoffed. "If I call you, it means I'm out of a job."

Otto didn't argue. She left without looking back.

Outside, she climbed into the car and called Smithers. He picked up immediately.

"Got something," she said.

"Same here."

"You first."

Smithers sounded grim. "Sinclair was digging into classified intelligence reports before she left the NSA. High-clearance financial records. She was looking for something buried."

Kim tightened her grip on the wheel. "Sinclair and Hooper met inside the consulate. They accessed an archive room."

Silence. Then Smithers exhaled. "Swell. They're working together. On something very specific."

"That's how I see it," Kim said.

"Any chance whatever they're doing connects to Reacher? Because if it doesn't, we need to turn our attention in a different direction," Smithers replied.

"You have another lead we can pursue at the moment?"

Smithers groaned and muttered a curse. "So what's our next move?"

Kim pulled up a flight log database on her phone. She ran Sinclair's name. Then she ran Neagley. Both had acquired a last-minute flight, which had already departed.

Kim started the engine. "Pack up. We're leaving."

Smithers didn't hesitate. "Where to?"

Kim pulled into traffic. "Miami."

She pulled out her phone and called her boss, something she rarely did willingly. She needed transportation and intel. Cooper was the man most likely to have the answers to her questions, too.

After five rings, she hung up.

Cooper didn't answer, which was fine with Kim. She didn't have the time or the inclination to fill him in at the moment. Her second call was to her former partner, Carlos Gaspar.

He answered instantly. "Good morning, Suzie Wong. What's going on in your world today?"

Kim smiled. Gaspar could always raise her spirits. "I'm headed your way. Looking for Cuban coffee. Got any?"

"Always," Gaspar replied. "But you want something else. You never call just for grins."

"True." She nodded, even though he couldn't see her. "First, I need two plane tickets to Miami from Logan on the next flight. First class if you can swing it. We'll have our weapons. Me and Smithers."

"Yeah, I know what you like, Sunshine." He clacked the computer keys for a couple of seconds and then said, "Done. What else."

"Background, if you can get it. Marian Sinclair and Bradley Hooper," she said. "I'm looking for points of intersection. They know each other and they're working together. I'm just not sure how, when, or why."

Gaspar paused a minute as if he were considering the request, but she knew he was thinking it through. "So this is about Reacher."

"Isn't it always?"

"Yeah," he sighed, as if her mission was impossible. Which, so far, it had proved to be. "What else?"

"Frances Neagley is also involved in this. Which means Reacher's not far away," Kim said.

"Okay. I'm on it. Get going. You'll miss your flight. See you when I see you," Gaspar replied before he disconnected.

One thing Gaspar could be counted on for was not to scold her when she was moving fast. He'd give her an earful when he had the chance.

She picked up Smithers at the motel's curb and headed for Boston Logan. She filled him in on the way. Traffic was light and they arrived well within time parameters.

They dropped the car in the long-term parking lot and hustled into the terminal. She'd get someone to pick it up and return it later.

At the TSA checkpoint, they showed their badges along with the boarding passes Gaspar had emailed. The agent took a quick look and escorted them around the metal and bomb detection devices.

A quick hustle through the terminal to the gate and they were able to board at the very last minute before the gate agent closed the jetway door. The jet's engines were already rumbling when she took her seat and quickly stowed her bags.

The captain announced heavy weather and turbulence ahead. Passengers were told to remain in their seats for the duration of the flight. Before she had a chance to freak out too much, they were in the air.

After what seemed like the longest few hours of her life, Kim gripped the armrest as the plane touched down at Miami International. Hot sun blazed through the window, which was a welcome contrast to Boston's damp gray skies.

Her phone buzzed with an update from Gaspar.

She scrolled through his message.

Sinclair had checked into the Mandarin Oriental under her own name. Either very confident or very careless. Kim always bet on overly confident bureaucrats.

Inside the jetway felt like a sauna. A thin film of perspiration formed on her upper lip as Kim loosened her collar while she headed for the air-conditioned terminal and then the rental counter.

Gaspar had arranged the wheels. She wasted no time collecting the SUV. When they were inside the vehicle, she checked the time.

Sinclair had a three-hour head start.

Her phone buzzed again. She glanced at the screen. A text from Chen. "Archive room inventory shows nothing missing."

Kim frowned. Could that be true? They hadn't taken anything at all?

She shook her head. Made no sense.

More likely, Sinclair had found what she came for and managed to remove it without setting off any alarms.

"Landed early," she said as she picked up the incoming call from Gaspar.

"My contact at Miami PD spotted Sinclair headed toward Coconut Grove."

"What about Neagley?"

"No visual. But there's chatter about private security presence. Very professional. Very discreet."

"That's Neagley's style." Kim glanced at Smithers who was behind the wheel.

"What about Hooper?" Smithers asked.

"Nothing yet. But if the pattern holds, he'll be around somewhere."

"He'll show." Smithers pulled the SUV out of the garage.

Kim ended the call and merged onto the highway.

Whatever Sinclair had found in that archive room, it was worth killing for.

The bigger question was, why did Reacher care?

CHAPTER 24

Sunday, July 10
Miami, Florida

KIM OTTO ADJUSTED THE SUV's air-conditioning as she and Smithers rolled into Coconut Grove. The relentless Miami heat bore down like an oppressive weight. The ocean breeze barely stirred the palm trees lining the narrow streets.

Kim had been here many times before. The neighborhood was a mix of old money and new ambition. High-end boutiques, trendy cafes, and historic mansions tucked behind gates everywhere she looked.

Smithers checked his phone. "Gaspar's guy spotted Sinclair's car turning onto the main street twenty minutes ago. No sign of Neagley."

Kim kept her eyes on the road, scanning. "What about Hooper?"

Smithers shook his head. "Still nothing."

"Stay alert. Sinclair and Hooper worked together inside the consulate. They accessed the same archive," Kim replied. "With Sinclair in Miami, Hooper's probably nearby."

"Neagley, too," Smithers said.

"Right."

Smithers pulled the SUV to the curb near a café with shaded outdoor seating. Gaspar's contact had last seen Sinclair heading toward the waterfront, but there were too many possible routes. They needed to move fast.

Kim grabbed her sunglasses from the dashboard. "Let's walk it."

Smithers climbed out, scanning the sidewalk as they crossed the street. The midday heat pressed down like a hot, wet paperweight.

They moved past a row of upscale shops, weaving between tourists and locals. Sinclair wasn't a tourist. She had a destination in mind.

Two corners down, Kim spotted a small marina tucked behind a row of palm trees. Slips filled with million-dollar yachts. A few charter boats. A fuel dock.

Kim tilted her head toward the marina. "The water's an easy exit."

Smithers followed her gaze. "You think she's running?"

"Not yet." Kim shook her head. "But she's setting something up."

They approached the marina office, a small white building with tinted windows. A man in a faded polo leaned against the counter, scrolling through his phone. His name tag identified him as Ricardo.

"We're looking for a woman who came through here in the last half hour." Kim flashed her badge quickly enough for him to recognize it without a thorough review that might lead to questions she wouldn't answer. "Blond, mid-fifties, sharp dresser. Might've been meeting someone."

Ricardo barely reacted. "This is Miami. Half the people I see look like that."

Kim pulled out her phone and brought up a photo of Sinclair. "This one."

He frowned, then nodded. "Yeah, she was here. Didn't ask about a boat. She stood by the fuel dock for a few minutes, looking around."

Smithers leaned in. "Did she talk to anyone?"

Ricardo cocked his head and thought for a second. "A guy pulled up in a dark SUV. They didn't talk long. Then he left, and she walked off toward the market."

Kim's pulse ticked up. "What kind of SUV?"

"Black. Tinted windows. Looked government or private security." He shrugged. "Or maybe drug dealers. Hard to say."

Smithers exchanged a glance with her. "Could be Hooper."

Kim turned back to the dockworker. "What about the guy driving it? Did you get a look?"

Ricardo shook his head. "He didn't get out of the car."

"You got CCTV here?" Smithers asked, craning his neck to look for cameras.

Ricardo shook his head again. "We don't need it. All these yacht owners have their own security and insurance."

Smithers replied, "In that case, we'll need your manifests. We'll ask the owners for access to their CCTV."

"Got a warrant?" Ricardo asked.

"Easy enough to get one," Smithers bluffed.

Ricardo shrugged as he turned to walk away. "Just let me know when you have it."

"One more thing," Kim said as she pulled up Reacher's head shot on her phone. "Have you seen this guy around here?"

Ricardo took the phone and studied Reacher's photo carefully. "Possibly. Is this old? The guy I'm thinking of is about fifteen years older."

"He give you his name?" Smithers asked.

Ricardo shook his head and returned Kim's phone. "Nah. No need. We're not starting a rock band."

Kim exhaled. Reacher was here. Somewhere. Her stomach thrashed around like a cornered animal. Unobtrusively, she slid an antacid under her tongue.

"Where is he now?" Smithers pressed.

Ricardo shrugged as he looked at his phone screen. "I gotta go. Customer needs assistance."

Sinclair had been meeting someone, and now she was on foot. That meant she wasn't done here yet.

Kim and Smithers walked along the sidewalks, scanning the crowd.

Kim's phone vibrated in her pocket. She pulled it out to read. "Gaspar says Sinclair's credit card was used two blocks away. Small café."

"She getting sloppy?" Smithers asked.

Kim started moving. "Doubtful. Feels more like a summons."

The café had shaded outdoor seating and a back entrance that led toward an alley. Inside, it was cool and quiet. The scent of fresh espresso lingered in the air, but Kim ignored it.

Sinclair sat at a small table near the rear, a cup of tea in front of her. A paperback lay open on the table, but she wasn't reading. It was a prop. She was waiting.

She didn't look surprised when Kim slid into the chair across from her.

Smithers stood to the side, arms crossed.

Sinclair smiled faintly. "Took you longer to find me than I expected."

"You should have left a shorter trail. Better yet, you could have called," Kim replied.

Sinclair sipped her tea. "Haven't you heard? I'm retired. I've got all the time in the world."

Kim let that sit. "Who did you meet at the marina?"

Sinclair's smile didn't waver. "I have a lot of old friends."

Kim leaned forward. "Bradley Hooper?"

For the first time, something flickered in Sinclair's eyes. Not surprise. Recognition.

Smithers caught it too. "That's a yes."

Sinclair sighed, setting down her tea. "You're persistent, I'll give you that."

Kim didn't break eye contact. "Why Miami?"

"I'm retired." Sinclair sat back.

"So you said."

She shrugged. "I like the weather."

Smithers scoffed. "It's a million degrees out here in this sauna. Cut the crap."

Kim kept her voice even. "The consulate in Boston. The archive. You found something. And whatever it was, it brought you here."

Sinclair folded her hands on the table. "And what if I did?"

A voice from behind cut in.

"Then you should stop talking." Neagley stood near the exit, a to-go cup in one hand, the other resting near her hip. Not on a weapon. Not yet.

Smithers tensed, but Kim did not.

Neagley looked calm, like she had all the time in the world, too.

Sinclair barely reacted. "I was wondering when you'd step in."

Neagley shrugged. "I give people room to avoid mistakes before I correct them myself."

Kim's pulse ticked up. "You working with her?"

Neagley's expression didn't change. "What do you think?"

Kim measured her. "I think you don't back the wrong people."

Neagley let that hang.

Smithers glanced between them. "So what's the play here?"

Neagley glanced at Sinclair. "We're leaving."

"Looks like we are," Sinclair smiled slightly.

Kim stayed seated. "You can go. But we'll find you again."

Neagley gave her a look Kim had seen before. "I'm counting on it."

She tossed a ten-dollar bill on the table and ushered Sinclair toward the door.

Kim didn't stop them. She wanted to, but this wasn't the place.

Smithers exhaled. "That could've gone worse."

"Yeah? How so?" Kim asked as she rose from the chair.

"Shall we follow Sinclair or Neagley or keep looking for Hooper?" Smithers asked on the way out.

"Neagley's the obvious choice. She's most likely to know where Reacher is," Kim replied. "And she'll probably lead us to Hooper, too."

"Why?"

Kim shrugged and stepped across the threshold. "Too much to explain right now. Let's go."

CHAPTER 25

Sunday, July 10
Miami, Florida

NEAGLEY WENT UP FIRST to secure the location. She stepped off the elevator into a place where no real people actually lived.

The hotel's penthouse reeked of anonymous wealth, all chrome and glass and hollow luxury. Ocean salt mingled with expensive perfume, creating an artificial atmosphere that matched the space perfectly. Meaning, the place was sterile and cold, which Neagley preferred.

Sinclair said she had chosen the penthouse because it was the kind of place where off-the-books meetings happened behind soundproof walls. Visitors came and went on a short-term basis, leaving nothing behind that might identify them.

Neagley figured Sinclair thought the choice gave her control.

She was wrong.

While Sinclair waited in the elevator, Neagley cleared all nine rooms of the apartment. She pressed her shoulder against the cool window frame, feeling the subtle vibration of the building's air system through her jacket. She signaled Sinclair to enter.

Miami's lights pulsed below like a fevered heartbeat, reflecting off the bay. The ocean stretched endlessly. The surface was deceptively peaceful. No surveillance teams. No watchers in the shadows. Not yet. But the night was young.

Sinclair hunched over the sleek coffee table. Her finger tapped rhythmically against Wiley's map as she studied it as if she'd never seen it before. The weathered paper crackled softly with each touch.

"Routing codes," she murmured as if she'd solved an ancient puzzle. Which, in a way, she had. "After he died, Wiley's money was moved from the Zurich bank where he'd hidden it. Then his plan must have been implemented at the same time as the purchase of his ranch in Argentina. Whatever his plan was, the seed money he started with has increased substantially."

Hooper had been invited to join them. Neagley figured Sinclair had invited him. He remained still as stone, but Neagley caught the microscopic tightening around his eyes.

Hooper had changed. When she'd first met him in Hamburg, he'd been one of the team.

Now, he seemed like an adversary.

Which was fine with Neagley.

She could handle enemies with one hand tied behind her and not break a sweat.

Friends and colleagues were much more difficult for her. Put succinctly, she sucked at relationships of all kinds.

Reacher was the only friend she'd made while in the Army, and maybe in her entire life, come to think of it. Neagley had never traded her life for approval of others. She was satisfied with her choices.

Ice clinked against crystal as Sinclair swirled her drink. The sound was sharp enough to slice the tension. "The bank that acquired Wiley's assets has a big office here. Tomorrow morning, we pay them a visit."

"You think they'll just hand over whatever you ask?" Hooper's voice carried an edge of skepticism. "You're not the NSA anymore. You have no muscle or leverage here."

Sinclair's lips curved into a predator's smile.

"Why Miami?" Neagley studied her body language, reading the absolute certainty in her posture.

Sinclair met her gaze. "Because Wiley's 'process' wasn't a simple payout scheme. It was a machine. Self-perpetuating and always in motion. The money flowed through this bank, then others, like blood through veins. Never stopping, never slowing, never settling."

"Presumably, Wiley planned to access the money at some point. But he died before he could perform the next step," Hooper said.

"So the bulk of the cash is just sitting there." Neagley frowned. "How much money are we talking?"

Sinclair sipped her amber drink, savoring the moment. "We're looking at ten times Wiley's original deposit. Maybe more."

Hooper's sharp exhale cut through the room. "Wiley's hundred million turned into a billion?"

"At least." Sinclair set her glass down with a decisive click.

Neagley had her doubts, but she said nothing. She was good with money and investing. She knew what the legal limits were. Wiley's results were well beyond normal limits.

"And if the money is already gone?" The muscles in Hooper's jaw danced beneath his skin. "What's your plan B?"

Sinclair's shoulder rose in an elegant shrug. "Then we follow the breadcrumbs."

Hooper's phone buzzed. Only one short, decisive vibration, but Neagley noticed.

His fingers moved quickly to close the screen as if he were worried they might see and steal his secrets.

Sinclair leaned forward. "Problem?"

"No." Hooper's response came too fast, too flat.

Sinclair's perfectly shaped eyebrow arched.

Neagley let the silence stretch. She didn't mind Hooper keeping secrets. Hell, she was much less transparent.

But some secrets were more dangerous than others.

Bottom line? Hooper made Neagley uneasy, and she was reasonably sure Hooper's secrets could get them all killed. Which meant the more distance she kept between them, the better.

The elevator dinged.

Neagley noted their reactions. Sinclair didn't stir and Hooper barely glanced up.

The elevator doors slid open quietly. A man stepped out.

He seemed vaguely familiar. Lean, hard, sun damaged. Moved like he owned the ground under his feet.

He didn't give Neagley so much as a quick glance.

His attention went straight to Hooper, and he dropped into a chair nearby like he belonged there.

"You call me in to babysit?"

Hooper didn't look at him.

Which meant Hooper wasn't surprised, but he wasn't exactly happy about it.

Neagley clocked the tension. She sized the guy up and caught the bulge of his holster beneath his jacket.

"Didn't think I'd be back on your payroll so soon, Sinclair," he said.

Sinclair shrugged. "We needed an extra pair of hands. Hooper suggested you."

After a curt nod of acknowledgment, he said, "Good to see you again, Neagley."

"Do I know you?" Neagley replied.

"Paul Bennett," he said, leaning back to stretch as if this were a routine social visit. "We met once a long time ago when we were a lot younger. Hamburg. When we were both in the Army. You were working with Reacher, as I remember."

The mention of Reacher's name caused Sinclair's eyes to widen, Neagley noticed.

Waiting to see where all of this was going, Neagley nodded and let the silence drag.

Sinclair watched the exchange but offered nothing. Hooper kept still.

Bennett drummed his fingers on the table, which emphasized his impatience. He flashed a grin. "Do I have spinach in my teeth or something?"

"You're early, Bennett." Hooper exhaled. Then he shifted, refocusing. "We have a timeline to keep."

Bennett's smirk deepened into something uglier.

Sinclair said, "Let's get back to it."

Neagley let the conversation roll forward. The situation had changed, and the vibe was more hostile than before.

What the hell was really going on here?

CHAPTER 26

Sunday, July 10
Miami, Florida

THE MANDARIN ORIENTAL GLEAMED in the Miami heat, all tinted glass and moneyed silence. Sunlight ricocheted off the windows, casting diamond patterns on the marble steps. The kind of place where people like Sinclair operated.

Kim Otto stepped inside. The blast of air-conditioning after the sweaty heat outside raised goosebumps on her arms. Her senses immediately cataloged the space.

Italian marble floors reflected the crystal chandeliers overhead. The quiet hum of discreet wealth surrounded everything. Too quiet. Places like this weren't truly silent. Muted conversations in hushed tones floated from the bar where ice clinked against crystal. Through the floor-to-ceiling windows came the faint murmur of ocean waves.

Kim caught her reflection in the polished brass elevator doors and ignored the concierge's assessing glance. The woman's eyes lingered on Kim's sensible clothes as if department store origins were a crime against fashion. Which they probably were.

Smithers loomed at her side. His broad shoulders, rigid posture, and practical stance marked him as law enforcement from fifty paces.

The message was both clear and final. They didn't belong here among the Hermès scarves and Cartier watches. They weren't the type to sip hundred-dollar cocktails on balconies or wrap themselves in five-star luxury bath towels.

Sinclair, though? She'd play the part perfectly. Kim could almost see her gliding through the lobby, turning heads without seeming to notice.

Kim moved toward the front desk, plastering on her best disarming smile. The woman behind the counter had the sharp eyes and perfect posture of someone trained to remember faces and forget names. The navy blazer she wore probably cost more than Kim's annual home mortgage bill.

"Good evening," Kim said, placing her Bureau credentials on the marble surface. The badge caught the overhead light briefly before Kim dropped it into her pocket. "I'm looking for a guest. Dr. Marian Sinclair."

The woman didn't react, but Kim caught the microscopic flicker of recognition in her perfectly mascaraed eyes that lasted less than a heartbeat.

"I'm sorry, ma'am, but we can't give out guest information." Her practiced neutrality had no doubt denied kings and criminals alike.

Kim nodded as if she understood. Which she did. That didn't mean she cared. This wasn't a social call.

"She checked in under her real name." Smithers's voice rumbled like distant thunder. "That means she's not hiding."

Or she wants to be found. The thought slithered through Kim's mind like ice water.

The woman behind the counter smiled to reveal the kind of perfect teeth that only money can buy. "I'm afraid I can't help you."

Kim leaned in just enough to make it personal. "We're not here to bother her. We just need to know if she's in the building."

A beat of hesitation. The woman's French-manicured nails tapped once against the counter. "She checked out an hour ago."

Kim absorbed that, feeling the investigation shift beneath her feet. "Alone?"

The woman's eyes darted to the security cameras mounted in the corner. "She had visitors earlier today."

"Names?"

"I don't have that information."

Probably a lie.

Kim kept her expression neutral, but she felt Smithers tense beside her like a guard dog catching a scent. Sinclair was traveling with others. Which meant the operation was planned, choreographed, and every move calculated.

Gaspar's intel was solid. Sinclair had been here. She'd met someone here. Then she vanished into the Miami heat like morning fog.

Kim took a half step back. "We'd like to see her room."

The woman's fragile smile hardened into diamond. "I'm afraid that's against policy."

Kim let the silence stretch. The fountain in the lobby trickled to fill the silence, each drop of recycled water providing rhythmic ticking like a game show clock.

"We can get a warrant. It'll take about an hour," Kim said, selling the bluff. "Maybe some of the other guests will have better information. We'll ask around while we wait."

The woman held her ground for three long seconds. Then she exhaled, just slightly, and glanced toward the security desk where two men in tailored suits pretended not to watch.

"Give me a moment."

She disappeared through a door behind the counter, her heels clicking a precise rhythm like a flamenco dancer.

Kim turned to Smithers. Sweat had begun to darken his collar despite the arctic air-conditioning. "She's waiting for clearance."

"Which means Sinclair was flagged and they're watching her," Smithers replied flatly. "Question is who's watching and what they want to gain."

Kim's gut tightened like a fist. Sinclair had left behind a trail. On purpose. Like breadcrumbs for children in a fairy tale. Except this was no fairy tale, and Sinclair was no fairy godmother.

A bellman followed the woman as she returned. "Thomas will take you to the suite you're interested in," she said dismissively as she returned to her desk.

"This way," Thomas said, making friendly conversation, as he led them into a private elevator. He used his keycard to unlock security controls and pushed the penthouse button on the panel.

The elevator lifted gently off the ground and made its way up the outside of the hotel, allowing a breathtaking panoramic view of the city and the Atlantic.

When the elevator car stopped, Thomas waved his keycard again and the doors opened like magic.

He stood beside the doors after they'd closed again. "I'll wait for you here."

The suite wrapped them in climate-controlled luxury. Notes of Sinclair's brand of pricey perfume lingered in the air. Everything gleamed. Chrome fixtures, glass tabletops, the ocean view beyond floor-to-ceiling windows.

Nine rooms. Four were bedrooms. The others were for socializing. They found no discarded clothes or personal effects. But trace evidence remained like shell fragments after the tide retreats.

Kim moved to the mahogany desk and trailed her fingers across its polished surface. No room service receipts. No airline confirmations. No scattered papers or forgotten pens.

She opened one of the drawers. A single matchbook inside that seemed to wait for her like an invitation.

She picked it up, the cardboard rough against her fingers. *Sabal Marina*. Gold letters on black.

Smithers caught her look from across the room where he was examining the curtains. "Someone left that on purpose. Neagley?"

Kim flipped the matchbook open. No markings. No writing. Just pristine matches waiting to spark.

"Could be a dead end," Smithers said from deeper in the suite. His voice echoed eerily off the marble that covered floors, counters, and walls.

"No chance," Kim replied as she tucked the matchbook into her pocket. "NSA Sinclair doesn't do random. Everything here is calculated, measured, precise."

Smithers returned with a discarded hand towel stained with heavy streaks of makeup foundation and mascara. He held it up to the afternoon light streaming through the windows.

Kim frowned. "Sinclair wasn't wearing that much makeup when we saw her at the cafe."

Smithers tossed it onto the counter where it landed with a soft thump. "Confirms she wasn't here alone."

"Four bedrooms. Maybe one each for Hooper, Sinclair, and Neagley. Have all four been used?" Visitors, the concierge had said. Plural. The word echoed like a warning. "Check the trash."

Smithers riffled through the chrome bins. He held up a torn corner of an envelope, cream-colored hotel stationery. He slid the envelope into an evidence bag and handed it to Kim.

The handwriting was sharp and deliberate. Each stroke was as precise as a knife cut.

Tomorrow. Then today's date.

She stared at it, feeling time compress around her.

Smithers's reflection watched her from the window.

CHAPTER 27

Sunday, July 10
Miami, Florida

KIM STEPPED OUT OF the Mandarin Oriental. The sun had shifted, painting the buildings in shades of gold and shadow. Cars crawled past on the street, dark windows tinted against the glare.

Smithers followed. "What now?"

Before she could answer, her phone buzzed. The screen showed an unknown number. She'd have ignored the call, but the digits were too random.

She answered. "Otto."

A pause filled with static and street noise. Then a low male voice, smooth as aged whiskey.

"You're late."

Kim's pulse kicked up, adrenaline flooding her system. "Who is this?"

The line went dead.

She turned in a slow circle, scanning the sidewalk where tourists sauntered while lugging dozens of designer shopping bags. Parked cars gleamed in the heat. Traffic flowed steadily past like blood in the city's veins.

She could feel eyes on her skin like laser sights.

She lowered the phone. "We need to move. Get out of the line of fire."

They cut across the street toward the underground parking garage.

Smithers touched his ear, head tilting. "You hear that?"

Footsteps. Matching their pace. The sound bounced off concrete pillars, echoing in the garage's artificial twilight.

She turned her head slightly, catching a reflection in a tinted window.

A woman. Compact as a coiled spring. Dark clothing that absorbed light. Moving with the precision of a synchronized swimmer.

Kim stopped abruptly. She tilted her head in the woman's direction because Smithers hadn't spotted her yet. "Neagley."

Neagley didn't break stride. She brushed past, close enough for Kim to smell gunmetal and leather. Her voice was low and calm as a snake.

"Go away, Otto," she said. "We don't need you. You're in the way."

Then she was gone, dissolving into the crowd outside like sugar in coffee.

Kim moved to follow, but Smithers caught her arm. His grip was tight enough to leave marks.

"She wanted you to see her. If she'd wanted you to follow, she'd have said so."

Kim inhaled sharply, tasting exhaust fumes and salt air. "Neagley said *we*. Could mean Reacher's here, too."

The thought raised the hair on her arms despite the heat.

"Or she might have meant Sinclair. We know Neagley is working with her," Smithers said reasonably as he slid behind the wheel of the rental.

Kim plopped onto the passenger seat as the leather burned through her clothes. She recalled the matchbook. *Sabal Marina.*

Smithers started the engine and flipped the AC up as high as it would go. "What's the angle?"

Kim replied, "Sabal Marina."

Smithers pulled into traffic, moving toward the water that shimmered like broken glass on the horizon.

Kim's phone buzzed again. This time, it was Gaspar. His name on the screen felt like the first friendly thing she'd seen all day. "Tell me something good, Chico."

"Wish I could, Sunshine," Gaspar replied. "Sinclair's name popped up at a private bank there in Miami. Meeting scheduled for tonight."

Smithers looked over, sweat darkening his temples. "Where?"

Gaspar read the address. Kim checked the matchbook again, though she didn't need to.

Same location. The pieces clicked together like a gun being assembled.

Kim exhaled. "We're in the right place."

Sinclair had left breadcrumbs. Questions hammered in Kim's mind. Did Sinclair want to be followed, or was she laying out a trail that led straight into quicksand?

Smithers pulled onto the highway where heat waves danced on the asphalt between slow moving vehicles. "So what's the plan?"

Kim shrugged. "We watch. Wait. Figure it out."

Smithers tapped his fingers against the arm rest in a nervous rhythm. "And if Sinclair gets what she came for?"

Kim didn't answer. The sun caught the rearview mirror, flashing like a warning.

And she had a feeling Reacher was already ahead of them, moving through Miami like a storm front, impossible to stop and dangerous to ignore.

She punched in the address for *Sabal Marina* and waited for the GPS to start talking.

CHAPTER 28

Sunday, July 10
Miami, Florida

SMITHERS FOLLOWED THE GPS to Sabal Marina. He muttered, "What the hell is going on here?"

Whatever was planned for tonight had drawn a significant crowd. Which, Kim figured, was the reason Sabal Marina had been chosen for whatever Sinclair was doing here.

The parking lot was full. Families piled out of SUVs bringing their entire homes with them, like they were going to Disney World for a month.

Smithers pulled in behind a long line of vehicles lined up at the entrance while a single agent checked ID and tickets at the gate. The attendant must have recognized some of the families because he waved them through as they approached. Others, presumably strangers, were subjected to a more thorough and time-consuming check.

The line moved slowly until Smithers reached the guard shack.

"Tickets, please, sir," the attendant said after Smithers buzzed down the window.

Smithers showed his FBI credentials. "We're not staying for the show. We need to take a look around and then we'll go."

The attendant's eyes widened. "Are you immigration enforcement? We called asking for help tonight, but we never heard back."

"No, sorry," Smithers replied firmly. "Something else."

"Okay, well, while you're here, help us keep a lid on the crowd, will you? We're shorthanded," the attendant said before he waved them through the gate.

Smithers gave him a quick wave in response and buzzed the window up while he rolled the SUV into the marina parking lot. He pulled up to the front door and parked nearby, as if the valet had done the job for him.

Kim climbed out of the passenger door and landed with both feet on the ground. "Half of Miami must be here tonight," she said when she had a chance to scan the crowd.

"Mostly families. Could be a fireworks display planned for later," Smithers replied as they moved deeper into the crowd.

"Yeah. Let's do what we came for and go before they get too rowdy," Kim said, swiveling her head to scan her surroundings. Yachts, docks, and speed boats still on their hoists filled most of the available spaces.

She caught a glimpse of the entrance where a sleek black sedan crept into the lot, gliding through the heat like a predator in the shallows. The kind of car meant to blend in but not disappear. Tinted windows, spotless finish, no plates visible from Kim's viewing angle.

"Check the entrance," she said, and Smithers shifted beside her, his stance easy but deliberate. He wasn't reaching for his weapon, but the readiness was there.

They observed the sedan ease into a parking spot near the entrance. The driver's door opened, smooth and controlled, like the man inside had thought about it before moving.

He stepped out.

Tall. Mid-forties. Angular features. His suit jacket, tailored but unbuttoned, framed an athletic build that suggested military. Or maybe he kept himself in shape for the kind of work that required top-notch conditioning.

His gaze swept the lot first, cataloging every detail, but not in a way that suggested nerves. He wasn't looking for an ambush. He was confirming.

He turned his attention to the marina and the crowds.

His eyes landed on Kim first. Then Smithers. Then back to Kim.

He smiled.

Not friendly. Not hostile. Just a measured expression, designed to test the reaction it got.

Smithers muttered, "Friend of yours?"

Kim didn't answer.

The man shut the car door behind him with the same deliberate ease and walked toward them.

Even pace. No hesitation. He moved like he always knew his next step before he took it.

Kim let him come. She stepped forward a fraction. Not enough to meet him halfway, but enough to establish that this was not the time or place for a confrontation.

"Agent Otto," he said, when he was close enough to speak at normal volume.

Kim's pulse stayed steady, but her muscles coiled. "Do I know you?"

He tilted his head slightly, like he was considering how to answer. Then he extended a hand. "Larry Knox."

Kim stared at his hand but didn't take it.

Knox smirked, dropping the offer without comment. He slid both hands into his pockets, casual but deliberate. His body language said he didn't rattle, didn't bluff, and wasn't here to waste time.

"I figured we should talk before you get too deep into this," he said.

Kim didn't move. "Too deep into what?"

Knox's gaze flicked toward the marina entrance, scanning for a moment before returning to her. His expression never changed, but Kim got the sense he was calculating his next words.

"Sinclair. Hooper. The bank." His voice was even, like he was reading a list off a grocery receipt.

Kim's stomach roiled. Whoever he was, he knew more than he should have. Which wasn't okay. Not at all.

"You think you're following the money," Knox continued casually.

Smithers exhaled loudly, but didn't reply.

Knox turned his head slightly, appraising Smithers. Kim caught the subtle shift in his stance. His weight moved slightly, no longer observing but assessing.

What did he want?

Kim stayed where she was. Knox's confidence wasn't arrogant. It wasn't overplayed. It was the kind of confidence that came from experience and competence.

Men like that didn't show up out of nowhere for no reason.

"That's not a warning," she said, keeping her tone neutral.

Knox pressed his lips together a moment before he advised, "You're watching the wrong people."

Kim crossed her arms. "We're satisfied with our approach."

Knox nodded like that was fair. "Sure."

She waited.

His eyes locked on hers. "But ask yourself this, why are you here?"

Kim felt the weight of his words settle on her shoulders. The question was a seed. One meant to take root. Meant to make her doubt. It was the sort of thing Cooper did all the time.

Knox let the silence stretch. He was watching her now, waiting for a reaction.

Kim didn't give him one. "You have something to say, say it."

His expression sharpened, easy posture vanishing for the briefest moment. "What you're doing here? Your whole assignment? It's not about Reacher."

Kim felt a minute flicker of doubt before shoving it aside. That was bullshit. Of course, this was about Reacher. Cooper wouldn't have sent her all over the planet otherwise.

Smithers shifted. "You expect us to take your word for that?"

Knox didn't answer right away. He checked his watch. Then his gaze flicked back to Kim. "You think Cooper sent you to Arizona and Boston and now here to find Reacher. But that's just the part he told you."

Kim's jaw tightened.

Knox pressed on. "Cooper knows where Reacher is. Probably always has."

Kim felt a sharp jolt in her gut.

"He sent you here anyway," Knox said matter-of-factly. "You should ask yourself why."

Kim held his stare. She didn't have an answer, and she was sure he knew as much.

Knox glanced at the crowd. Darkness was gathering while the families spread their blankets on the ground facing the water where the fireworks display would be. "You're looking for Reacher. But maybe Cooper wants you to find something else."

Kim's pulse ticked up.

"Think about that. What does Cooper really want?" He let that sit while he pulled a burner phone from his pocket and dropped it into hers. "Call me when you figure it out. Clock's ticking, Agent Otto. Don't waste too much time."

Knox turned and stepped away, headed to his sedan with the same casual confidence he'd walked in with.

Kim didn't stop him. Didn't call after him.

Because Knox wasn't trying to convince her. He wanted to shake her.

And she had no idea which part of his warning was true. If any.

She slid her phone from her pocket and pressed the button to call the only intel source with the actual facts.

Once again, Cooper failed to pick up her call. She didn't bother with a message. Instead, she retrieved the dedicated burner phone and pressed the redial to call the only reliable source she had.

"What's the problem, Suzie Wong?" Gaspar asked when he picked up.

She filled him in and they agreed on a long list of tasks to be completed.

"When I'm done granting your wishes, how about I wave my magic wand and create world peace?" Gaspar teased.

"Works for me. But do it quick. I'm playing beat the clock here," she said before she disconnected.

CHAPTER 29

Sunday, July 10
Miami, Florida

THE NIGHT AIR IN Miami carried the scent of sea salt and gasoline, thick with the oily residue of sunbaked asphalt. The sidewalk beneath Kim's boots radiated leftover heat, a slow burn against the cooling breeze rolling off the water.

Global Continental Bank, a sleek glass and steel fortress built for the ultra-wealthy, stood across the street. Mirrored windows reflected the city lights, warping them into a jagged mosaic while concealing everything inside from casual watchers walking the streets.

Smithers leaned against the SUV, arms crossed, scanning the street like a bored pedestrian. The air settled on his shoulders like a steam towel. He ignored the sweat and maintained his focus.

He muttered into his coms, "Sinclair's late."

"Copy that." Kim exhaled. Her stomach stayed steady, but something felt off. A weight pressing everything flat. The kind of quiet that came before a situation went sideways.

A sleek black SUV rolled up near the curb. The engine was barely audible. Tinted windows, no plates visible from her angle. The back door swung open with a faint mechanical hiss.

Marian Sinclair stepped out wearing a tailored cream blazer, sunglasses perched on her head, her expression unreadable.

Her heels clicked against the pavement, sharp and deliberate. She presented herself as she had been for so long, a woman used to power, who expected doors to open before she even reached them.

Her entitled demeanor was ingrained in her DNA and nurtured over a lifetime of clandestine operations.

Behind Sinclair, Brad Hooper emerged from the SUV. His movements were precise but not rushed. He scanned the street the way a bodyguard would. Like he knew threats could come from any direction.

His shirt sleeves were rolled up and exposed forearm tendons flexed beneath his skin. His gaze locked on Sinclair, but his attention never stopped searching as if he were shooting a video of the entire scene.

Sinclair and Hooper were not equals. Not even close. She led the way and he followed. Until they reached the front entrance. Hooper reached forward and pressed a button. A few moments later, a well-dressed man ushered them inside.

"You've heard of impeccable customer service. Banks that open on Sunday night, just because you ask. What next?" Gaspar said in her ear.

Kim rolled her shoulders. Quietly, she murmured into the coms, "Showtime."

Smithers pushed off the car, hands loose at his sides, tension thrumming just beneath the surface.

Before he could make a move, Neagley appeared.

She came from the opposite direction, gliding like a ghost in dark clothing. Her silhouette was barely distinguishable from the shifting shadows of the street and passed a group of pedestrians without drawing a second glance.

Kim kept eyes on her.

Neagley didn't appear to be with Sinclair or Hooper. She didn't follow them into the bank through the front. Instead, she stopped near the bank's side entrance, watching.

"Neagley's here," Kim muttered, her voice barely above the rustle of palm fronds shifting in the breeze.

Smithers followed her line of sight. "But not going in."

"Nope. Not yet," Kim said. "Which means they're not expecting trouble."

"At least, not the kind Neagley is infamous for," Gaspar replied through the coms from his home office. "You've read her Army files. Watch yourselves out there."

The distant whine of a siren, muffled through the humid air, faded as the emergency vehicle turned away. Kim's focus stayed locked on Neagley.

Gaspar's voice in her ear, "Operative on the sidewalk across the street. Running him through facial recognition now to get a name. Be careful."

"That's just what we don't need," Kim replied under her breath. The faint taste of metal coated her tongue, caused by the surge of adrenaline coursing through her.

Gaspar came back almost instantly. "Name's Bennett. Definitely an operative. Could be on either side, though."

Smithers shifted his position for a better view. "Stay sharp. That operative is also in play. Which means there's four of them and two of us."

Kim tapped her earpiece. "Gaspar, you set up yet?"

"Yep." Gaspar's voice came through crisp, underscored by the faint clicking of keys. "Been looking around inside for the past hour. They've got good security, but not as good as they think. I'm patched into the feed. No audio yet, but we've got real-time eyes and we're recording, just in case we miss something or need to go back through it."

Kim flexed her fingers. "Tell me what you see."

A pause, then Gaspar muttered, "Sinclair's in a private meeting room. Third floor. They walked her back without making her wait. That's a sign of either fear or respect. Maybe both."

"And Hooper?" Smithers asked, voice low.

"Standing outside the door like a damned gargoyle."

Kim absorbed that. "Who's she meeting?"

"Bank director. Shiny plate on the door says his name is Fred Schafer. Looks like he's had a bad day."

Kim's stomach twisted. "Define 'bad day.'"

"She handed him a sheet of paper and told him it contained routing codes. His face went white as a snowman."

Kim's fingers curled. "What's she saying?"

"Can't hear, but she's pressing. Hard. He's resisting. She just handed him a demand and a phone." Gaspar exhaled. "Yeah. This is not a social call."

Kim's eyes locked onto the bank entrance. A subtle shift inside. A guard adjusted his stance. A second one repositioned.

Something was happening.

Then Neagley moved.

A single step backward.

Kim tensed. "Neagley just received some sort of signal. Any clue what it was or where it came from?"

"Schafer returned and handed Sinclair a flash drive. A few words were exchanged. She dropped the drive into her right jacket pocket," Gaspar reported in real time. "He's not thrilled at all. Now she's leaving."

"Here we go," Smithers replied as he pushed away from the vehicle. "I see Sinclair and Hooper at the rear exit."

"Where's Bennett?" Kim asked as she moved in the same direction.

"Not sure," Smithers said.

They crossed the street fast, the distant thump of bass from a nearby club pulsed against the sidewalk.

Bennett appeared out of nowhere like a magician's rabbit.

Not toward Sinclair and Hooper. But to block Kim.

Kim reached for her weapon just as Neagley stepped into her path.

Neagley's expression was unreadable as always, but her stance was clear.

"Move," Kim ordered.

Neagley didn't. "Wrong target."

Kim clenched her jaw. "You helping them now?"

Neagley was stern and carried a level of menace Kim hadn't caught before. "You think Sinclair is the biggest problem here?"

"What the hell are you talking about? Get out of the way." Kim's pulse pounded against her ribs.

"Can't do that."

"Why not?"

"Orders," Neagley replied.

"Orders from whom?" Kim demanded.

She shifted her weight to move around the obstacle, but Neagley's gaze locked onto hers.

"Think about it, Otto. You're here because of Cooper. Sinclair and Cooper travel in the same circles. They are not friends," Neagley said, laying out a few bare facts. "You know the players as well as anyone. In this situation, what would Reacher do?"

Kim froze.

A chill that defied the relentless weather wrapped around her spine.

"How the hell would I know?" Kim cocked her head. "Reacher's not here."

Neagley narrowed her eyes to give Kim a steady stare. "You sure about that?"

The words landed like a gut punch.

Kim hesitated. Just for a second.

And that was all the time Neagley needed. Her gaze met Bennett's, and he moved quickly to step between them.

Kim didn't have a clean path anymore. Smithers was too far away. Gaspar was a superhero, but he couldn't transport himself instantly from Coconut Grove.

The opportunity was lost.

Sinclair and Hooper slid into the waiting SUV, and it peeled away from the curb, tires hissing against hot pavement.

Neagley exhaled like she'd just averted a disaster.

Kim seethed. "You let them go."

Neagley didn't gloat. Didn't smirk. She just watched.

Then she stepped back. "Why did Cooper send you here?"

"I suppose you've got a theory about that, too," Kim snapped angrily.

"Reacher doesn't want you dead, Otto. He won't like it if you get yourself killed. You should know that by now," Neagley said. "Can you say the same thing about Cooper?"

Before she could follow up, a loud crash filled the air, followed by car alarms and honking horns and screaming pedestrians. Briefly, Kim glanced toward the melee. Two vehicles had slammed into each other when one blew through the red light.

When she returned her attention to the bank, Neagley was gone, slipping into the shadows with effortless grace as if she had done it a thousand times before.

"Anybody see where she went?" Kim asked.

"No," Smithers said.

"I'll check street cams, but it'll take me a minute," Gaspar replied. "I'll look for Reacher while I'm at it."

"Thanks," Kim said.

The black SUV carrying Sinclair and Hooper was already long gone.

First responders had arrived to handle the traffic crash and direct traffic around it.

Kim exhaled. "That could've gone better."

"Roger that." Smithers said. "Now what?"

"Hard to say. The pieces aren't fitting together," Kim replied. "Too many holes in our intel. We need to fix that and figure out what to do next."

"Or we could go back to DC and camp on Cooper's doorstep until he tells us what we want to know," Smithers said angrily. "I'm tired of being a pawn in his game."

"Yeah, well, welcome to my world," Kim deadpanned. "Let's get out of this heat. Gaspar, we're headed your way."

CHAPTER 30

Sunday, July 10
Miami, Florida

THE PRIVATE JET LIFTED off from one of Miami's private executive airstrips, slicing through gravity's resistance to float above the ocean. Below, the city sprawled amid the humid haze. Neon rays were bleeding across the skyline in shimmering, pulsing ribbons.

Sinclair leaned against the cool leather of her seat. Her laptop was open and the screen glowed pale amid the dimmed cabin lights.

"You've been staring at that screen for twenty minutes," Hooper said from across the cabin, fingers laced over his hard stomach. "Did you find something?"

Bennett sat off to the side, idly flipping a pen between his fingers.

"Bennett, if you don't stop with that pen, I might have to shoot you," Neagley called from the rear of the cabin, where she sat with her arms crossed and eyes closed.

"I thought you were sleeping," Bennett shot back.

"I sleep when I need to," Neagley replied. "Right now, I'm listening to you fidget."

"Some of us cope with tension differently," Bennett said, though Sinclair wasn't fooled by his casual posture. The man was wound tighter than a precision stopwatch.

Sinclair plugged the flash drive into her laptop and keyed in a secure decryption sequence. The screen flickered. Columns of transactions filled the display. Numbers rolled like cascading dominos, displaying far more than she had expected.

"This can't be right," she muttered, hitting the stop button after a few minutes. "There's too much here."

"Care to share with the rest of us?" Hooper asked, leaning forward.

Sinclair kept scrolling. "I've never seen anything like this. It's a machine, an ecosystem. Self-sustaining transactions operating for decades without human intervention."

"English, please," Bennett interjected.

"I expected to find a dormant slush fund," Sinclair said. "This is alive."

Hooper shifted, his sharp eyes catching the change in her expression. "What exactly do you mean by 'alive'?"

"It's still running," Sinclair said, keeping her voice even.

"Wiley's money is still there, you mean?" Bennett asked, suddenly alert.

"Yes. And it never stopped growing. Exponentially." Sinclair tapped a key, scrolling through pages. "No oversight. No intervention. Pure automation."

"Someone has to be controlling it," Hooper insisted, straightening in his seat.

Sinclair flicked a glance at Neagley before answering. "No one is."

"That's not possible," Hooper scoffed.

"Actually, it is," Sinclair replied, eyes still on the screen. "It's a closed system. Wiley didn't need a human manager. He built it to feed itself."

"Show me."

"Funds cycle through shadow holding companies. Reinvest. Multiply. Buy assets. Sell them," She rotated the laptop toward him. "Funnel cash into secure accounts and start over."

Hooper studied the screen, flipping from one document to another. After half an hour, he said, "Okay. It's not exactly feeding itself. But it is multiplying at amazing rates."

"How?" Sinclair replied.

"Looks like income far exceeds expenses. Which is the way money usually grows, isn't it?" Hooper said. "Deposits come from all over the globe. A day or two later, the money goes out again. Minus a very hefty chunk that might be a brokerage fee of some sort."

"How hefty?" Neagley asked.

"Millions in. More millions out," Hooper replied. "The first transaction was one hundred million dollars deposited in Zurich. Sixty million of that was sent by wire transfer to Argentina."

"Presumably to pay for Wiley's ranch," Sinclair explained. "There was forty million left, and that was moved to the Zurich bank branch in Miami before being transferred to the Caymans."

"Is the money still there?" Neagley asked.

Hooper nodded. "And millions more."

"You're telling me whatever this process is, it's actually still generating that much money?" Bennett whistled low.

"It's self-propelled. No expertise required," Neagley said, voice quiet but firm. "Which means someone can hijack it at any time."

"They'd need to know the fund existed first," Hooper replied.

"Yep. But how hard is that? Dozens of people must know the money exists after all these years," Neagley replied. "Over time, more than one person could hijack it, if they knew where to find it."

"And someone already has," Sinclair said, pulling up a folder labeled *Active Asset Acquisitions*. "Look at these purchases. Freight vessels, logistics firms, security companies. Mercenary groups. Arms shipments."

Hooper muttered an astonished curse.

"Not normal passive investing, is it?" Bennett said tightly.

"No," Sinclair confirmed. "It's a pipeline."

"A pipeline for what exactly?" Bennett pressed.

"These security firms? They're shells," Sinclair said, continuing to scroll through the screens. "The freight ships are marked 'inactive' in international shipping lanes."

"Meaning what?" Hooper demanded.

"Meaning they're ghosts," Sinclair said grimly. "Perfect for moving illegal cargo."

"So Wiley's self-sustaining money machine is now someone's personal black-market ATM?" Bennett said, as if he wholeheartedly approved.

Hooper scanned the transactions. "These numbers are staggering."

"Over a billion in movement," Sinclair confirmed. "And that's just what we can see."

"The real question is who's behind all of this," Neagley said.

"They're not controlling it," Sinclair surmised. "They're riding it."

"We'll learn more tomorrow morning at the Cayman Islands bank," Hooper said, a hard smile forming. "The bank manager is an old friend. He'll tell us what we need to know."

"Always good to return to the Caymans," Bennett said, stretching.

Sinclair turned to Neagley. "You haven't said much about all this."

Neagley met her gaze, calm and steady. "I don't like puzzles with missing pieces."

Sinclair let it go. Neagley knew more than she was saying. That much was clear.

CHAPTER 31

Sunday, July 10
Miami, Florida

KIM PACED THE LENGTH of Gaspar's home office and back, thinking. From the leather couch, Smithers rested with his eyes closed. Gaspar was working the keyboards.

She'd also given him the drives from the Lone Wolf box to work on. So far, he hadn't cracked the encryption, either.

A hint of salt air crept in from the bay, carrying with it the promise of another sticky Florida summer night. Air-conditioning labored against Miami's relentless heat and humidity. Muffled sounds of traffic filtered through the closed windows.

Gaspar glanced up from his screen. "You're making me nervous, Sunshine."

"Sorry." Kim ran a hand through her damp hair, feeling it cling to her neck. "I'm thinking."

"You're worrying," Smithers corrected, his voice rough with fatigue. "There's a difference."

Gaspar's fingers striking keys carried like distant rainfall. "I've been running through the bank's CCTV footage again. Looks like Sinclair took more than data. She took history."

"What does that mean?" Kim's frown deepened, creating a sharp line between her brows.

"Yeah," Smithers added, leaning forward. "Let's skip the drama and get to it so we can move forward."

Kim grinned when Gaspar leaned back, extended his legs and folded them at the ankles. She'd seen him adopt the same posture many times. It was his way of stretching his bad leg without acknowledging the constant pain.

"Sinclair went into the bank in Miami with some sort of plan. Walked straight to a meeting room like she owned the place. No delays. No waiting," Gaspar said thoughtfully. "Bank director met with her personally, no intermediaries."

"Meaning what?" Smithers asked.

"In that world?" Kim replied. "That's like the Pope giving you a private audience. Nothing like that happens without advance planning and lots of it."

"She wasn't alone. Hooper, Bennett, and Neagley were with her," Smithers said, thinking about it. "That's a lot of fire power for one meeting where not much of anything seemed to happen."

"Right. But the key words are 'seemed to.' We missed something," Kim said slowly. "So what was she after and did she get it?"

"Sinclair handed the bank guy a sheet of paper. I can't read it, but when I zoomed in as far as I could get, I'd say it looks like it could contain routing codes," Gaspar smiled as if she were a particularly apt pupil. "Then the banker left the room. Came back two minutes later with a flash drive. Like he only had to collect it from somewhere. As if he were expecting her and had prepared for her visit."

Kim digested the intel and nodded. "So the drive was preloaded. And he didn't plug it into a computer while she was there. Which means she knew what was supposed to be on it and she trusted him to deliver what she came to collect."

"Exactly. He had it ready to go." Gaspar replied easily. "She didn't have to negotiate, search, or pressure him for records. She knew exactly what to ask for and she probably asked in advance of the meeting. To do all of that, someone has been feeding her intel."

Kim exhaled slowly. The implications crystallized in her mind like ice forming on a window.

If he had pointed Sinclair in the bank's direction, did that mean he was working with Sinclair or against her?

Smithers caught the same idea at the same time. "Cooper?"

"Possibly." Kim's jaw tightened until she felt her teeth protest and she eased off.

Cooper had sent her after Reacher. That had always been her mission. But now, somehow, Sinclair was in the mix. An ex-NSA deputy's rogue operation and a growing pile of unanswered questions confounded and confused the operation.

Smithers shifted his weight. "You think Cooper sent us here for Sinclair?"

"It's the sort of thing he would do," Gaspar replied. "Sinclair walked out of the bank with something. Could've been a contract, financial records, a name. But whatever it was, she was sure as hell happy to have it."

Kim's pulse ticked up. "Where's she going?"

"Hard to say," Gaspar admitted. "But she mentioned the Caymans in passing when they were leaving. Looked like they were making travel plans."

Kim's fingers tightened around the phone. "So Sinclair's next stop is Grand Cayman."

"Wouldn't bet against it," Gaspar confirmed.

"The hell with it. Let's find out." Kim fished the dedicated burner phone she kept for private calls with Cooper from her pocket and pressed the speed dial. The phone barely completed its first ring before he answered.

"Otto," he said, voice crisp as fresh currency. "What have you got?"

"We've got a few problems," she replied, putting the call on speaker so Smithers could hear.

"You usually do."

Kim paced to the window, watching heat ripple off the pavement below. "Sinclair is out of Miami. She left the country an hour ago."

A pause hung between them like smoke. "Where?"

"Cayman Islands," Kim replied, testing the words like placing weights on a scale.

Cooper's silence stretched just a beat too long, heavy with unspoken knowledge.

"You don't seem surprised," Kim said, pressing her free hand against the cool glass. "In fact, you already knew Sinclair was in Miami, didn't you?"

"Of course."

"Care to tell me why you sent me after her?" Kim asked, watching a bead of condensation track down the window. "Is this connected to her getting passed over for NSA director?"

Cooper's tone remained unchanged, professional as polished steel. "A scorned agent at her level isn't something to be trifled with, Otto. She's spent decades inside the deepest intelligence corridors around the world. She knows where all the bodies are buried, including the ones you and Reacher put in the ground."

Kim leaned against the desk, feeling the solid wood ground her. "So she's a loaded weapon."

"She's a threat," Cooper confirmed. "One that needs to be contained."

The air-conditioning clicked off, leaving the room in sudden, heavy silence.

"What about Reacher?" Kim asked, the name falling like a gauntlet. "Any connection between them?"

Another measured pause. "It's possible. They were both in government service for a long time. Could have crossed paths. The details are unclear."

"Convenient," Smithers murmured softly from the couch.

Kim waited, but Cooper offered nothing more.

"Sinclair's digging into that is making you nervous," she said.

"A scorned agent at her level is nothing to be trifled with," Cooper said. "Sinclair spent her entire career inside one of the most secretive agencies in the government. She knows things we'd rather she didn't share."

Kim's pulse ticked up. "So this isn't about Reacher?"

A beat of silence. Then Cooper said, "It's likely they knew each other."

"Likely?" Kim pressed. "That's all you've got?"

Cooper's voice stayed even. "Follow Sinclair to Grand Cayman. See where it leads."

"And if it leads to Reacher?"

"Then you'll know what to do." Cooper's voice stayed neutral as Switzerland. "Follow the money."

"That's what this is really about," she said. "The money. Sinclair's a vector. Means to an end."

Cooper didn't confirm or deny it. His silence was answer enough.

"So we follow Sinclair until we know whether Reacher is involved?" she pressed.

"Correct."

The word landed like a full stop.

The dead air confirmed he'd hung up.

Kim exhaled as she returned the burner to her pocket.

"Cooper's not telling everything he knows about all of this," Kim said, tasting the staleness of the office air.

Smithers snorted a sharp sound in the quiet room. "Shock of the century. Man treats information like kids treat candy. Only shares when he's forced to."

Kim pushed off the desk. Her muscles fairly hummed with tension. "We need to know more about Sinclair. Everything there is to know."

"Where do we start?" Smithers asked, already reaching for his gear.

Kim grabbed her jacket and settled the familiar weight across her shoulders. "By doing what Cooper just told us to do. We follow the money."

Smithers arched both eyebrows. "Cayman Islands?"

"Yeah. And she's got a team with her. From the manifest, it looks like Hooper, Bennett, and Neagley," Gaspar said.

Kim's eyebrows shot up, almost of their own volition. "Guess Neagley really is working with Sinclair now. Could mean Reacher's closer than expected."

"You'd better get going," Gaspar said, nodding. "Cooper's got a jet waiting."

"Good thing we've packed light. Place like that, heavy luggage draws attention." Smithers rose off the couch, pulled open the door, hinges whispering as he left the room.

"Thanks, Chico. Let us know when you find out what's on those flash drives." Kim stepped out behind Smithers into the humid Miami night.

The scent of rain hung heavy in the distance, promising a storm coming across from the Gulf. She shuddered. Storms and small planes were never an easy combination for her.

Sinclair was chasing something. Cooper was keeping secrets. And Reacher?

She still had no proof he was even in play.

But if he was?

He was already ahead of them all, moving like a shadow just beyond their reach.

The first drops of rain began to fall as she followed Smithers along the path into the darkness.

CHAPTER 32

Monday, July 11
Grand Cayman

NEAGLEY WATCHED AS THE Gulfstream touched down with barely a whisper and its wheels rolled smoothly across the tarmac in Grand Cayman. The descent had been flawless, as expected.

Neagley was literally fearless, meaning she felt no fear. Air travel was the safest form of travel in the world. Not one thing to concern herself about on that score.

Not that her fear or the lack of it mattered much. Air travel safety wasn't affected either way.

A mosaic of streetlights and moonlit coastline sprawled in the darkness outside the window. Even at this hour, the July heat pressed down like thick syrup. The scent of salty sea and tropical plants combined to create a compost vibe of rotting fruit and decomposing fish.

Sinclair closed her laptop and pinched the bridge of her nose. The last few hours had been a sprint, deciphering Wiley's financial network while cross-referencing data against what she already knew. But heavy and unanswered questions still hung in the air.

Across from Sinclair, Hooper checked his watch. His forearm flexed as he adjusted the band. The veins in his forearms stood out against tanned skin.

Bennett sat farther down, arms crossed, watching the cabin door as if expecting trouble to step through it. Neagley, quiet as ever, leaned back with her eyes half-closed, though she wasn't resting.

The intercom crackled, the pilot's voice calm and clipped. "Welcome to Grand Cayman, Dr. Sinclair. Customs has been cleared. You're good to go."

Sinclair stood, rolling her shoulders to shake off the stiffness of travel. The cabin air was cool, sterile, but the humidity beyond the sealed door was already creeping in.

"No reception committee?" she asked.

"Just as planned," Hooper said, pulling out his phone. His fingers danced over the screen before he dialed.

Sinclair slung her bag over her shoulder and adjusted the strap, listening with mild interest as Hooper spoke.

"We need access. Tonight." His voice was low, controlled.

A pause.

Sinclair caught the faintest edge of annoyance in his expression.

"I don't care about security protocols," Hooper said, voice sharpening. Another pause. "Not before five? That's the best you can do?"

He exhaled sharply through his nose and snapped the phone shut.

Sinclair arched a brow. "Problem?"

"Bank director can't disable overnight security before five a.m.," Hooper muttered. "Earliest he'll meet us is five-thirty."

Sinclair's lips pressed into a thin line. It wasn't unexpected, but she hated waiting.

"Guess that gives us a few hours," Bennett said, standing and stretching with deliberate ease. "Could be worse."

The pilot shut everything down and a few minutes later, he opened the door and lowered the stairs. The passengers filed through the door, one at a time.

Neagley was the last one out except for the pilot. She stepped onto the hot tarmac, feeling the heat through the soles of her boots.

Outside, the low rumble of the jet engines faded, replaced by the rhythmic chirr of insects and the muted roar of waves crashing against the beaches beyond the airport's perimeter.

Neagley was already moving toward the terminal. "Let's go."

The moment the aircraft door was unsealed, the Caribbean night seemed to swallow them whole. The tarmac stretched ahead, glowing under floodlights that threw sharp shadows across the concrete. Beyond the airport fence, palm trees swayed lazily in the warm breeze.

A black SUV idled just beyond the private hangar. Tinted windows obscured the driver. The soft rumble of the idling engine filled the silence as they approached.

Sinclair slid into the backseat first. Hooper followed, then Bennett and Neagley. The interior smelled of sun-baked leather and faintly of cigars, probably reflecting the last passenger's vice.

The driver, a nondescript man wearing a dark polo shirt, waited until they were all inside before easing onto the narrow road leading away from the airport.

Neagley gazed out the window as they sped through the quiet island streets. The town was a study in contrasts—beach front resorts with opulent balconies not far from modest homes. Windows were mostly dark, but a few showed dim lighting glowing softly in the quiet darkness. An occasional neon sign advertising rum bars and late-night cafés flickered.

The SUV's tires hummed against the pavement. Hooper checked his watch again.

"You think the banker's going to cooperate?" he asked.

Sinclair turned her gaze back to him. "He'll do what's required."

Hooper studied her, something unreadable in his expression. "And if he doesn't?"

Sinclair replied, "Then we find someone else."

The SUV made a sharp right, veering onto a quieter road lined with palm trees and high, wrought-iron gates. The destination ahead was a private villa, secluded and discreet. The kind of place arranged for people who didn't want to be noticed.

The driver pulled through the gate and up the curved driveway. Soft exterior lighting cast a warm glow over the modern façade. Sleek clean lines and massive windows overlooked the ocean.

Bennett exhaled as he stepped out. "Well, it's not exactly the Ritz, but it'll do."

"Rest while you can," Sinclair replied as she pushed the villa's door open and stepped inside.

Neagley moved past her. The interior was cool, scented with citrus and fresh linen. She made a quick tour of the villa while securing the entry points with quick efficiency.

Bennett tossed his bag onto a chair, already making himself comfortable.

Hooper leaned against the wall, arms crossed. "You're not planning on sleeping, are you?"

Sinclair dropped her bag onto a glass-topped table. "No."

Hooper's jaw tightened slightly, but he didn't argue.

Neagley watched the dynamic. Hooper knew Sinclair better than Neagley had realized. Which changed the situation significantly.

"Fine," Hooper said. "Just don't let your brain fry before morning."

Sinclair ignored him, already pulling out her laptop. The Cayman bank held the next piece of the puzzle.

And by sunrise, she intended to have it in her hands.

Neagley pushed off the chair and stretched. "I'm going for a walk."

Sinclair lifted her head. "Not a good idea."

Neagley's expression remained neutral. "Been cooped up too long."

"We're not on vacation," Sinclair said.

Neagley gave her a level stare. "And I need fresh air. Won't be long."

Sinclair didn't like it. She'd already figured out Neagley wasn't the type to take casual strolls alone in the moonlight.

Sinclair turned to Bennett. "Go with her."

Neagley's gaze flicked to Bennett, then back to Sinclair. "That won't be necessary."

"Not up for debate." Sinclair's voice was steel. "We can't have any trouble here tonight."

Bennett pushed himself upright and stretched. "Fine by me. I'm kinking up here myself."

Neagley exhaled annoyance but didn't argue. She pulled open the villa door and stepped out into the humid night with Bennett close behind.

CHAPTER 33

Monday, July 11
Grand Cayman

EVEN IN THE DEAD of night, Grand Cayman refused to cool. The air was thick as molasses and twice as sticky. Sweat trickled down Neagley's spine, sticking to her lightweight shirt as she moved through the darkness.

Closer to the ocean, she noticed the heavy scent of salt, sun baked stone, and something sweet like rotting mango hanging in the air. Her nose wrinkled when the faint trace of diesel from the boats mixed with the perpetual lingering scent of suntan lotions.

The quiet streets were mostly empty. Visibility was bathed in the sickly yellow glow of sparse streetlights. Slipping between shadows, she saw tourists sleeping it off and locals minding their own business. All appearing and disappearing like ghosts in the tropical night.

Neagley moved efficiently, smooth and silent. Her boots barely made a sound against the cracked pavement. Stealth was second nature to her. Each step was careful and calculated. Her breathing was measured and controlled.

Behind her, Bennett was not smooth and silent. He made more noise than a moose during rutting season.

His footsteps dragged more than enough to broadcast his location. His shoulders rolled with the subtle stiffness of a man who knew a fight was coming. He was comfortable with it. Expected it. Maybe even welcomed it, judging by the way his fingers kept flexing at his sides.

"Still not buying this 'just a walk' excuse," he muttered, his voice a rough whisper that seemed to hang in the stagnant air. "People don't take casual strolls in neighborhoods like this in the wee hours just for grins and giggles."

Neagley didn't answer.

"You know," Bennett continued, wiping sweat from his brow with the back of his hand, "a little heads-up would've been nice. 'Hey Bennett, we're going hunting tonight.' See? Not hard."

"You want to discuss this, that's fine. But not now," she finally said, low and controlled. "Just keep your eyes open and your mouth shut."

"I see you're as charming as you've always been," Bennett muttered, tugging at his damp collar.

They turned a corner onto a narrow, dimly lit street. The pavement was uneven beneath her feet. A flickering neon sign cast intermittent blue-red shadows across the weathered buildings. An electric buzz mingled with the steel drum music floating on the air.

The local Seven Fathoms rum bar windows glowed with friendly amber light. Silhouettes of late-night drinkers were visible through smoky glass. A single streetlight buzzed out front as if it might flicker out at any moment.

Which was when Neagley felt the shift.

A change in the atmosphere.

Like something waiting to spring.

The hair on the back of her neck rose and her skin prickled. The air seemed to thicken as if it were charged with potential energy.

She didn't slow her stride. Didn't stop to look. Just noted the angles, escape routes, and threats. Her fingers brushed against her concealed weapon's warmth against her skin.

Bennett's pace shortened. His hands shifted slightly, loose but ready. The subtle movement of a man preparing for impact.

"We've got company," he whispered, his breath hot against her ear as he moved closer.

Neagley nodded. She'd already noticed they weren't alone anymore.

Two men stepped from a side alley, emerging from the darkness like apparitions.

Not tourists. Not drunks.

Movements were too deliberate, too coordinated. Eyes scanned with professional assessment. The taller one's jawline flexed.

Every move was intentional.

Bennett noticed too. His shoulders squared and muscles tensed beneath his sweat-dampened shirt.

"Great," he muttered, the word dripping with sarcasm. "This night was getting boring. I was afraid I'd have to settle for a mai tai and an early bedtime."

"Stay focused," Neagley warned quietly, barely audible above the distant sounds of the ocean.

Two threats.

One was built thick, all arms and chest. Muscles didn't quite fit his off-the-rack dress shirt and the fabric strained across his broad shoulders.

Private security or ex-military. The scent of expensive cologne couldn't mask the underlying smell of gun oil and cigarettes. His knuckles were scarred, telling their own story.

The other one was lean and quick. A knife glinted in his right hand. The blade reflected the neon from the bar sign in pulsing flashes of crimson.

Neagley said cooly, "Before this gets messy, you might want to reconsider."

The thick one laughed, a sound like gravel being crushed. "Pretty sure of yourself, lady."

"I'm the one you should worry about," Bennett said, shifting his weight to the balls of his feet.

Without further warning, the lean one's knife moved first.

A glint of steel in the dim light. A blur of practiced motion. The air whistled as the blade cut through it.

Bennett dodged left. The knife missed his torso by inches. But he didn't see the third man emerging from the shadows behind a parked car.

A heavy object, maybe a pipe or a club, slammed into his skull with a dull thud.

He hit the pavement hard. The impact forced air from his lungs in a harsh gasp.

The smell of Bennett's blood filled Neagley's nostrils, metallic and warm.

"Son of a bitch," he growled, cut short by pain.

Neagley was already moving.

Knife guy came at her fast, the blade weaving complex patterns in the humid air.

"Don't make this worse than it needs to be," he hissed, his accent thick, Caribbean with something else underneath. European maybe.

Neagley weaved aside and then stepped in, caught his wrist, twisted hard.

Bone ground against bone beneath her grip.

He howled and his knife clattered onto the stones.

"Who sent you?" she demanded, applying more pressure to the captured joint.

He didn't respond.

Another set of footsteps approached from behind, the scuff of leather against concrete. The meaty smell of sweaty aggression grew stronger.

She turned, expecting the next attacker, muscles coiled to spring.

But the second man was already down, sprawled on the pavement like a broken doll.

Neagley hadn't touched him.

And she saw she wasn't the only one here anymore.

The big man moved from the shadows.

Tall. Deliberate. Controlled. The air around him seemed to vibrate with contained energy.

The pipe-wielder never saw him coming.

One second, he was upright, pipe raised for another strike.

The next, he was slammed against the wall with bone-jarring force and crumpled to the ground like discarded trash. The sound of his collapse echoed off the surrounding buildings.

Neagley didn't see him, but she didn't need to.

She could guess who had stepped in.

Right on time.

CHAPTER 34

Monday, July 11
Grand Cayman

BENNETT GROANED FROM THE pavement. Blood trickled down his temple, black in the dim light.

Neagley crouched, grabbed his arm, hauled him up. His skin was clammy beneath her fingers. His shirt was soaked with sweat and blood.

"You good?" she asked, scanning his pupils in the meager light.

Bennett wiped blood from his face with the back of his hand, leaving a dark smear across his cheek. "If 'good' means 'feeling like my skull just had a close encounter with a lead pipe,' then yeah, I'm fantastic."

Neagley glanced down the alley, her eyes adjusting to the deeper shadows.

No sign of Reacher.

She hadn't expected him to stick around with Bennett here. But he'd been there. Like a thunderstorm that passes quickly but changes the landscape.

"Did you see—" Bennett started, then winced, touching his head gingerly.

"See what?" Neagley asked, her tone deliberately neutral.

Bennett squinted into the darkness. "Third man. Big guy. Moved like...hell, I don't know what he moved like. Something not normal."

Neagley looked at him as if he'd sustained a concussion and was talking nonsense.

Bennett shook his head, immediately regretting it as pain lanced through his skull. "What the hell just happened? One minute we're taking your mysterious midnight stroll, the next we're in *West Side Story*."

Neagley dusted herself off, feeling the sting of scraped knuckles. "Someone sending a message would be my guess."

"Never heard of texting?" Bennett grumbled, probing the growing lump on his scalp.

He dusted himself off and exhaled sharply, eyes narrowing as he surveyed the fallen attackers. "You think Sinclair's got locals on her payroll? This feels like her style. Subtle as a sledgehammer."

"Not likely. We're here at her expense. Why would Sinclair send goons after us?" Neagley replied, the taste of adrenaline still sharp on her tongue.

Because Sinclair wasn't the only one with enough reach to organize an attack on foreign soil. Neagley had a long list of candidates far more likely than Sinclair.

"You know something you're not sharing," Bennett said, studying her face in the half-light. "Something about that third guy. The one who disappeared."

She shrugged. Reacher had been here waiting. He didn't leave a plan to connect later.

Neagley wasn't worried. Reacher would find her again. Not that she'd share any intel with Bennett.

"Let's get back," she said, avoiding his question as she headed toward the villa. "That head needs looking at."

"My head's fine," Bennett insisted, though his unsteady gait said otherwise as he followed. "It's the rest of me that's pissed off."

The villa was bathed in soft lighting, casting long shadows across the stone driveway. The scent of night-blooming jasmine hung in the air, incongruously delicate amid the lingering smell of violence that clung to them both.

Sinclair was waiting at the door, her silhouette sharp against the warm interior light. Her white linen blouse remained crisp despite the humidity and her posture ramrod straight.

Arms crossed. Expression unreadable.

But her gaze missed nothing, Neagley was sure.

Bennett limped past her, the sole of his shoe leaving a smear of blood on the polished floor. His scowl deepened with each painful step.

"You look like hell," Sinclair said, cool and measured.

"Wouldn't if you hadn't sent me out there," Bennett shot back, wincing as he lowered himself into a chair. "Or did you think I wouldn't figure out that little excursion was your idea?"

Sinclair's gaze flicked to Neagley. Assessing. Calculating.

"I didn't authorize any late-night reconnaissance," Sinclair said.

"Could've fooled me," Bennett muttered, pressing a towel to his bleeding scalp.

Hooper stood off to the side near the large windows overlooking the darkened beach. Arms crossed. Watching. His reflection in the glass created the illusion of two of him, both equally inscrutable.

He took stock of their condition. "Professionals?"

"Enough to be a problem," Neagley replied. "Not enough to solve it."

"Solve what, exactly?" Sinclair pressed, her fingers drumming against her forearm.

"I need a shower." Neagley brushed past them all without further comment.

In the pristine bathroom, Neagley washed the blood from her knuckles until the water ran pink then clear down the white marble sink. The skin was unbroken, but the impact still lingered in her bones. The familiar dull ache of violence absorbed and dispensed.

The mirror reflected a face composed, controlled, betraying nothing of the calculations happening behind her eyes.

She reached for a clean shirt in her bag and paused when she spied a disturbance in the precise arrangement of her belongings. Subtle. Almost imperceptible. But to Neagley, it was a flashing neon sign.

A small, folded note nestled between her spare magazine and her satellite phone.

No signature. No explanation.

Just four handwritten words in precise, block lettering she'd seen many times before.

See you in Argentina.

Neagley exhaled, slow and measured, feeling the weight of those words settle into her consciousness.

As always, her pulse remained steady, breathing unchanged.

She folded the note and tucked it away in her pocket until she had a chance to discard it where Sinclair and her crew wouldn't find it.

She glanced once more at her reflection, noting the hardness in her gaze.

"Game on, Reacher," she whispered to what appeared to be the empty room because she was certain Reacher could hear her.

CHAPTER 35

Monday, July 11
Grand Cayman

EVEN IN THE EARLY morning, Sinclair felt Grand Cayman's oppressive heat thick and heavy as she scanned the scene from the sidewalk. The bank's subdued façade waited patiently. It had been designed to protect power with discretion as it handled closely guarded secrets and the cash that came with them. All for a hefty fee, to be sure.

"Ready?" Sinclair asked.

"Yeah." Hooper led the way toward the entrance.

Bennett lingered a step behind, scanning for threats. The man never stopped watching. Which was exactly why Sinclair kept him around.

Neagley had slipped away somehow. Sinclair had no idea where she'd gone. The woman was uncontrollable. Which was not okay but there was nothing Sinclair could do about it.

Inside, the cold sterile bite of recycled air clashed with the warm humidity still clinging to her skin. The bank's lobby was sparsely furnished and almost totally unoccupied. White marble covered the floors. A highly polished desk manned by a single receptionist wearing a professional smile rested in the center of the room.

Sinclair approached the desk while adjusting her blazer cuff. "Dr. Marie Keating."

The man's gaze flickered with recognition before he nodded smoothly. "Mr. Gibbons is expecting you.

He pressed a button beneath the counter. A door to the right emitted a low, mechanical hiss as the lock disengaged. "This way, please."

Sinclair followed and stepped through the doorway first. Hooper was close behind with Bennett trailing like a shadow.

The conference room was exactly as she expected. Soundproofed, windowless, and designed for private discussions. Walter Gibbons, the bank director, waited behind a sleek glass desk. Sinclair sized him up in one glance. Late fifties, suit crisp, tie perfectly knotted, and posture so rigid he might have fallen over in a stiff wind.

Sinclair took the chair across from him. Hooper remained standing with his arms crossed. Bennett positioned himself near the door, back against the wall, expression unreadable.

Gibbons cleared his throat. "Dr. Keating, your request was unusual."

Sinclair didn't blink. "Unusual but necessary."

Gibbons hesitated, then tapped a few keys on his tablet. A moment later, the embedded screen in the table flickered to life. Columns of financial transactions scrolled rapidly in real-time. The sheer volume of numbers was staggering.

Sinclair leaned forward. "It's still running."

Gibbons exhaled sharply. "It never stops."

Sinclair traced the numbers with her gaze, watching the figures shift and evolve like a living thing. Money flowed through the system in bursts. Each entry was converted, reinvested, funneled through shell companies. Every transaction was an untouchable ghost in the system.

Hooper stepped closer and locked his gaze locked on the screen. "We need access to the account."

Gibbons stiffened. "That's not possible."

Hooper's fingers drummed against the back of Sinclair's chair. "You don't seem to understand the urgency of this situation."

Gibbons met his stare. "I understand perfectly. But this institution operates under strict legal protections. I have no authority and no ability to circumvent the systems. No one controls this fund directly. Not even us."

Sinclair narrowed her eyes. "Then who is moving the money?"

Gibbons shrugged to indicate his ignorance.

Hooper's jaw flexed. "That's bullshit."

"Mr. Wiley designed it this way," Gibbons said, voice smooth but firm. "His intention was for the account to remain functional throughout his lifetime and beyond."

Sinclair's stomach tightened. If Wiley had indeed created an untouchable system, she was screwed.

Hooper wasn't ready to back down. "You're telling me that billions of dollars are just moving on their own? That no one has a kill switch?"

Gibbons folded his hands. "That's two questions. No one has a kill switch. That's exactly what I'm telling you."

"But the billions of dollars in movement?" Hooper pressed.

"It's not possible that the money is actually moving on its own." Gibbons shrugged. "What I'm attempting to convey is that Mr. Wiley's system operates independently of bank personnel. Everything is handled electronically. We have no control and no access to the underlying assets."

Sinclair studied him. He was telling the truth as far as he knew it.

Bennett shifted, arms still crossed. "Then someone must be benefiting from this system. Otherwise, it would have been changed long ago."

Gibbons hesitated. A crack in his composure. Sinclair caught it immediately.

"Who is benefitting?" she asked.

The banker scanned the room and its occupants, probably checking for listening ears. Then he leaned in, voice low.

"There's activity," he admitted. "The account's performance is being steered. Not controlled but influenced, I'd say."

Sinclair held his gaze. "Who is doing this steering?"

Gibbons hesitated again, then turned the screen slightly, scrolling through recent transactions. He stopped on a name buried in layers of encrypted transfers.

Sinclair's pulse kicked up.

Hooper swore under his breath.

Bennett shifted just enough for his expression to change, something between realization and calculation.

Sinclair exhaled slowly, absorbing the weight of the revelation.

On the screen, hidden within the layers of financial movements, was a name she hadn't expected to see.

"Davy Crockett?" she said, not as incredulously as Gibbons might have expected.

The moment stretched.

Hooper's low, controlled reply came next. "That's impossible."

Gibbons looked uncomfortable. "You asked for answers. That's the one I can give you."

"Then we've got a much bigger problem," Bennett said. "Davy Crockett has been dead for almost two hundred years."

Sinclair felt the shift, as if the entire situation had changed. She felt it settling in, suffocating, undeniable.

On the screen, the name *Davy Crockett* sat buried in financial transactions worth billions. An absurdity. A name that shouldn't be there. Couldn't be there. And yet, there it was.

Hooper leaned over the table, his presence looming over Gibbons. "Whoever is using that name, what are they doing with the money?"

Gibbons swallowed hard. "The account cycles through various investments, but it never stops moving. Every transaction runs through the pre-programmed pathways Mr. Wiley set up decades ago."

"Bullshit," Hooper snapped. "Money doesn't move itself."

The banker's hands remained steady, but his jaw tightened. "No human oversight. That's what makes it untraceable. It regenerates, multiplies, moves between offshore holdings. There's no paper trail that leads to a single person. It was designed that way."

Sinclair narrowed her gaze. "Then how did *Davy Crockett* leave a fingerprint?"

Gibbons exhaled, pressing his fingers against his temple as if the headache behind his eyes was finally catching up to him. "It's not a fingerprint. It's a shadow. The system recognizes transactions linked to an origin point. An old authorization key buried in Wiley's original framework."

Sinclair's pulse ticked up. "Which means?"

Gibbons hesitated. "Someone is using a legacy access code to interact with the system. Not to control it. But to steer it."

Silence stretched.

Bennett shifted with his arms still crossed. "Then that means someone, somewhere, has been touching this money for a long time."

"And they didn't want anyone to notice," Hooper muttered.

Sinclair studied Gibbons, watching the way his throat moved as he swallowed again. "Who is Davy Crockett?"

The banker shook his head. "I don't have a name."

"Then give us something else," Sinclair pressed. "Whoever has been using that access code had to retrieve it from somewhere. Where does that authorization key link back to?"

Gibbons hesitated. He was sweating now, even in the icy cold of the air-conditioned office.

"There's a vault," he finally said.

Sinclair tilted her head slightly. "Vault?"

His fingers tapped a quiet rhythm against the desk. "A physical storage archive. Certain high-value accounts were granted secured storage upon request. Documents, bearer bonds, safety deposit holdings. Things of that nature."

Sinclair caught the evasive tone. "And?"

Gibbons exhaled sharply. "Mr. Wiley had one."

Bennett let out a low whistle. "Of course he did."

Sinclair frowned. "You're saying Wiley stored something here? Something that might explain all this?"

"I'm saying that if there are answers, that's the only place they'd be."

Hooper cut through the tension sharp and fast like a guillotine. "Then we need access."

Gibbons shook his head immediately. "That's not how this works."

Sinclair leaned forward. "Then explain how it works. Because you either open that vault for us right now, or we walk out of here and this bank gets a level of attention from which it will never recover."

Gibbons considered his options. His fingers moved to his tablet. "I can grant you access. But once you're inside, you're on your own."

Sinclair didn't hesitate. "Let's go."

CHAPTER 36

Monday, July 11
Grand Cayman

THE GULFSTREAM'S WHEELS TOUCHED down smoothly on the private airstrip in Grand Cayman, skimming over the tarmac like a stone skipping across water. The descent had been quick and clean. The pilot knew what he was doing. No wasted movement. No unnecessary time in the air.

Kim exhaled as she powered down her phone while the screen reflected her own tired eyes back at her. The flight had been a straight shot from Miami.

She was two hours behind Sinclair, and it felt too long. Every second counted now. Sinclair was moving fast. Which meant she and Smithers had to move faster.

The cabin door opened, and the night heat rolled in thick and oppressive. Sticky tropical humidity coated everything like a film.

Smithers shifted beside her, rolling his shoulders to loosen up. He shot her a look as they moved down the stairs to the waiting car. "Where to first?"

Kim didn't answer right away. The car was a sleek black sedan, parked just off the runway with the engine idling. The windows were tinted so dark they might as well have been painted. The driver, a local man in a pressed linen shirt, gave them a nod as he pulled the door open.

They slid inside. Cool air blasted from the vents, artificial and sharp against the humidity. The sedan moved smoothly onto the quiet, palm-lined road leading away from the airstrip.

Kim said, "Sinclair left Miami. She's here for money. That suggests she's here for the bank."

"Makes sense," Smithers nodded as he scanned the dark streets. "You think she's staying put or passing through?"

Kim's fingers tapped a steady rhythm against her knee. "My guess is that she's headed somewhere else after she collects her payday."

The driver turned onto a quieter road toward the island's financial district. Low, sleek buildings loomed ahead. The kind of structures that had no real address, no signage, just a row of tinted windows hiding the wealth inside.

"So you're thinking we should wait for her at the bank?" Smithers asked.

"I'd like to find her before she shows up at the bank." Kim pulled out her phone, checking the last GPS ping they had on Sinclair.

Smithers grinned. "You got a plan, or are we knocking on every door in every high-end hotel in town?"

Kim tapped the driver on the shoulder. "You know the luxury rentals in the area? The private ones?"

The driver's hands stayed steady on the wheel, but she caught the flicker of recognition in his eyes. "Few places like that. Depends on what kind of people you're looking for."

"The kind who fly in on private jets and don't want anyone to know they're here," Kim said.

The driver gave a low chuckle. "Yeah. I know those places."

The sedan made a sharp right onto a winding road leading toward the coastline. The properties here were gated, secluded. The kind of locations that catered to people with something to hide.

He pulled up in front of a villa with clean architectural lines and inviting exterior lighting. A black SUV was parked in the driveway.

Smithers leaned forward slightly, studying the scene. "We don't know that Sinclair and her posse are inside this particular house, do we?"

Kim shook her head as she replied, "If she's in there, she's not going anywhere for a while. Let's do a bit of recon."

She gave the bank's address to the driver, and he nodded.

Soon, the black sedan glided through the narrow streets of Grand Cayman's financial district. The engine was barely a whisper against the early morning quiet. Kim watched the buildings blur past. Unmarked structures with security tighter than some embassies.

After a few trips around the immediate area, Kim directed the driver to return to the airport. They climbed into the plane and Kim ordered an SUV for later. Then, they sacked out for a few hours.

Shortly after five o'clock, a black SUV was parked at the bottom of the jet stairs, as requested. Kim and Smithers hustled down the stairs and climbed inside.

Smithers scanned the road ahead, his fingers tapping idly on his thigh. "We should assume Sinclair's already inside the bank."

Kim nodded.

Smithers slowed the SUV to a smooth stop a block away from the entrance of Cayman Global Holdings. It was a charming but well-fortified structure designed to blend in with the island's Caribbean vibe. The kind of place built for discretion and absolute deniability.

No visible signage. Just a reinforced door and a security panel visible from the street. Two guards were stationed near the entrance, dressed in crisp suits that failed to hide the bulk of weapons beneath their jackets.

Smithers exhaled sharply. "Not exactly a friendly neighborhood credit union."

Kim reached for her bag, adjusting the strap across her chest. "We go in quiet. Nothing aggressive. Just clients looking for a banker."

Smithers gave her a skeptical look. "At this early hour? Who's gonna believe that?"

Kim smirked. "You clean up well enough to pass for a hedge fund manager on vacation. Everybody knows those guys can't turn it off and relax."

She pushed the door open and stepped onto the sidewalk. The sun, barely cresting over the horizon, cast long shadows across the pavement. The scent of morning rain hung in the air. No storm had come through yet, but rain was expected later.

The bank's entrance was deliberately uninviting. The glass was tinted so dark that the inside was impossible to see. The guards tracked their approach, expressions unreadable.

Kim stopped in front of the security panel. A small, stainless-steel intercom was embedded in the wall. She pressed the call button. A sharp chime sounded, followed by a clipped, emotionless voice.

"State your business."

Kim kept her tone neutral. "We have an appointment."

A pause. The voice returned, slightly more measured. "Name?"

Kim didn't miss a beat. "Gerald Weaver."

Smithers barely contained his surprise.

Another pause. Then a low beep. "One moment."

The guards shifted slightly, their hands still loose at their sides, but their attention sharpened.

Kim exhaled slowly, keeping her gaze steady. The name she'd given wasn't random. Gerald Weaver was a real client of Cayman Global Holdings. One who had been flagged in

FBI records for suspected financial crimes. Kim figured he was the kind of client who moved money the same way Wiley had. Meaning, by wire transfer from an offshore institution.

Smithers leaned in slightly. "You planning to walk out of here with someone else's money?"

"We've got to get inside first. Do you have a better idea?"

The glass door gave a soft, mechanical hiss as it unlocked. One of the guards gestured them to enter.

Inside, air-conditioning scraped against her skin. The bank's interior was all cold polished marble, high ceilings, and recessed lighting that cast everything in a crisp, sterile glow.

A receptionist in a fitted gray suit greeted them with a practiced, professional smile. "Mr. Weaver?"

Kim returned the smile easily. "His assistant, actually. He's delayed, so he sent us ahead."

The receptionist's smile barely faltered. "Of course. If you'd follow me."

Kim and Smithers exchanged a quick glance. They had a foot in the door. Now they had to find out what was happening behind the scenes. Before Sinclair walked out with whatever she came for.

CHAPTER 37

Monday, July 11
Grand Cayman

SINCLAIR STOOD BEFORE A steel-reinforced vault door, deep in the lower level of the bank. The air was even colder here, recycled and sterile. Fluorescent lighting buzzed faintly overhead.

Gibbons was positioned at a biometric panel, inputting codes, pressing his thumb against a scanner.

The door groaned as the locking mechanisms disengaged, one by one. The sound was deep, mechanical, layers of security peeling away under the weight of approval.

Gibbons watched the process with the quiet unease of a man who knew he was opening something that shouldn't be opened.

Then, with a final, heavy clunk, the vault door released. A blast of cold, stale air hit Sinclair's face, laced with the scent of aged paper, polished metal, and preservation chemicals. The room beyond was nothing like what she had expected.

No rows of neatly stacked files. No safety deposit boxes filled with financial records, codes, or authorizations.

Instead, the space resembled a private museum—silent, reverent, untouched.

Glass display cases lined the walls, containing items placed with deliberate care. A few heavy-duty chests sat along the edges, bolted in place. There were no signs of regular use—no clutter, no dust or other signs of neglect. Everything inside had been preserved. Curated.

Sinclair took a slow step forward, her boots making no sound against the polished floor.

Neagley had caught up and moved beside her, silent, scanning every corner with sharp, assessing eyes. Bennett hung back near the entrance, arms crossed, unreadable as ever. Hooper stayed near the door, shifting his weight impatiently.

Sinclair studied the room again, now understanding exactly what she was looking at.

"Artifacts. Tributes," she murmured as she catalogued the contents. "A token of respect. A bribe. A gift to a ghost."

The kind of things criminals sent to people they owed.

Wiley's money machine had never been about one person. It had been a lifeline for warlords, mercenaries, and arms dealers who needed cash to move as fast and far as their trade. They hadn't simply used Wiley's system. They had worshipped it.

And this was how they showed gratitude.

Sinclair approached the nearest display case. Her gaze shifted across the artifacts inside.

She stopped in front of a painting.

The colors had begun to fade, and the edges of the canvas were rough and torn. The frame was gilded, too new, a modern attempt to hide the damage of history.

Sinclair knew exactly what it was.

A battle painting from Afghanistan.

Rough brushstrokes. A depiction of warriors on horseback, swords drawn, charging into the fray. An artist's attempt to capture the chaos of war.

Sinclair's pulse ticked up.

This painting had been looted from the National Museum in Kabul before one of the bloodiest battles of the war.

Stolen. Sold. Passed through hands drenched in blood.

And now it was here.

Sinclair glanced at Gibbons. "This was never meant to be in a bank vault."

Gibbons's jaw flexed, but he offered no reply.

Neagley stepped beside her, eyes on the painting. "They were using Wiley's system for money, moving stolen art, and who knows what else."

Sinclair agreed as she turned away from the painting to the next chest. She knelt, unlatched the reinforced lid, and pushed it open.

Inside, she found more pieces of the past.

A ceremonial dagger. Blade blackened with age, its handle wrapped in dyed leather and gold filigree. Pashto script carved into the steel. The kind of weapon that belonged to an insurgent leader.

Beside it, a gold-plated pistol. Engraved with a name she didn't recognize. Cartel markings. The kind of gift exchanged between men who brokered death for profit.

Neagley exhaled wearily. "This is a monument to crime."

Sinclair let the words settle.

Neagley was right.

This was a legacy.

It meant Wiley's system had never been limited to arms dealing.

It was a marketplace. A guarantee. A pipeline for dirty cash, stolen goods, weapons, and power.

Wiley's plan was to increase his own wealth from the comfort of his Argentina ranch by offering his money machine to criminals and thieves as well as legitimate businesses.

Which meant Wiley was a lot smarter than Sinclair and the rest of her team had given him credit for at the time.

Hooper cut into the silence with sharp impatience. "You two done playing historian?"

Sinclair shot him a look. "You're standing in the middle of a bank vault filled with gifts from the world's most dangerous criminals. You should be asking what else this bank is hiding."

Hooper didn't answer.

Sinclair turned back to Gibbons. "Who sent these?"

Gibbons held her gaze, face blank. "Clients."

"Which clients?"

He hesitated.

Gibbons shifted and his eyes flicked toward the transaction records stacked neatly in a separate drawer near the wall. "I can't tell you what I don't know."

Which Sinclair took as an invitation. She stepped toward the drawer and flipped open the top ledger.

The numbers meant nothing on the surface. A long list of coded transactions, accounts rerouting through shell companies, offshore holdings, and back again.

Until she saw the pattern.

Sinclair's breath stilled.

A series of payments, all tied to Argentina.

They started small, a few thousand at a time. Then the payments grew. Hundreds of thousands. Then millions.

Sinclair exhaled. Argentina. Again.

She turned to Gibbons. "Who's receiving these payments?"

Gibbons didn't blink. "I don't know."

"Liar."

Silence stretched.

Neagley closed the ledger. She didn't take it. Didn't need to. She had memorized every key detail.

Hooper stepped forward. "We're done here. Let's go."

Sinclair wasn't finished. "This money is still moving. Which means someone is controlling it."

Gibbons's expression flickered for just a second. A crack in his resolve. He knew exactly who was behind the payments.

Sinclair stared him down. "Tell me."

Gibbons set his jaw, squared his shoulders. "I have nothing to tell."

Neagley spoke quietly. "That's not the same as not knowing."

Gibbons shrugged.

Sinclair exhaled. This wasn't the end of the trail. But it was proof they were on the right path.

She turned, heading for the exit.

Bennett lingered, watching. Silent.

Sinclair didn't trust him. Not entirely.

They stepped into the main bank lobby. The hot Cayman sun pressed against the floor-to-ceiling glass windows.

Hooper walked ahead, lifting his phone, murmuring low.

Sinclair caught a single word.

Not enough to know who he was calling. But enough to know he was reporting to someone.

She let the tension settle. Didn't react. Didn't ask.

They stepped outside. The sun-bleached air was thick with salt and the faint scent of gasoline.

Sinclair was already thinking ahead. Argentina. The payments. The connection. She had answers. But others had them, too.

Neagley fell back three steps. Her move looked casual. Natural. But Sinclair recognized the tactical adjustment. A better position. A clearer line of sight.

Hooper pocketed his phone. His shoulders tensed. The change was subtle. A shift in posture that spoke of violence held in check.

"The car will be here in five." Hooper scanned the street. His movements were sharper now. More focused.

Sinclair kept her voice neutral. "Who did you call?"

"Transport."

A lie. Simple. Direct. The kind of answer that revealed nothing while saying everything.

Bennett moved closer to Hooper. The gesture marked his allegiance.

A black SUV pulled to the curb. The windows were tinted dark. No plates.

"Get in." Hooper's tone had changed. An order, not a suggestion.

Sinclair looked at Neagley. A quick glance. An entire conversation without words.

The pieces clicked into place in Sinclair's head. The bank vault. The Argentina connection. Hooper's call.

Someone else pulled the strings. Someone who wanted what they had found.

Hooper reached into his jacket. The movement was smooth. Professional. The kind of reach that ended with a weapon.

Neagley acted first.

Her hand shot out, catching Hooper's wrist. Bone met bone with a crack.

The fight exploded in a burst of movement. Hooper twisted from Neagley's grip. His free hand whipped up toward her throat.

Neagley blocked. Countered. Her knee drove into his side.

Bennett drew his weapon. The gun snapped up. Centered on Sinclair.

"Stop." His voice was cold. Different. The mask had fallen away.

Neagley released Hooper. Her hands rose slowly.

Two men stepped from the SUV. Combat stance. Military training obvious in their movements.

"The ledger." Hooper straightened. Blood trickled from his lip. "Give it to me."

Sinclair kept her voice steady. "No ledger."

"The numbers. The accounts. You memorized them."

"Wrong again."

Hooper smiled. The expression never reached his eyes. "You know what happens next."

Traffic moved past on the street. Normal life continued only a few feet away. Unaware.

"Cooper sent you." Sinclair watched his face for reaction. Found none.

A car horn blared. Close.

The sound broke the tension.

Neagley moved. Fast. Fluid.

Her elbow caught the first man in the throat. Her foot swept the second man's legs.

Bennett fired. The shot went wide.

Sinclair dove. Her shoulder hit concrete. She rolled behind a parked car.

More shots cracked the air. Glass shattered. Metal pinged.

Sinclair heard running feet. Tires squealing.

She looked up. Saw Neagley sprinting down an alley.

Hooper shouted orders. The SUV's engine roared.

Sinclair pushed to her feet. Ran. Each step precise. Calculated. Her focus stayed sharp through the burn in her lungs.

An engine revved behind her. Tires squealed.

She cut left between buildings. The alley was narrow. No room for vehicles.

Footsteps pounded the pavement. Two sets. Getting closer.

A door stood open ahead. Service entrance. Steel frame. Industrial.

Sinclair grabbed the edge. Swung inside. The darkness swallowed her.

Voices carried from the street.

Sinclair strained to hear. Hooper's tone was clipped. Professional.

"Target mobile. Heading east." He paused. "No. They saw everything." Another pause. "Understood."

The call ended. Boots scraped concrete.

Sinclair moved deeper into the shadows. The pieces formed a new pattern in her head.

Hooper wasn't acting alone.

But who held his leash?

She needed to find Neagley. The accounts. The Argentina connection.

She'd come too far to step aside now. Wiley's assets were Sinclair's now. That's how she saw it. If Hooper or anyone else viewed things differently, that was not her problem.

CHAPTER 38

Monday, July 11
Grand Cayman

THE ASSISTANT LED THEM to an office inside the bank. The name plate said the office belonged to Walter Gibbons.

A man stood beside the desk, his tie loose, sweat darkening his collar. His fingers tapped absently against a leather portfolio, as if he were contemplating the end of the universe as he knew it.

"This is highly irregular," he said once the assistant departed after making introductions.

"So is the activity in your vaults," Kim replied flatly. It was a solid guess. A bluff because she hadn't actually seen Sinclair inside the vaults.

Sweat beaded on his forehead. "I've had enough unscheduled visitors today."

Kim shrugged. "Those visitors seemed to get what they wanted. We're interested in what they found."

The banker's eyes widened, and he gripped the desk phone's receiver. "I don't discuss client matters. Security will show you out."

Kim leaned forward to get a better view of his computer screen. She pointed to the video feed. "Is that the private vault they accessed?"

The banker's gaze darted to his computer screen. Gibbons seemed mildly terrified. He punched a keyboard button, and the video feed disappeared.

"That's an active feed, I see." Kim moved closer. "What's in the Wiley vault that needs constant monitoring?"

"Leave now," Gibbons replied, still holding the phone receiver. "Or I'll have you removed."

"Your security cameras caught everything your earlier visitors saw and did down there, right?"

Gibbons stabbed the intercom. "Security to my office."

Kim held his gaze. "Who is pulling your strings, Gibbons?"

His face drained of color. Footsteps approached in the hall.

Kim and Smithers moved quickly. Smithers reached the door first as Kim backed away from the desk.

The corridor was empty. They walked briskly toward the elevator. Footsteps echoed behind them.

"Stairs," Smithers said, pushing open the fire exit door.

They descended two flights and heard the door above them bang open. More footsteps.

Kim took the last flight of stairs two at a time. They exited through a side door into the bright Cayman sun.

The guards were close behind.

They reached the black SUV just as the guards emerged into the parking lot. Smithers started the engine while Kim slammed her door shut, closing them inside the steamy sauna. Tires squealed as Smithers pulled away, narrowly missing a security vehicle.

Smithers took the first right, then another. He checked the mirror. "Clear."

"For now." Kim released her breath. "That vault video feed was labeled *Wiley Holdings*. I didn't get much of a look at it."

"Wiley? The same name as the rental agreement in Arizona?" Smithers asked. "That's a little crazy, isn't it? A guy who rents a wreck from a discount shop but owns a Cayman bank vault?"

"There's more," Kim nodded. "I spied the Lone Wolf Security emblem in the banker's office, too. The same logo we found on that buried box at Ted's place in the desert."

The Cayman sun heated the narrow streets and sidewalks. Wavy heat rose from the pavement distorting her vision.

"Where are they now? Sinclair and her crew?" Kim asked.

Smithers glanced across the console. "They got a head start. Could be on their way to anywhere by now."

Kim nodded as she settled deeper into the passenger's seat. She focused on the road ahead, but she felt watched from every corner.

"We don't need to catch Sinclair yet. We do need to know where she's going," Kim said. "If she got what she wanted from Wiley's vault, she'll be leaving Grand Cayman."

Smithers replied, "But if she didn't get everything she came for, she'll be looking for it now."

"Yeah, let's try to eliminate that option before we jump on a plane to follow her," Kim replied.

Smithers drove along Bay Street, weaving through sparse traffic. He cocked his head like a quizzical retriever. "Sinclair's not bossing this thing alone is she?"

"I suspect she is. She's always been uncontrollable, according to her NSA personnel files. No reason to believe she's turned into a different animal at this point," Kim replied while keeping watch. "Sinclair's got an agenda, but so does everyone in her orbit. Hooper. Bennett. Even Neagley. They're all playing their own angles. At this point, we don't have enough intel to define them."

"Neagley's a question mark," Smithers said after a couple of minutes. "Why is she here?"

Kim's jaw tightened. "For Reacher."

Smithers raised an eyebrow. "You sure he's involved?"

Kim didn't answer. The truth was, she wasn't sure. Not yet. But wherever Neagley went, Reacher wasn't usually far behind in Kim's experience. She and Neagley had worked together a couple of times before. She claimed she couldn't find Reacher and had no idea where he was, but Kim didn't believe her.

Smithers turned down a side street, looping toward the marina. Sinclair had to resurface eventually. These streets were a maze, but they all led to the same Caribbean Sea.

Kim ticked through the possibilities in her head. "This *Wiley Holdings* setup. Whatever it is, Sinclair wants it. Which means it's worth something to her."

"For what?"

Kim shook her head. "That's what we need to find out."

Ahead, the marina came into view. Rows of sleek yachts and fishing boats rocked gently in the turquoise water.

"Want to head directly to the villa?" Smithers asked.

"Let's stop at the marina first. It's on the way and they could have been there before."

"Your wish is my command," Smithers replied with a mock salute as he pulled the SUV into the parking lot.

Smithers stepped out, stretching his legs. "Think they're here?"

"Possibly. Let's take a quick look and if we don't see them, we'll head to the villa." Kim scanned the docks for any sign of Sinclair's team. She pointed toward a cluster of small storefronts along the marina. "Let's check there."

They moved quickly, blending into the sparse foot traffic. Kim kept her head on a swivel. Every shadow felt heavier and every glance from a passerby seemed to linger too long.

Inside a bait shop the air was cooler, and the smell of saltwater was replaced with the stench of last week's fish. A bored clerk leaned against the counter flipping through a fishing magazine.

Kim approached. "We're looking for a group that came through here earlier today. Four people. One or two women, two or three men. Black SUV."

"We get lots of people through here." The clerk barely looked up with a shrug. "Don't know what you're talking about."

Kim leaned closer, lowering her voice. "I think you do. And I think you saw where they went."

The clerk shrugged as if he had no interest in her questions or her suppositions. He ignored Kim and turned his attention to the next customer.

She walked outside and Smithers fell into step beside her. "No help?"

Kim shook her head and quickened her pace. "Let's take a quick look around. If we don't find them, we'll check the villa before we head back to the airport."

The docks creaked underfoot as they walked toward the water. Boats bobbed gently, masts swaying against a cloudless sky.

"You notice anything unusual with the people around here?" Kim asked, still wearing her dark sunglasses.

Smithers scanned the marina. "Too many eyes. Not enough questions."

Kim nodded. "Exactly."

No one stared directly at them. But everyone seemed to know they were there. Whatever had happened, the news seemed to have rippled through the local community.

A flash of movement caught Kim's eye. She paused, focusing on a small charter boat at the end of the dock. A man in khaki shorts unloaded gear from the stern. He swayed with the easy rhythm of a man accustomed to living and working on the water.

"Let's see if this guy knows anything," Kim said, walking in his direction. When she approached, he paused his work.

"Interested in a fishing trip today?" he asked with a broad smile when she was close enough to hear.

"No time today, I'm afraid," Kim shook her head. "We're looking for a group that came through here earlier today."

The captain kept working. "Lot of people pass through every day."

His hands stilled for just a second. Just long enough.

"Right. They were here," Kim pressed, nodding encouragement. "What happened?"

The captain straightened. Salt stained his shirt and sun had weathered his face. Kim saw the calculation in his eyes. Weighing risk against whatever someone else had paid him, probably.

"There was a woman. Ran through here maybe an hour ago." He kept his voice low. "Alone."

"Which direction?"

He jerked his chin toward a path leading away from the marina. "Beach road. She was moving fast. Like someone was after her."

"And the men with her?"

He shrugged. "Never saw them."

Kim held his gaze. "What else?"

"Gunshots." He shrugged again.

"Did you get a good look?" Kim pulled out her phone and showed him a photo of Marian Sinclair. She swiped through photos of Hooper and Bennett.

"Sorry," he said as he shook his head. "I mind my own business."

"Just two more," Kim said as she pulled up Neagley's head shot. "Did you see her?"

He cocked his head and peered at the photo. "Yeah, I think so. She was having coffee with a guy. Big man. Massive. Fair hair. He seemed preoccupied."

"Was it this guy?" Kim asked, showing him a fifteen-year-old photo of Reacher because that was all she had been able to find in months of searching.

He nodded. "Yeah, that's him. They had coffee and then went their separate ways."

"Did they connect up with the other woman and her two friends?" Smithers asked.

The fisherman shrugged again. "Dunno, man. I didn't see those three."

Kim handed him a twenty. "Thanks for your help."

They backtracked to the SUV. Kim checked her phone. Nothing from Cooper. Nothing from Gaspar.

"The group split up," Smithers said along the way.

"Or someone split them up," Kim replied, climbing into the passenger seat.

Smithers started the engine and drove toward the beach road and up toward the villa. Houses thinned out. The terrain grew wilder. Dense tropical plants crowded the narrow road.

Kim's phone buzzed. Gaspar.

"Talk to me," Kim answered, putting him on speaker.

Gaspar's voice crackled across the miles. "Airport chatter says a private plane filed a flight plan ten minutes ago. Destination Miami. Passenger list includes Dr. Marie Keating."

"That's the alias Gaspar found. She used it to gain access to the Wiley vault," Kim said. "And the others? Are they on the manifest?"

"Just her."

Kim frowned. "When does the flight leave?"

"Thirty minutes. You want me to delay it?"

"Not until we confirm Sinclair's actually on board."

She hung up. Looked at Smithers.

"Sinclair's name is booked on a private flight to Miami."

"You think it's real?"

"Not a chance. It's a diversion. There's nothing more for her in Miami." Kim checked her watch. "Let's head to the villa first. We still have time."

Smithers turned the car around. Kim punched the address into the navigation system. Twenty minutes northeast. A private rental near the cliffs.

"If they split up, something went wrong," Smithers said.

"Or everything went exactly according to plan," Kim countered.

The road wound upward. Houses grew larger. More secluded. The kind of places people rented when they wanted privacy.

Nothing about this felt accidental. Sinclair either assumed or knew she was being followed, which was why she was being cagey. Bennett reported to Hooper and Hooper worked for someone else. Neagley was tracking Reacher.

"Sinclair went into that vault for a specific reason," Kim mused aloud. "Whatever it was, did she find what she wanted?"

Smithers slowed as they approached a gated property. High walls. Security cameras. A black SUV parked out front.

"That's the villa," Kim confirmed.

Smithers parked down the road. Out of view of the cameras.

Kim checked her weapon. "We go in fast. Try to stay alive."

Smithers grinned. "Sounds like a plan."

CHAPTER 39

Monday, July 11
Grand Cayman

THEY APPROACHED ON FOOT. The gate code panel had been smashed. The gate itself stood partially open. No guards outside. The black SUV waited in the driveway. The hood was still warm.

"Security's compromised," Smithers said quietly.

Kim moved through with slow precision. Smithers kept pace, both moving as silently as possible as they reached the villa. The front door hung ajar. Glass littered the entry steps.

She assessed the building. Two floors. Glass doors at the back opened onto a terrace. Security cameras mounted at the corners swept the perimeter.

Smithers pointed to the camera above the terrace. It was tilted at an odd angle, as if someone had adjusted it to create a blind spot.

"Someone didn't want to be seen," Smithers murmured as he moved to flank the entrance.

Kim drew her weapon and entered the property first.

Voices carried from inside the house. Sharp. Angry.

A man shouted. She recognized the voice. Bennett.

Kim edged closer, positioning herself at the side terrace. From her angle she could see through the glass doors into a large living room.

Bennett stood with his back to the window, gun drawn, pointed at Sinclair who sat on the couch. Her posture was rigid, but her face remained neutral.

"I won't ask again," Bennett snarled at Sinclair. "Where is it?"

Neagley was nowhere in sight.

Hooper stood in the corner, watching. His stance suggested he was ready to move in any direction depending on how the situation played out.

"We need a diversion," Kim whispered, drawing her weapon.

Smithers nodded. "How long?"

"Thirty seconds."

"On it. Watch your six."

Smithers moved away, circling back toward the front entrance. Kim kept her focus on the scene inside.

Bennett paced in front of Sinclair. His movements were agitated. The gun in his hand never wavered.

"Where is Neagley?" Bennett demanded.

Sinclair didn't answer.

"Your silence won't save her." Bennett stepped closer. "The account data. Where did she go with it?"

"I have no idea what you're talking about," Sinclair replied coldly.

Bennett shifted position, moving toward the hallway. His right hand hovered near his weapon.

"Someone's here," Bennett warned. "I heard something."

A crash sounded from the front of the villa. Smithers had made his move.

Bennett whipped around, muscles tense like coiled wire.

"Check that," he barked at Hooper, who peeled away toward the hallway, weapon in hand.

"If she moves, shoot her," Bennett called after him.

Kim seized the moment. The glass door was already spider-webbed with cracks. She launched a precise kick at the weakest point and put all of her weight behind it.

The impact sent shards exploding inward with a monstrous crash. The villa's cool air rushed against her face as she tucked her shoulder in tight and broke through.

"Federal agent!" Kim shouted. "Drop your weapon!"

Time slowed. Bennett pivoted back, his expression morphing from surprise to deadly focus in a heartbeat.

His weapon came around quickly. "Too late for that."

Kim registered everything in vivid detail. The slight widening of his pupils, the white-knuckle grip on his gun, the minute adjustment of his stance.

His first shot cracked past her left ear, so close she felt the air displacement on her skin.

She dove right and rolled behind a heavy leather chair as splinters of wood erupted where she'd stood a split second before. The acrid smell of gunpowder filled her nostrils.

"Otto, down!" Sinclair shouted as she launched herself forward in a controlled tackle, driving into Bennett's legs. Her shoulder connected with his knees producing an audible crack.

Bennett's second shot punched into the ceiling, releasing a shower of plaster dust that drifted down like snow. He snarled something incoherent as his face contorted with rage.

Kim steadied her breathing while still gripping her weapon. She peered around the edge of the chair, calculating angles, identifying threats.

"Sinclair, clear!" Kim called out.

The leather upholstery by her face exploded as Bennett sent another round through it. She jerked back, feeling the sting of leather fragments on her cheek.

"You're dead," Bennett threatened through clenched teeth. "All of you."

Bennett fought to regain his balance, but his powerful movements were off-center. Sinclair had driven a knee into his ribs with brutal efficiency. He'd doubled over momentarily, then recovered with frightening speed. His hand swept out in a vicious backhand that connected with Sinclair's face. The blow knocked her sideways onto the glass-strewn floor.

"Hooper!" Bennett shouted. "Where the hell are you?"

Sweat trickled down Kim's back. She shifted position, seeking a clean shot, but Bennett and Sinclair were too close, their movements too erratic.

The front door crashed open. Smithers entered low, weapon extended in a perfect weaver stance. He fired two quick, controlled shots aiming to force Bennett to seek cover. The bullets thudded into the wall inches from Bennett's head, sending fragments of plaster flying.

"Drop it!" Smithers commanded. "Now!"

Kim saw Bennett regaining control, his weapon swinging back toward her position. His eyes were cold, calculating, like a predator who'd cornered helpless rabbits.

"You should have stayed out of this," Bennett said, suddenly calm.

A flash of movement in the hallway snagged Kim's attention. Neagley stepped forward. Her stance rock-steady, weapon raised with deadly intent. The moment she was in place, she squeezed the trigger.

"Bennett!" Neagley called out.

The shot cracked through the chaos. Bennett jerked when the bullet grazed his shoulder, tearing through fabric and flesh. The impact sprayed blood in a fine mist that caught the light from the terrace windows.

"You," Bennett gasped, recognizing Neagley. For a moment, time seemed suspended.

Bennett stood motionless, shock registering on his face. Then he twisted back, bringing his weapon to bear on Neagley.

"Should have killed you when I had the chance," he spat.

Neagley's second shot struck Bennett center mass. His body absorbed the impact. The gun wavered in his grip, suddenly too heavy to hold. It slipped from nerveless fingers, clattering as it landed on the expensive tile floor.

Bennett's eyes showed a moment of distant surprise, as if this outcome had never occurred to him.

"Cooper will—" He started but never finished.

His knees buckled. He dropped to a kneeling position, swaying slightly, as blood spread across his chest.

Then gravity claimed him completely. He toppled forward, face down on the Moroccan rug, one arm trapped awkwardly beneath him.

The room fell into momentary silence broken only by ragged breathing and the distant whine of the air-conditioning.

"Hooper," Neagley said urgently. "Where is he?"

Hooper was gone. The sound of a door slamming echoed from the back of the villa.

"He must have grabbed the intel at some point. Maybe a copy of the flash drive we collected in Miami," Sinclair said, pushing herself up from the floor. Blood trickled from her lip. "We need to go after him."

Kim kept her weapon raised. "Not so fast. What intel?"

Smithers moved to check on Bennett. "Dead."

Neagley lowered her weapon but didn't holster it. "Hooper is headed to Argentina. With that data he has access to the entire system."

"Who are these guys working for?" Kim demanded.

"Cooper," Sinclair said, spitting blood. "Who else?"

A noise from outside pulled their attention. Footsteps pounded across the terrace.

Kim moved to the broken glass door. An engine roared to life on the service road behind the villa.

"He has a vehicle," Kim said as she turned to Sinclair. "Talk. Now. What did Hooper take for Cooper?"

Sinclair wiped blood from her mouth. "The key to Horace Wiley's money machine. A system that's been running for years, generating billions. Cooper wants control of it."

"And Reacher?" Kim pressed. "Where does he fit in?"

Neagley stepped forward. "Reacher has nothing to do with this."

Kim gave her a glare and shot back, "Then what the hell is going on?"

Sinclair and Neagley exchanged a look.

"We don't have time for this," Sinclair said. "Hooper is on his way to Argentina right now. If Cooper gets control of Wiley's system, he has access to nearly unlimited funds."

"For what?" Smithers asked, joining them.

"Does it matter?" Sinclair snapped. "A man with Cooper's connections and unlimited money? Use your imagination."

Kim kept her weapon steady. "You stole classified intel. You're working with a known felon. You just killed a man. Give me one reason why I shouldn't arrest you right now."

"Because Cooper sent you here to fail," Neagley said steadily. "He knew Sinclair would find what he wanted. You were the canary."

Kim stared at her. "That's not true."

"Then why did he send you to Arizona? To Ted's cabin?" Neagley pressed. "Ted was killed because he knew about Wiley's system. Cooper needed to flush out anyone who knew about Wiley. He used you. Again. Or Still. Either works."

Smithers looked at Kim. "She might have a point."

Kim's phone buzzed. Gaspar.

"Talk to me," she said keeping her eyes on Sinclair and Neagley.

"Tracking a private jet that took off," Gaspar said. "Small craft. Single pilot. One passenger."

"Hooper," Kim guessed.

"Got him on the security cam," Gaspar confirmed. "Flight plan says Buenos Aires."

"You're sure no one else is on the plane?" Kim asked.

"No."

Kim ended the call. Argentina. Just like Sinclair said.

She lowered her weapon. "We need to move."

Smithers checked his watch. "We can catch the next commercial flight. Six hours."

"Too long," Sinclair said. "Hooper will be gone by then."

Kim made the call. "Gaspar. Get us a plane. Fastest route to Buenos Aires."

She turned to Sinclair and Neagley. "You're coming with us."

"Gladly," Sinclair replied.

Neagley nodded once. "After you."

Kim holstered her weapon. "Hooper has the data. Bennett is dead. What exactly are we chasing in Argentina?"

Sinclair's eyes hardened. "The truth."

"About what?"

"About who Wiley was really working for."

Kim studied her face. "You think it was Cooper all along."

"I know it was," Sinclair said. "And now I can prove it."

Kim wasn't so sure, but she didn't argue. No point. Instead, she looked at Neagley. "And Reacher? What's his angle?"

Neagley's expression gave nothing away.

Kim turned to Smithers. "Call local police. Report the shooting. Then get our gear. We're wheels up in thirty."

Sinclair moved toward the door. "I'll get cleaned up."

"I'll keep an eye on her," Neagley said, following.

Kim stood alone in the room. Bennett lay dead on the expensive carpet. The laptop with the Wiley data was gone. Argentina loomed.

Cooper had played her. That much was clear now. The question was why.

The bigger question was what she would find waiting in Argentina.

Her phone buzzed again. Unknown number. A simple text message:

See you in Argentina.

Kim stared at it for a long moment.

He knew she was coming.

And he would be ready.

CHAPTER 40

Monday, July 11
Grand Cayman

THE GULFSTREAM'S ENGINES SCREAMED as it punched through another wall of turbulence. Neagley braced herself against the leather seat, watching the others react.

Otto sat stiffly in her seat, reviewing notes while the Gulfstream powered through the night. The jump from Grand Cayman to Buenos Aires was nearly eight hours, factoring in refueling at a private airstrip.

Smithers dozed beside Otto, exhaustion overtaking even his usual vigilance.

Sinclair remained awake, her fingers drumming on a folder marked with Wiley's name.

Neagley stared out the window. Below them, the dark expanse of the South Atlantic stretched endlessly toward Argentina.

They'd endured the storm system stretching from takeoff in Grand Cayman. More than six hours of calculated silence punctuated by violent drops in altitude.

So far.

They weren't down yet.

Sinclair sat across from Neagley, impassive now despite the constant, stomach churning bounces. Sinclair hadn't spoken in over an hour.

Her right hand kept checking her pocket. Neagley had noticed the gesture three times now. Whatever Sinclair carried there mattered to her, at least.

Otto's face had a greenish tint that hadn't improved since takeoff. Neagley was tempted to grin or give her a fist bump for bravery. Maybe both.

Otto white-knuckled the armrests in her rear-facing seat over the wing. The safest seat on the plane, according to the pilot. Otto had insisted on it. Her lips moved silently with each drop and surge as if she were praying. Perhaps she was.

Smithers maintained his professional calm beside Otto, but the turbulence had reduced even his attempts at conversation to terse nods.

Neagley clocked the subtle shift of his jacket. He'd kept his weapon accessible despite the gut-churning flight. Smart move. If the plane went down, the last thing they needed was to lose their weapons.

The smell of ozone and jet fuel permeated the cabin. Ice crystals ticked against the fuselage like distant gunfire.

Neagley checked her watch. Another hour to Buenos Aires.

The plane dropped suddenly, sending loose items rattling across the cabin floor.

This time, she grinned. Neagley loved flying through turbulent weather. She liked fast cars, skydiving, helo-skiing, and almost anything that streamed adrenaline through her veins.

Extreme living had always appealed to her. Which was one reason she'd joined the Army and Reacher's 110th Special Investigators Unit. Always something exciting going on.

Otto's phone lit up. She read the screen with narrowed eyes, then looked up at Sinclair.

"We found something." Otto shouted intro her headset to be heard over the roar of the engines and the constant buffeting.

Sinclair leaned forward, visibly reluctant to unbuckle even slightly and shouted back, "What?"

Otto held up her phone.

A purchase record from an outdoor supply shop in Buenos Aires, timestamped four hours earlier. Paul Bennett's name on the platinum card used to make the purchase.

Which, of course, was not possible.

Bennett was dead.

"Looks like Hooper bought climbing gear, clothing, satellite phones," Otto shouted to be heard while she kept her eyes on Sinclair. "Equipment for high-altitude mountain terrain, possibly. Where exactly is he going?"

Sinclair's expression didn't change. Neagley read the slight tightening around her eyes as confirmation without admission.

The plane jolted again. Otto closed her eyes briefly, swallowed hard, then fixed her gaze back on Sinclair.

"Cut the crap." Otto's voice carried despite the noise. "You know exactly where Hooper's going. Tell me now or I'll have the authorities waiting to arrest you when we land."

Sinclair made no effort to reply.

"Obstruction of justice. Interfering with a federal investigation," Otto kept going, listing the charges she could make stick. "Whatever immunity you once had expired with your career."

Neagley watched the calculation in Sinclair's gaze.

They needed Otto's resources, at least for now.

Her threats were credible, although Neagley didn't believe for a moment that Otto would actually do any of it. Cooper would have her head if she tried. Neagley didn't know a lot about Cooper, but she knew he was no fool.

Otto wasn't supposed to be out of the country or even working this case. She couldn't explain her actions to a cop or a judge or a jury and they all knew it.

"A ranch," Sinclair finally said, perhaps realizing she needed Otto on her side for now. "La Pampa. Near the center of Argentina."

The plane dipped again. Otto gripped the armrests tighter but kept her focus. Sweat beaded on her upper lip.

"Whose ranch?" she asked.

"Originally, it belonged to a shell corporation Wiley set up before he died. Through a series of transfers, it's now owned by a holding company called Davy Crockett Enterprises."

Otto's phone buzzed again. She answered, pressing it hard against her ear.

Neagley caught fragments. A male voice, barely audible. A vehicle rental in Bennett's name, he said. Heading southwest out of the city three hours ago.

Otto ended the call. "Good guess. Hooper rented a Range Rover this morning. We've traced his rental SUV heading southwest toward La Pampa."

The plane lurched, harder this time. Metal groaned. An overhead compartment popped open, spilling a laptop bag into the aisle. Nobody unbuckled a seatbelt to reach for it.

"Still want to tell me you don't know where he's going?" Otto challenged once the plane stabilized.

Sinclair glanced at Neagley. A silent question.

Neagley gave an imperceptible nod. They had reached the point where partial truth served better than none.

But Sinclair was still holding back. The constant touching of her pocket. The careful phrasing.

Which was when Neagley realized that Sinclair had an endgame she hadn't revealed.

"Wiley's process needed a physical location," Sinclair explained. "Somewhere remote. The ranch served as a hub for the entire operation."

"What operation?" Smithers asked.

Another pocket of turbulence hit before Sinclair could answer.

The plane dropped sharply, causing Otto to clamp her lips together. She was definitely green around the gills. Neagley stifled a grin. Everyone fell silent until the aircraft leveled out.

When the plane recovered, Otto looked directly at Neagley. "What does Reacher have to do with any of this?"

The question hung in the cabin. Unexpected. Pointed. As if Otto had run out of patience, too.

Neagley kept her face neutral. She'd already planned how they would approach the ranch compound. Two entry points. High ground for overwatch. The terrain would require splitting their forces exactly as she planned to suggest.

"What makes you think Reacher is involved?" Neagley asked.

"A fisherman back in Grand Cayman ID'd him with you."

Neagley didn't confirm or deny. She'd learned from Reacher long ago that silence often revealed more from others. Some people talked simply to fill the silence.

A while later, Otto's phone vibrated with another message. She read it and frowned.

"Found security footage for a hotel not too far from Wiley's ranch. Reacher checked in late yesterday. CCTV confirms." Otto's eyes never left Neagley's face. "He's already there."

The revelation didn't surprise Neagley, but she raised her eyebrows as if this was new intel. It wasn't.

Reacher worked methodically, always a step ahead.

But she hadn't expected Otto to have confirmation so soon. Otto's resources were deeper than Neagley had been led to believe.

The pilot's voice crackled through the cabin speakers. "Beginning our descent to Buenos Aires. Weather clearing slightly. Remain seated with seatbelts fastened."

The plane banked as it began the approach.

Turbulence eased marginally when the Gulfstream dropped beneath the worst of the storm system. The persistent rattling of the cabin quieted enough for conversation without shouting.

Otto leaned forward, looking ill but determined. "I need to know what we're walking into."

Sinclair adjusted her position and deadpanned, "Cooper didn't tell you? What a shock."

Otto's silence was confirmation enough.

"Get a clue, Otto," Sinclair chided, shaking her head.

CHAPTER 41

Tuesday, July 12
Buenos Aires, Argentina

"THE RANCH IS A strategic location." Sinclair explained, despite the plane's continued rocking. "Wiley set up his system to operate from the actual physical infrastructure there."

"What infrastructure?" Smithers asked.

"I don't know exactly. Could be servers. Tracking systems. Communication arrays." Sinclair's explanation was deliberately vague.

Neagley caught the lies immediately. Sinclair knew precisely what waited at the ranch. Why was she lying?

"From there, Wiley planned to move money anywhere and everywhere without detection. The system's still operational," Sinclair said.

Otto's phone lit up again. She examined it, then turned the screen toward them.

Satellite imagery showed a sprawling compound nestled in a broad valley. Multiple buildings. Security perimeter. Private airstrip.

"This the place?" Otto asked.

Sinclair nodded once.

"What's Hooper's plan?"

"Same as Cooper's. Mine, too. Control," Sinclair said simply. "Whoever controls the ranch controls Wiley's billions and his system, now and in the future. Imagine the freedom that comes with all of that. Wouldn't you like to be out from under Cooper's thumb, Otto?"

Otto studied the satellite image more closely, zooming in on sections of the compound. "We need vehicles that can handle mountain terrain and get us on site quickly."

"Commercial flights will take too long," Sinclair said. "Hooper's already at least eight hours ahead of us. Possibly more."

"We're arranging a helo," Otto replied. "But it can only take two of us."

"We've got transportation," Neagley caught Sinclair's eye. "We'll meet you there."

Otto looked skeptical.

"Don't worry. You'll get there first. You won't miss anything," Neagley countered with a grin. She'd had enough interference from the FBI on this project already. "We can approach from a different angle. Tactical advantage. The compound has multiple buildings. We may need to secure them simultaneously."

Neagley was already mapping the terrain and various approaches in her head.

Miles of grasslands. Limited access routes.

The place was designed to be defensible. A proper assault would require coordinated entry from at least two points.

The plane hit a pocket of unexpected turbulence, ending the conversation momentarily. When it stabilized, Otto was checking another message.

Her expression changed. Shock first, then focused determination.

"Cooper," she said by way of explanation. "Orders to secure the asset."

"What asset?" Smithers asked.

She looked up. "He doesn't specify if that means Hooper or the ranch."

"Does it matter?" Smithers asked. "Either way, we need to get there."

Otto nodded. "Neagley and Sinclair can take ground transport, since it's already arranged and waiting. Smithers and I will take the helicopter when it arrives. We coordinate positions once we're all in range of the compound."

The plane began its final descent, breaking through cloud cover into clearer skies. Buenos Aires spread out beneath them, a sprawling grid of roads and buildings stretching across the miles.

Neagley watched the city approach.

Somewhere out there, Reacher was moving toward the same destination.

But his goal wasn't to recover Wiley's money.

Reacher didn't care about money.

She knew what no one else on the plane did. For Reacher, this was about finishing what started in Hamburg.

Hooper's betrayal had compromised an operation and leaked intelligence. Which Reacher would have overlooked.

But Hooper had enabled the transfer of portable nuclear weapons, so called "Davy Crockett backpack nukes," that later cost hundreds of lives.

People had died screaming in radioactive fire because of Hooper's greed. He'd played both sides.

Reacher considered Hooper's treachery a personal failure that he would correct and never let happen again.

Neagley approved of Reacher's opinion as well as his refusal to let Hooper get away with it.

The plane finally touched down with a jolt, tires screaming against the tarmac.

As they taxied toward the private aviation terminal, Neagley caught Sinclair watching her.

"Something you're not telling me?" Sinclair asked quietly so Otto and Smithers couldn't overhear.

Neagley met her gaze. "Plenty."

"About Reacher?"

"He's not after what you think."

Sinclair processed this. "Will it interfere with our objective?"

Neagley considered the question as the plane rolled to a stop.

"No," she said finally. "But Hooper won't be leaving Argentina alive."

"Cooper won't like it," Sinclair nodded with a slight grin before she nodded to accept the calculated risk. "As long as we get Wiley's system first."

The pilot rolled to a stop and cut the engines. The sudden silence felt oppressive after hours of unrelenting noise and vibrations strong enough to shake the bravest flyers.

Otto unbuckled quickly as if she absolutely could not wait one more second to have both feet on solid ground.

As they gathered the minimal gear they'd brought aboard, Neagley felt the familiar tension building.

The stillness before violence erupted.

The pressure change before the storm.

She'd felt it countless times before, in deserts, mountains, and cities around the world. With and without Reacher.

She knew the signs.

Reacher was hunting Hooper, but he really wanted answers. About the weapons Wiley and Hooper had smuggled from Hamburg.

About who still controlled them.

About how many remained unaccounted for.

And when Reacher hunted, blood always followed.

Anyone who stood between Reacher and the truth would be collateral damage in a private war most of them didn't even know he was fighting.

"Bring it on," Neagley muttered aloud.

CHAPTER 42

Wednesday, July 13
La Pampa, Argentina

SINCLAIR GRIPPED THE DOOR handle to steady herself as Neagley jounced the Range Rover over rocks and scrub. There were no roads leading to Wiley's ranch. Brutal terrain. Unforgiving. Perfect for hiding secrets.

They'd driven four hours from the Buenos Aires airstrip on dusty backroads without landmarks. Nothing but endless grassland stretching to distant mountains.

Until the ranch appeared without warning. A compound of low buildings sprawled across the valley floor. No fences. No barriers. Just isolation. Which was okay. More than okay, actually. The fewer eyes and ears on the ranch, the better, as far as Sinclair was concerned.

"Stop here," she said.

Neagley braked behind an outcropping of rock five hundred yards from the main structure and turned off the ignition. The engine ticked as it cooled. Wind whistled through scrub grass. Neagley heard nothing alarming blowing in the wind.

Sinclair scanned the compound through binoculars. Six buildings. Concrete and steel. One larger than the others with solar panels covering the roof. A satellite dish pointed skyward.

No vehicles visible.

No movement.

"Looks abandoned," she said.

Neagley took the binoculars. "Too well-maintained to be abandoned."

Sinclair studied Neagley's face. She had been unnervingly quiet. Watchful. Alert. Like she was waiting for something. Or someone.

"We thought we'd put Hamburg to bed," Sinclair said quietly. "You think this connects back there?"

Neagley handed back the binoculars. No confirmation. No denial. Shared history in the Hamburg situation hung between them.

Dust plumes rose in the distance. Two people moved at the compound's perimeter. One the size of a linebacker and the other tiny.

"Otto and Smithers," Neagley said, adjusting the binoculars. "They've been here at least an hour. Maybe longer."

The helicopter that brought them would be gone by now. The pilot returned to Buenos Aires. No witnesses. No escape vehicle. Except the Range Rover, now that Neagley and Sinclair had arrived.

Sinclair watched their methodical movements. "They're still searching the compound."

"We should move," Neagley said, already reaching for her weapon.

Sinclair patted her jacket pocket, checking her secure satellite phone. Whatever Wiley had hidden here contained the prize she wanted. She wouldn't leave without it.

She said, "Let's go."

The sun beat down mercilessly as they approached on foot. Heat waves distorted the air above the scrubland. No shade. No cover. Just open ground and the constant wind carrying grit that stung exposed skin.

Otto and Smithers spotted them, moving to intercept at the halfway point, weapons lowered but ready.

"No signs of current occupants," Otto reported. "But someone's been maintaining the place."

"Generators are fueled," Smithers added. "Water system functional. This place isn't abandoned."

Sinclair gestured toward the main building. "What did you find inside?"

"Offices. Living quarters. All empty." Otto's eyes narrowed slightly. "But the computer systems are operational. On standby mode."

"So we've found Wiley's financial network," Sinclair confirmed. "The hub of the entire operation."

"Cooper wants it," Otto said. It wasn't a question.

"Yeah. Who doesn't?" Sinclair replied flatly.

Smithers pointed to the ground near the main building. "Fresh tire tracks. Double tread pattern. Heavy vehicle."

He crouched to examine them. "Recent. Came through here in the last twelve hours or so."

"Hooper arrived ahead of us as expected," Sinclair said.

"Or someone was here and left in a hurry," Otto replied.

Neagley remained still. Her head slightly tilted, like a predator catching a scent.

"Something's off," she said quietly.

"What?" Otto asked, scanning the perimeter.

"Feels like we walked into a setup."

Sinclair recognized the signs too. Trained instinct never faded, no matter how long you'd been behind a desk. Someone was watching them. She was certain of it.

"We push forward?" Smithers asked, looking to Otto for direction.

Otto nodded once. "Yep."

They moved as a unit, weapons drawn now. Otto took point with Smithers covering the rear. Combat formation. Automatic. Instinctive.

The main building's door was intact. No forced entry. Sinclair punched a code into the keypad.

"You know the access code?" Otto asked sharply.

"Lucky guess. Wiley's birthdate," Sinclair replied, not meeting her eyes. "I memorized everything about him and his operation."

The door unlocked with a hydraulic hiss. Climate-controlled air rushed out. The smell of electronics and recirculated air.

Inside, the building was a single large room. Rows of server racks lined the walls. Old technology mixed with newer equipment. A deliberate upgrade path suggesting the system had been maintained for decades. Cables snaked across the floor, connecting to a central workstation.

Sinclair moved to the console. Three monitors. One displayed lines of code. Another showed a satellite map.

"All active," she said. "Fully operational."

Her phone buzzed in her pocket. She pulled it out. No service bars. No incoming calls or messages.

"Electronics interference," she noted, showing the others. Their devices were all experiencing the same issue.

"It's a signal jammer," Neagley said. "Recent installation. Not part of the original security system because it's newer tech."

"Someone doesn't want us communicating," Sinclair added.

"Or someone's monitoring our electronics," Otto suggested.

Neagley moved to the back wall. "There's another door here."

The door led to a wide tunnel. Concrete walls. Motion-activated lights flickered on responsively as they moved through it. Sinclair noted the whole setup was too responsive. Too well-maintained for a supposedly abandoned facility.

"Someone's keeping everything running," Smithers said, noting the fresh scuff marks on the floor. "Dragging heavy equipment through here recently."

The tunnel sloped downward, then leveled out, ending at another reinforced door. This one hung partially open.

"Bunker," Sinclair said.

Their footsteps echoed as they entered a large chamber carved into the bedrock. Empty weapons racks lined the walls. Steel tables. Equipment for assembly and testing.

"This is where they prepared the devices," Sinclair murmured.

Otto examined a workbench. She identified tool marks in the dust. "Looks like recent activity."

"What devices were they preparing here?" Smithers asked.

Sinclair and Neagley exchanged a look. Hamburg. Were there assets they failed to recover? No. Not possible.

So what was all of this?

"Back in Hamburg, we worked Wiley's case. He had discovered a cache of portable nuclear weapons," Sinclair finally said. "Soviet-era tactical nukes nicknamed Davy Crocketts. Wiley was brokering sales from his base in Hamburg."

"We knew about all this?" Otto asked incredulously.

"Not exactly. It was a covert operation. We were tasked with stopping Wiley's plans," Neagley answered for both of them. "Wiley died before we could get to him. But not before at least one sale was completed."

"Which is where his money came from," Sinclair explained.

A monitor on the far wall blinked to life as they moved deeper into the bunker. This one was a security feed. Multiple camera angles of the compound exterior were displayed on the screens.

"Security systems shouldn't be active if the place is abandoned," Sinclair said, approaching the screen.

"Meaning someone's watching when they aren't here," Neagley confirmed.

They followed another door which led them outside where they emerged on the far side of the compound. They followed a worn path up a gentle slope.

At the top of the hill, they saw the shockingly barren land below.

Vegetation struggled to grow in an irregular patch about fifty yards across. Vegetation struggled at the edges but refused to take root inside.

The soil was darker, almost black, baked hard by something stronger than the sun. The soil was discolored, too. Darker than the surrounding earth.

Years of weather had softened the boundaries, but the pattern remained distinct.

Sinclair walked to the edge of the dead zone. Her radiation detector remained silent, though she knew residual traces might still exist beneath the surface.

Time had done its work. But she recognized the signature.

She'd seen the after-effects of tactical nuclear weapons twice before. Once in training. Once in the field after a recovered device was detonated.

She crouched down and ran her fingers through the soil, feeling a strange, brittle texture beneath the top layer. The earth wasn't simply dry, it was different. Glassy fragments mixed with the dirt. The result of intense heat fusing sand and minerals together for a fraction of a second. Another signature.

"This is an old nuclear detonation site," she said tightly. "A low-yield tactical device."

Neagley whistled. "Someone demonstrated a nuke here? That's more than a little insane."

"When?" Otto stepped forward staring at the scarred earth.

Something crunched under her boot. She lifted her foot and found a small, half-melted fragment of metal, twisted and charred. Maybe a casing. Maybe part of an old delivery mechanism. Something left behind when the fireball ripped through.

"Twelve to fifteen years ago, probably," Neagley said. "Not long after Hamburg."

A breeze swept across the barren ground. The air smelled different here, too. Dry, sure, but also faintly metallic. Like scorched earth that never quite forgot what happened to it.

Neagley shifted her gaze toward the horizon. No birds flew over the site. No insects buzzed. Even they had abandoned this place.

Otto frowned. "Feels like a place people avoid."

Sinclair stood up, brushing her hands off. "They should."

Otto holstered her weapon. "You're saying Wiley's system wasn't only moving and laundering money. It's also selling portable nuclear devices."

"And someone kept his system running long after he died," Sinclair added with a firm nod. "The money. The weapons. All of it."

"That's why Cooper's involved," Otto said. "He wants total control."

"Cooper's not the only one," Sinclair replied. "Hooper. Bennett. Everyone who knew or discovered Wiley's operation."

Smithers had moved to the edge of the ridge, surveying the valley below. "Multiple access points. Limited cover."

He turned back toward the group. "If someone wanted to trap us here, it would be simple to do."

He let the words hang in the air.

The wind shifted. Carried the faint sound of an engine starting somewhere in the distance.

Neagley's hand moved to her weapon. "Let's go."

"Why?" Otto demanded.

"Because we're not alone."

Sinclair felt it too. Whoever had deliberately maintained this facility kept the systems running. Updated the technology. Added new security measures.

This wasn't abandoned property. It was an operational base.

They'd walked into something. A trap. A test. A demonstration.

A setup.

CHAPTER 43

Wednesday, July 13
La Pampa, Argentina

KIM CONTINUED TO STARE at the damaged landscape after Sinclair returned to the bunker. She soaked up the truth of what she saw. The aftermath of a small nuclear explosion was less damaging than the bombs dropped on Hiroshima or Nagasaki. But it was an awful sight to behold.

"It's easy to understand why no one has been living on this ranch. It's potentially dangerous still to groundwater and soil," Smithers said. "The Argentine government must know the nuke was detonated, though. It would have been obvious at the time. Easily detected."

"Cooper knows, too," Kim said. "Or if he didn't know about it before, he does now. He watches every move we make. No way to keep it from him."

Smithers replied, "Hell, there's probably video of the original detonation stored somewhere at the Pentagon."

After a while, Kim inhaled deeply and took one long, last look at the scorched earth. "Let's see what she's cooking up."

She and Smithers followed Sinclair inside.

When Kim stepped into the bunker, she was instantly blinded by the darkness. She turned her flashlight beam to cut through the gloom.

Smithers followed close behind, sweeping his flashlight beam across the walls. A rat ran through the tunnel ahead, squealing against the spotlight.

"Could be a good sign," Smithers said with a grin. "At least the rats are still alive. Maybe the radioactive waste won't kill us all."

"Over here," Sinclair called from deeper inside the bunker.

Kim walked carefully over the uneven ground toward Sinclair, sweeping the flashlight beam in front of her as she went. Until she rounded a corner and froze when her flashlight beam landed. She stopped short and stared.

Four squat, cylindrical objects rested on a metal rack. Each bore faded stenciling: "M-28 or M-29 Davy Crockett."

Nearby, Sinclair stared, face ashen. "That's impossible. We got them all."

"Did we?" Neagley's voice cut like a knife. "I'd say not."

"You've seen these before?" Kim asked, cocking her head to cover the shock.

"Not exactly," Neagley replied. "We found ten Davy Crocketts during the Hamburg operation. Wiley planned to sell them to the highest bidder. That's how he made his big money. We believed there were only ten."

"You were wrong," Kim replied flatly.

"So it would seem," Neagley said. "Although these four and the one that detonated outside could have come from another source. After all, Wiley's been dead for more than fifteen years now. We know he didn't move these here before he died because he didn't own the ranch back then."

Sinclair flashed a hard glare in Neagley's direction in an apparent effort to silence her. Neagley shrugged off the warning.

"You were chasing Wiley's money, *the process* as you called it," Kim said. "But you also wanted these nukes? What the hell for?"

"No." Sinclair shook her head. "Who in her right mind wants to take responsibility for nuclear weapons? That would be insane."

"And you're saying you're not insane, Sinclair?" Neagley interjected. "You're standing in a bunker in Argentina because you're chasing a dead man's money, and you think that's not insane?"

A heavy pause settled over the bunker as they continued to stare at the bombs, until Smithers finally spoke. "Now what? Anybody got any bright ideas?"

Kim raced through the possibilities. "Disable the warheads. Destroy them. Call it in to get a hazmat team out here?"

Before she could act, a man's voice stopped her cold.

"None of the above," Larry Knox said as he stepped from the shadows, hands raised placatingly.

Kim snapped her weapon up, leveling it at Knox's chest. "Hands where I can see them."

Knox complied, a wry smile playing at his lips. "You're gonna shoot me and risk a stray bullet damaging those nukes?"

"I won't miss my target," Kim said flatly. "I'm not worried."

Smithers moved to cover the entrance while Neagley circled behind Knox.

"Start talking," Kim demanded.

Knox's gaze swept the room, lingering on the warheads. "Quite the discovery, isn't it? Nice little insurance policy. No red tape. No permissions. Just make a deal with the right people, charge a hundred million each or so, and there you are. Wealthy beyond your wildest dreams."

"Can't spend money when you're dead. Ask Wiley," Kim replied, still holding the weapon.

Sinclair found her voice. "You knew about this, Knox."

"Of course we knew," Knox replied. "Did you really think we'd let four nuclear devices vanish without a trace?"

Kim's finger tightened on the trigger. "We?"

Knox's smile widened. "Agent Otto, you're in way over your head here. Surely you realize that by now."

Kim kept her gun trained on Knox, muscles taut, fully prepared. The bunker's stale air pressed in around them.

Sinclair stood frozen, eyes locked on the warheads. Neagley circled silently behind Knox, ready to strike.

"Explain," Kim said.

Knox shrugged. "These nukes never left US control. We moved them here and we've been keeping an eye on them."

"Why?" Smithers asked from the doorway.

"Insurance," Knox said. "Keeps our options open."

Kim's jaw clenched and she jerked her thumb over her shoulder. "What about the detonation out there?"

"We needed to be sure they still worked, didn't we?" Knox shrugged. "These puppies are old. Who knew if they'd even fire?"

Neagley's voice cut through the tension. "Where's Hooper?"

Knox's eyes narrowed. "He'll be along shortly."

Kim caught Sinclair's slight head shake. A warning.

Just then, a loud crash echoed from outside. Smithers spun toward the sound.

"That'll be him," Knox said. "Right on time."

Otto kept her weapon steady. "Last chance. Surrender now, Knox."

His smile vanished. "I'm afraid that's not an option."

Kim glared at Knox. "How long have you been waiting here?"

"Long enough." Knox's eyes swept the room.

Kim's jaw clenched. "We need to call this in."

"Cooper will handle it. I've already talked to him," Knox said in response.

Neagley stepped forward. "So what's the plan, Knox? Cooper sweeps this back under the rug? And then what?"

Knox shrugged. "Not your problem."

"Everything's my problem." Neagley moved closer.

The door creaked. Hooper sauntered in, cocky grin fading as he spotted Knox.

Tension crackled.

Neagley's gaze assessed the threats.

Knox remained unnaturally calm. "Stand down, Hooper. It's all good here. Our guests were just leaving."

Hooper laughed. "Over? I'm just getting started."

A huge shadow passed the bunker's exit, briefly blocking the sunlight.

Kim whipped her head around to catch sight of him, but he was already gone. Neagley gave her a knowing look and a nod of confirmation.

Reacher.

Was Reacher showing up here good news or bad?

CHAPTER 44

Wednesday, July 13
La Pampa, Argentina

NEAGLEY HEARD THE ENGINE before she saw the vehicle. A low, throaty rumble outside the bunker, idling just long enough to send a vibration through the thick concrete walls. She quickly scanned the bunker to confirm. The others heard it too.

"Hooper." Otto stiffened, weapon steady, but her grip shifted slightly.

The bastard was finally here.

The entrance to the bunker filled with dim afternoon light as the door swung open, revealing a tall silhouette against the bright outside glare. Hooper stepped inside like he owned the place, head held high, shoulders squared.

He carried himself like a man who expected to be in control. Fortunately, he wasn't. Nor would he ever be, as long as Neagley had anything to say about it.

Neagley watched his reaction as his eyes adjusted to the darker interior. He expected to see his men standing guard. Instead, he saw Otto, Smithers, Sinclair, and Knox.

His eyes flicked to the rack against the far wall. Four squat nuclear warheads, the faded M-28 Davy Crockett stenciling barely visible in the dim light.

Neagley saw the moment he understood.

His men should have been in this room. Should have been standing beside him, securing the nukes.

But they weren't.

A subtle shift in his stance revealed that his confidence flickered, just for a second.

Hooper's jaw clenched. He took a slow, deliberate scan of the room, cataloging people, places, things.

Sinclair had edged slightly behind Otto, coiled like a bedspring.

Smithers held steady near the entrance, half-turned toward the outside, one eye on whatever was happening beyond the bunker walls.

Otto was all business. Her weapon level and face impassive.

Knox was the only one who moved. He took a casual step forward, hands loose at his sides, offering Hooper a slow, knowing smirk.

"Took your time, Hooper."

Hooper didn't answer. His eyes swept the bunker a second time, sharp and searching. The air inside had shifted.

His gaze locked onto Neagley for half a second before shifting past her, toward the tunnel leading deeper underground.

She didn't move. Held his stare. No expression.

Finally, he spoke. "Where the hell is my team?"

No one answered.

Hooper's hand twitched slightly, fingers flexing near his weapon. A small, but clear gesture. He wasn't as sure of himself now.

He'd had backup in place. Reacher told Neagley he had counted three men. He didn't say where they were now.

The silence stretched.

Then Neagley heard an unmistakable sound from outside.

A single gunshot. Distant. Muffled by the walls.

What was it? Reacher eliminating one of the guards? Or Hooper's backup?

Smithers turned slightly toward the noise. Otto barely reacted, keeping her focus on Hooper.

Neagley had worked with Hooper before. She glanced quickly in his direction and saw his reaction before anyone else.

Hooper's shoulders shifted. Spine locked straight. His fingers flexed again, this time forming a tight fist.

Finally, his mouth parted, but no words came out.

He seemed to understand the distant gunshot, even if no one else did.

Neagley took a step, enough to close his easiest escape route. Her boots barely made a sound against the concrete.

Hooper's sharp gaze flicked to her.

She met his stare, dead calm. "You're out of time."

Hooper didn't move again. Not right away.

Neagley could see his mind working, cataloging every possible play. His breathing stayed even, but his gaze shifted.

First to the bunker entrance, then to Knox, then back to Otto, who held her weapon steady, leveled at his chest.

He hadn't drawn his gun yet. Which meant he was still thinking. Still processing.

The silence continued.

Smithers turned his head toward the tunnel, checking their blind spots. Otto stood stock-still, waiting.

Knox's smirk hadn't altered, as if he were enjoying the show.

Sinclair had backed into the shadows, out of Hooper's immediate line of sight, but Neagley knew she was watching everything.

Hooper finally spoke. "You have no idea what you're doing."

His voice was measured, steady. No panic. Firm certainty.

Neagley didn't blink. "Enlighten us."

Hooper's lip curled slightly, but not with amusement. More like frustration. "You think you can walk out of here with those warheads? Like this is just another op?" He shook his head. "This isn't your fight."

"I'm standing here," Otto said. "That makes it my fight."

Hooper exhaled loudly. "Cooper wants the nukes intact. Knox is here to make sure of it. So why don't you lower the damned gun and let the professionals handle it?"

"Meaning you?" Otto asked.

Hooper didn't answer. His gaze flicked to Knox again. Something unspoken passed between them.

Neagley didn't like it.

Knox wasn't standing like a man ready for a fight. He had his hands in his pockets, like this was all going exactly the way he expected.

"Knox, you're Cooper's man on the scene," Neagley said flatly. "What's your plan?"

"Same as yours, I assume. Nobody wants a shootout next to four live nukes." Knox finally moved, just a fraction. A slow, deliberate shift of weight. "Especially because they are old and possibly unstable. Who knows what might happen?"

Smithers made a small noise, something between a snort and a breath. "You could have led with that."

Knox ignored him. "We secured the warheads. Cooper already gave the green light. I don't see a problem."

Neagley did. In fact, she saw too many problems.

So did Hooper.

His whole body was rigid now, muscles coiled. He was still standing, but Neagley knew that wouldn't last.

Hooper had been a member of the 110th Special Investigators Unit. Trained the same way she'd been trained. He was good back in Hamburg. But he'd been well supervised.

When and why had he changed? What caused him to go rogue?

Outside, the wind shifted. A faint creak echoed through the bunker entrance.

Hooper's jaw twitched. Then, for the first time since he walked in, he took a step back.

Not a retreat.

A recalculation.

Neagley adjusted her weight on the balls of her feet.

Otto's grip on her weapon didn't waver.

Hooper inhaled slowly.

Then he exhaled a long, even breath.

Then he moved.

His hand flashed toward his weapon. He pulled the gun from its holster and swung it toward Neagley.

Too slow.

Otto fired first.

One shot.

A clean, perfect hit.

She followed it with two more, to be certain.

Hooper staggered, his body jerking once, legs buckling. His gun dangled at the end of his right hand when he collapsed, dead before he hit the ground.

The silence returned.

"Well." Knox exhaled sharply as he rocked back on his heels. "That's one way to handle it. Cooper won't like it, but I'll tell him Hooper drew first."

Neagley didn't move. She kept her focus on Knox and Sinclair.

Otto stepped forward, nudging Hooper's body with the toe of her boot to confirm he'd drawn his last breath.

Smithers was watching the entrance now.

Because Hooper said he had backup. If Reacher shot the lookout, what about the others?

Where the hell were they?

The air inside the bunker remained still, thick with the scent of dust and sweat. Hooper's body lay sprawled on the concrete, blood pooling beneath him.

Knox hadn't moved much, but his smirk had thinned as his gaze scanned the room, calculating.

Smithers kept his position near the entrance, watching the outside. The wind had died down again, leaving an unnatural silence in its place.

Neagley didn't trust it. Any of it.

Reacher told her to leave Hooper's men to him, which she'd agreed to do. She'd seen Reacher fight close quarters with groups of men all at once. Three, five, seven or more to one. Reacher always won. She wasn't worried about him.

But she'd feel better when she knew he'd succeeded on that part of the plan.

Otto's toe nudged Hooper's body again. Nothing. No last twitches, no final words. He was gone.

Neagley crouched and went through Hooper's pockets. A burner phone. A switchblade. Nothing useful. No radio, no earpiece, no indication he had been in contact with anyone before stepping into the bunker.

Which meant his backup either wasn't expecting trouble, or they were already dead.

Neagley wanted confirmation, but she'd bet her last five dollars that Reacher had done the deed.

Smithers turned slightly, tilting his head toward the open entrance. "We've got a problem."

No one spoke.

Neagley stood to brush dust from her knee. "Right. No follow-up after that last gunshot. No rush of approaching boots. No return fire."

"Meaning no sign of Hooper's men," Smithers said. "So where are they? How long do we wait before we go searching?"

Neagley moved toward the entrance, slow and deliberate, keeping to the edges of the wall. Otto followed, her weapon still raised.

Smithers was already a step ahead, his eyes narrowed as he scanned beyond the bunker.

They moved as a unit, clearing the way into the open.

The wind kicked up again, dry and hollow.

Neagley's gaze swept the area. The dirt road leading to the bunker was empty. The SUV Hooper had arrived in sat where he'd left it, driver's door wide open.

She took another step, eyes tracking along the side of the vehicle.

Then she saw it.

A boot.

Half-visible behind the SUV's back tire.

Neagley gave Otto a quick signal before advancing, weapon steady, angles covered. Otto moved parallel, Smithers taking position behind them.

Neagley rounded the SUV first.

Hooper's man lay flat on his back, throat slashed with his own knife, blood spreading under his body. Reacher hated knife fights, but he used whatever was at hand when he had the chance.

No gunshots. No struggle. A clean, quiet, efficient kill.

Otto exhaled quietly beside her. "I think we found Hooper's team."

Neagley didn't need to check the second body.

Smithers crouched next to the body, inspecting the wound. "This wasn't a panic move."

Neagley said nothing. Reacher never panicked. Simple as that.

She took one last look at the bodies.

Reacher's work. No doubt about it.

She exhaled, turning toward Otto. "So now what?"

Otto scanned the area. The bunker. The SUV. The vast, empty stretch of land beyond. "Lock this place down. Secure the warheads. Call it in. Let Cooper deal with it all."

Knox chuckled. "Call it in? You think Cooper doesn't already know?"

Smithers straightened, rubbing at his shoulder where he'd hit the bunker wall. "Well, he's gonna want confirmation."

Neagley's gut tightened. Something was off. A piece missing.

She turned toward the bunker entrance. Sinclair had been inside. She'd been standing right next to the nukes, taking it all in, rattled but not freaked out.

Now she was gone.

Neagley's pulse kicked into high gear. She moved fast, stepping into the bunker's entrance, sweeping her flashlight beam across the walls. Nothing.

Smithers was right behind her. He noticed Sinclair's absence immediately. "Where the hell is Sinclair?"

No answer.

Neagley strode deeper into the bunker. The rack of Davy Crocketts stood untouched. No sign of Sinclair. No tracks in the dirt leading toward the side tunnels that she might have made, either.

Otto said sharply, "She's not outside."

Neagley pivoted toward the main room, checking every shadow. The bunker wasn't big. Nowhere to go except outside or into the tunnel.

If Sinclair had come outside, Neagley would have seen her. Which meant she'd entered the tunnels instead of joining the others out there.

A sound. A scuffle. Distant. From deeper inside the tunnels.

Neagley sprinted toward the noise.

She moved fast, but Otto and Smithers were right behind her. The flashlight beams bounced off old concrete, rusted metal, heavy dust.

Then a metallic slam ahead. A heavy door locking into place.

Neagley skidded to a stop at a fork in the tunnel, scanning the walls, the ground, the air itself.

She turned to Otto. "Which way?"

Otto didn't answer. She was staring at the floor.

Neagley followed her gaze.

"Two sets of footprints. One probably belonging to Sinclair," Otto said, pointing to the floor. "The other one is much larger. More than a hundred pounds heavier, too."

Neagley nodded but made no reply.

She snapped the flashlight up, tracking ahead. The tunnel stretched into darkness, twisting somewhere deeper underground.

Then another sound. A vehicle engine, distant but revving fast.

Neagley turned and ran back through the tunnels to the bunker's exit. She burst out of the bunker, scanning the landscape.

Far out, just beyond the rise of the dirt road, taillights faded into the distance.

Sinclair was gone.

Knox stepped up beside her, hands still in his pockets. He looked amused.

Neagley didn't.

She knew what this meant.

Reacher had extracted Sinclair.

The question was why?

And where was he taking her?

CHAPTER 45

Wednesday, July 13
La Pampa, Argentina

KIM STOOD AT THE bunker entrance, staring after the fading dust trail as the vehicle disappeared over the ridge. The wind kicked up again, hot and gritty against her skin, carrying the metallic stench of blood from Hooper's body sprawled across the concrete floor behind her.

The harsh Argentine sun beat down on the landscape, distorting the air with heat waves that made the horizon shimmer like a mirage.

She scanned the horizon one more time, looking for pursuit options. Nothing. Just endless grassland stretching toward distant mountains. Visibility for miles with no cover except the occasional stand of trees here and there.

Whoever had taken Sinclair, or however she had managed to slip away, she was long gone.

She turned to find Smithers already on his phone, fingers tapping the screen.

"Who are you calling?" she asked.

"Cooper," Smithers replied, not looking up while he waited for the connection. "This is way above our pay grade. We've got dead bodies, missing nuclear warheads, and Sinclair's disappeared. We need backup yesterday."

Kim stepped forward and pressed her finger against the screen, ending the call before it connected.

"No Cooper yet."

Smithers stared at her, eyebrows shooting upward. "What do you mean, not yet? How much more do we handle before we get some help?"

"We don't want to start an international incident," Kim cut him off. "Think about it. We're standing in a secret bunker in the middle of Argentina with four aging nuclear weapons from the US and too many dead bodies."

"Exactly. We're in over our heads." Smithers scowled.

"We need to understand what we're dealing with first," Kim said firmly. "Cooper sent us here knowing what we'd find. He didn't warn us about the nukes. He didn't warn us about Hooper's endgame. He never mentioned Knox. Why?"

Knox leaned against the bunker wall, watching their exchange with a calculated indifference that set Kim's teeth on edge.

"Where did Sinclair go?" she demanded, turning to Knox.

"We have the nukes secured. That was the primary objective." Knox shrugged as if he were bored. "Does it matter?"

"It matters to me," Kim replied.

"Your priorities seem misplaced, Agent Otto." Knox straightened his jacket. "The warheads are secure. Hooper and his team are neutralized. Sinclair is gone, empty handed. Mission accomplished."

Something about his casual dismissal raised Kim's hackles. He wasn't concerned about a former NSA deputy director suddenly vanishing. Sinclair held enough secrets in her head to subvert the entire country many times over. Why didn't Knox care about that, if nothing else?

Neagley emerged from the bunker, her expression unreadable but her eyes alert. She'd clearly been searching the tunnels.

"Anything?" Kim asked.

Neagley shook her head. "Two sets of footprints in the tunnel dust. One smaller. Sinclair's, most likely. The other was significantly larger. Then nothing. It's like they vanished."

"Or found another exit," Smithers suggested.

"We're too exposed here," Neagley said, scanning the horizon. "Standing around won't bring her back."

"She couldn't have gotten far alone," Kim said, head cocked to think. Sinclair was resourceful, but this was the middle of nowhere. "Unless she had help."

"Help from who?" Smithers asked. "If Cooper sent someone, Knox would know."

Knox raised an eyebrow but said nothing, which Kim found more telling. Knox knew way more than he was sharing with them, for sure.

But now was not the time to push him with Neagley present. Neagley was a direct line to Reacher. Tell her, you're telling him. Which Kim would have gladly done, if she could. But adding Neagley to the conversation wasn't how Kim wanted it to go.

"Let's see what Hooper brought with him." She walked to Hooper's vehicle and pulled open the driver's door.

The interior was cluttered with tactical gear and empty energy drink cans. Kim checked under the seats, in the glove compartment, and along the console. Nothing immediately useful.

While she had her head close to the carpet, she heard a faint buzzing sound from beneath the passenger seat.

"What's that?" she murmured, reaching under. Her fingers found something small and solid.

She pulled out a burner phone. The screen flashing with an incoming message. Kim stared at it for a moment before swiping to read.

Intercept Sinclair at ranch, if possible. Imperative. Stop her. She must not reach safe deposit box at First National, Buenos Aires. C

The moment she finished the message she scrolled up to read it again. But the message was no longer there. It simply vanished faster than a poof of smoke.

Smithers had joined her, peering over her shoulder at the message for half a second before it disappeared. "C as in Cooper?"

"Looks like Hooper was supposed to stop Sinclair from reaching a safe deposit box in Buenos Aires." She tapped the phone thoughtfully against her palm.

Her phone buzzed. Gaspar. She'd sent him a quick text when Sinclair disappeared. Maybe he'd found her.

She put it on speaker. "Tell me something helpful for a change. We're not having much luck here."

"Maybe," Gaspar's voice crackled over the connection. "Sinclair's SUV has GPS tracking built into the rental. It's still online but encrypted. Give me time. I'll pinpoint her location."

"Do it fast," Kim replied. "We might know where she's headed. If you can confirm, we won't be running around like headless chickens."

"And why she left in such a hurry," Smithers added.

Knox approached them, posture relaxed despite the tension. "We've got satellite surveillance on this entire area. Insurance against unexpected developments."

Kim turned to him. "And you're just mentioning this now?"

Knox smiled flatly. "Need to know, Agent Otto."

"So we can see exactly what happened to Sinclair," Kim concluded.

"Most likely." Knox pulled out his own phone. "I can request the footage. Might take some time to get anything."

"Do it," Kim ordered. She turned back to Hooper's SUV, examining it more carefully, but she found nothing else of consequence.

Smithers moved closer to Neagley. "You've been quiet about all this."

Neagley shrugged and her expression remained neutral.

"Those footprints you found. The larger ones. Any guess who they might belong to?" Smithers asked.

"Could be anyone," Neagley replied.

"Could be." Smithers held her gaze a beat too long. "But probably not."

Kim didn't comment. Because Smithers was right. Neagley knew more than she was saying. Neagley always knew more than she revealed.

Knox stepped away, murmuring into his phone. His posture shifted subtly. The affected boredom vanished, replaced by tightly coiled intensity. He was probably talking to Cooper.

"I need clean-up at these coordinates," Knox said, just loud enough for Kim to catch as she approached. "Full containment protocol."

Hooper's body still lay sprawled inside the bunker. The others lay outside. Containment meant the bodies would disappear. No evidence. No questions. Just the way the special operations teams liked it.

What would happen to Kim, Smithers, Neagley, and the others?

CHAPTER 46

Wednesday, July 13
La Pampa, Argentina

KIM WATCHED KNOX CLOSELY. He was too calm about Sinclair's disappearance. The nukes were found and Hooper's crew along with his plans had been neutralized. But Sinclair vanishing didn't seem to concern him at all.

Why not?

Sinclair knew everything about the Wiley operation. She'd been there when it happened and continued to track it from the beginning. Sinclair knew about the money. She set this whole situation in motion.

Why didn't Knox seem to care?

The answer snapped into place.

"He already has what he wants," Kim said in a low voice.

Smithers frowned. "Which is what?"

"I don't know, exactly," Kim replied. "Knox. Cooper. They don't care about Sinclair because she can't touch what they're really after."

"Which is what?" Smithers asked again.

"Walk with me." Kim moved to the bunker entrance, keeping her voice low. "Sinclair chased Wiley's money for weeks. Maybe years. But what if it was never about the money? What if it was about what Wiley bought and sold with that money?"

"The nukes," Smithers said, eyes widening slightly. "The ones we secured."

"Exactly. Cooper's covered all angles. We've secured the warheads. Hooper's dead. But Wiley's secret compound has been discovered. Cooper won't like that at all." She paused, glancing toward Knox. "They're cleaning up loose ends. Including us if we're not careful."

"And what about Lone Wolf and Sinclair?" Smithers asked.

Kim's jaw clenched. "Sinclair's either in the wind or being pursued. Knox doesn't look worried. Why?"

"Because Cooper already knows all about the money and the nukes," Neagley said from behind them. "He's controlled everything all along."

Both agents turned toward her.

"You knew, too?" Kim kept her voice steady.

Neagley's expression revealed nothing. "I suspected. Sinclair figured it out in the bank vault in Grand Cayman. Certain transactions required authorization from a higher level."

Knox finished his call and walked back toward them after he tucked his phone away. "Good news. Cooper's sending the satellite feed. We'll know exactly what happened to Dr. Sinclair."

Kim nodded, maintaining a neutral expression. "How long will that take?"

"Twenty minutes. Maybe less." Knox checked his watch. "A team's also inbound to secure the warheads. ETA ninety minutes."

"Quick response," Smithers remarked, his tone carefully casual.

Knox's smile was thin. "The boss likes efficiency."

"And he hates to be thwarted," Kim said.

"That, too," Knox agreed.

"What about Lone Wolf?" Smithers asked.

Knox replied, "Leave Lone Wolf to the boss. He'll deal with them in his own time."

Kim's phone vibrated in her pocket. She pulled it out, glancing at the screen. Gaspar had sent a text.

GPS active. Moving southwest 85 mph headed for Chile.

She kept her expression neutral, though her pulse kicked up a notch. Chile meant mountains. Borders. Escape routes.

"I need to check something in the SUV," she said, stepping away from the group.

Once inside Hooper's vehicle, Kim quickly sent Gaspar a reply.

Keep tracking. Cooper knows.

Gaspar's response was instant. *No surprise there.*

She slipped the phone into her pocket and popped open the glove compartment again. Nothing useful. Just rental papers and the owner's manual, like most rental vehicles.

A sound caught her attention. Faint. Electronic. A quiet buzz from beneath the driver's seat.

Kim reached under the floor mat, fingers searching until they closed around something small and solid. A second phone.

The screen glowed with a single message.

Safe deposit box. Buenos Aires. Beneath the message, a series of numbers. Sinclair had left breadcrumbs. For whom?

Kim committed the numbers to memory and tucked the phone into her pocket just as Knox approached.

"Find anything?" he asked, his casual tone belied by the intensity of his stare.

"Nothing. Just double checking," Kim lied smoothly. "Measure twice, cut once, as my grandpa used to say."

Knox's phone chimed. He glanced at it, then looked up with a grimace. "Satellite feed's downloading now. Let's see what really happened to Dr. Sinclair."

Kim followed him back to where Smithers and Neagley waited. Knox turned his phone screen toward them, revealing grainy aerial footage of the ranch compound.

The timestamp showed an hour earlier. The image zoomed in on Sinclair walking rapidly toward the SUV she'd rented in Buenos Aries.

She seemed rushed, but not afraid.

She was not alone.

A man, tall and broad, waited behind the steering wheel of the vehicle. The camera angle didn't capture his face clearly. Which was okay with Kim.

"There," Knox said, pausing the footage. "Looks like our missing NSA deputy had an exit strategy after all."

Kim's gaze caught Neagley's. A flicker of recognition passed between them.

The man in the driver's seat was unmistakable, even from this angle.

Certainly obvious if you already knew who he was.

Jack Reacher.

"And who might that be?" Knox asked smugly, as if he already knew, too. Which he probably did.

Kim lied with a head shake and a shrug. "But now we know what happened to Sinclair."

"She planned this," Smithers said. "Used the chaos as cover for her escape."

Knox nodded, apparently satisfied with that assessment. "Cooper will want details. I'm calling now."

As he stepped away to make the call, Kim moved closer to Neagley, keeping her voice low.

"You knew Reacher was here."

Neagley's expression revealed nothing. "What makes you think so?"

"Cut the crap," Kim replied. "Sinclair left a message. A safe deposit box in Buenos Aires. She's not running with Reacher because she's afraid. She's after the money."

Neagley met her gaze, unwavering. "What are you going to do about it?"

"Get to that box before the others do."

Smithers joined them, keeping an eye on Knox, who was still on the phone. "We're assuming Sinclair went willingly?"

Kim nodded. "She left a phone for us to find in Hooper's rental. Hidden, but not very well. Where she knew we'd find it. She wants us to follow."

"Why?" Smithers asked. "If she wanted us, she could have stayed here. Or asked us to come along with her."

Kim had no answer, but Neagley's guess made sense.

"Because," Neagley said quietly, "Cooper's only worried about the nukes and the money. Sinclair uncovered something else she thinks we need to see."

"Something about Wiley and his money," Kim guessed.

Neagley shook her head. "Something about who's been controlling it all along."

"Sounds like a very dangerous thing to know," Kim replied.

The wind picked up again, sending a gust of sand swirling around them.

Knox finished his call and tucked his phone away before he rejoined them. "Clean-up team's ten minutes out. Extraction to DC in thirty."

"We need to get back to Buenos Aires," Kim said. "Check on Hooper's activities there, see if there are any other leads on the operation. Find Sinclair if we can."

Knox's expression remained neutral. "Cooper wants a full debrief first. You'll be on the extraction helo with me."

Kim felt the weight of Sinclair's phone in her pocket. Whatever was in that safe deposit box, she needed to reach it before Cooper's team snatched it from her grasp. Reacher might be there, too.

And Knox couldn't know they were going after them.

"Looking forward to giving my report," Kim said with a calm she didn't feel. "This mission's had enough surprises."

Knox's smile never reached his eyes when he said flatly, "Hasn't it, though."

As the helicopter sounds grew louder, Kim caught Neagley's gaze once more.

Neagley gave her a curt nod.

They agreed, for once.

Time was running out.

CHAPTER 47

Wednesday, July 13
La Pampa, Argentina

THE LOW, RHYTHMIC BEAT of rotors pulsed against the distance growing louder, closing in. Neagley felt the hair at the back of her neck prickle, a familiar warning crawling beneath her skin. She shifted her weight, gravel crunching softly underfoot.

Knox stood near the bunker entrance, tone clipped, eyes steady, unreadable. "Extractions inbound. Cooper wants a full debrief immediately."

"How many helos?" Kim asked. "You've got a lot of bodies here to transport along with those nukes."

"Two. Military transport," Knox said.

Kim shot a quick glance toward Smithers, the silent exchange clear as neon. Nobody trusted Knox. Which would make things easier.

Neagley let out a slow breath as she scanned the perimeter. Shadows danced at the edge of her vision. The wind tugged at her jacket sleeves, carrying with it the scent of scorched earth and tension.

"Neagley," Knox said, turning sharply. "You're with us."

"No thanks." She shook her head slowly, voice calm but firm. "I've got my own ride."

Knox's expression hardened, irritation breaking through his usual calm. "That wasn't the agreement."

"I didn't agree to anything," Neagley replied evenly. "You handle the nukes. I'll meet up with you later."

Knox took a step toward her. His eyes flashed with suspicion bordering on anger. "Cooper gave explicit orders."

"I don't answer to Cooper," Neagley said simply. "And I sure as hell don't answer to you."

Before Knox could respond, she turned away, stepping swiftly into the shadow of the closest outbuilding. She felt his stare burning between her shoulders, but he didn't follow.

Knox had other problems at the moment. Problems that came with ticking timers and armed warheads. He'd quickly realize that she wasn't a priority.

Neagley didn't look back.

Behind her, she heard Otto deliberately neutral, keeping Knox busy. "You're going to be here for a while. Smithers and I will take Hooper's SUV. We'll meet up later, too."

Neagley didn't wait to hear Knox's reply. She moved deeper into the shadows, feeling the dry, cool air against her skin, adrenaline still thrumming through her veins.

She had maybe ninety seconds to vanish before Knox noticed her again. Less if he grew suspicious faster.

Ahead of her, the darkness stretched empty and quiet, calling her forward.

Neagley moved swiftly along the ranch's perimeter. Her heightened senses scanning every shadow as she moved. Her boots whispered against dry, brittle grass, but the crunch was nearly swallowed by the steady drone of incoming helicopters.

Knox's extraction team was minutes out. He'd soon remember that she wasn't coming and he wouldn't like it any better now than he had before.

She shrugged the concern aside. She wasn't inclined to deal with him at all, and certainly not right now.

Neagley slipped behind a rusted storage shed. The cool metal wall was rough beneath her fingertips. A vibration against her thigh startled her. The phone was silent but insistent. She drew it carefully shielding the screen's faint glow with her palm.

A message from Reacher.

North fence. Vehicle waiting. Now.

She let out a slow breath to steady her heart rate. She'd expected contact, but not this soon.

Reacher never operated by anyone's expectations. He set his own rules, every time. It had taken Neagley a long time to reconcile his personality with the norms of her world and internalize it.

He was one of her heroes, to be sure.

But she wasn't blind to Reacher's faults, either.

One of which was his tendency to boss everybody like he was still in the Army and everyone reported to him.

Another was his frank and candid opinions about everyone and everything. Reacher considered himself the best man in every room. Every time.

He wasn't often wrong in his judgments about the men, either. He could separate the wheat from the chaff with less than a second's exposure to a male enemy.

But his track record wasn't so great with women. He seemed to have a blind spot.

Reacher had profound respect for his mother and, by extension, other women in his life. His mother had been a freedom fighter in the French Resistance.

From everything he'd said over the years, Josephine Reacher had been a true badass. A woman with fierce loyalties who backed them up with her life.

When Reacher's respect for women was misplaced, trouble came at him fast and furious.

Anyone standing with him when that trouble manifested was likely to get hammered in the process.

Because Neagley knew all of this, she realized Reacher's relationship with Sinclair back in Hamburg was one of those times when Reacher allowed his afterglow of maternal respect to shine on the wrong sort of woman.

They'd all been on the same team back then. Even Hooper. Reacher obviously believed they still were.

He was wrong. Sinclair would throw him under the bus in a hot New York second, as soon as she had the chance. Sinclair was running hard and she wouldn't let Reacher or anyone else thwart her now.

Neagley pocketed the phone, quickly assessing her surroundings.

Beyond the edge of the compound, the northern fence stood silhouetted in the moonlight, weathered and sagging. She made her way carefully toward it, skirting around piles of old machinery. She moved her body efficiently and quickly without wasted action.

She stayed in the shadows.

Knox's helos were coming closer. She listened closely to the vibrations. One skill she'd honed to perfection was the ability to count incoming aircraft.

Knox had said Cooper was sending two helos.

Neagley heard three. She allowed herself a quick grin. She hadn't called the third helo, but she figured Reacher did.

Knox might notice the third helo, but he probably wouldn't. He'd be focused on the mission as he had defined it. Which meant two helos and not three.

At the fence, she paused and scanned the scene.

Near the gate stood an old Land Rover. Dark, quiet, blending seamlessly with the terrain.

The windows were tinted black, making the driver impossible to see clearly. The engine idled low, barely audible over the growing helicopter noise.

Neagley approached cautiously, brushing her hand against the holstered pistol at her hip. Trust in other humans, places, and things was not one of her virtues. Not tonight. Not ever.

The only person she trusted implicitly was Reacher. With good reason.

When she was within a few feet, the passenger-side window lowered slightly. No words. No greeting. A silent invitation and a clear order simultaneously.

She kept her face forward, resisting the urge to glance inside. She knew who was behind the wheel. No need for confirmation.

She slipped into the passenger seat without a word. She pointed toward the sky to indicate that Cooper had eyes and ears on the ranch at all times. Then put her finger across her lips followed by placing both hands over her ears to confirm.

He nodded understanding and said nothing.

"Sinclair's headed to Buenos Aires, I assume," Neagley wrote on her phone and showed it to him. "Cooper won't wait. He'll be right behind her."

He gave her a firm nod, probably because he'd already surmised as much, and the Land Rover rolled forward without headlights.

Words had always been unnecessary between them. They understood each other in a way no one else did.

She twisted around to look briefly back toward the compound. Knox would come looking for her soon.

The vehicle moved instantly, smoothly pulling away from the ranch into the darkness, headlights off. She didn't look at the driver, didn't speak, didn't need to. His presence was unmistakable, steady and calm, reassuring in the silence.

On the seat between them rested a small, folded slip of paper. Neagley picked it up, unfolding it carefully. A handwritten note, precise and familiar.

She grinned. He'd written the note before she'd arrived because they couldn't talk without tipping off the electronic surveillance.

Sinclair already moving. Buenos Aires. Cooper closing fast. Hooper just one piece. Stay ahead.

Neagley folded the paper and slipped it into her pocket. Beside her, he remained silent, unseen in shadow.

Reacher didn't need to speak. He'd already said everything that mattered when they met up back in Grand Cayman.

The Land Rover accelerated gently, headed toward Chile, leaving the ranch and Cooper's approaching helicopters behind.

Neagley stared ahead through the windshield seeking confirmation of the incoming helo.

Her heart was steady, and her thoughts were sharp.

She was as ready as she would ever be.

CHAPTER 48

Thursday, July 14
Buenos Aires, Argentina

BEFORE COOPER'S HELOS TOUCHED down at Wiley's ranch, Kim had pulled Smithers aside. The rotors whipped dust across the compound, stinging her eyes as she leaned in close.

She said, low and urgent, "Sinclair is on her way to a bank in Buenos Aires. Safe deposit box."

"Knox won't like it," Smithers warned.

"He won't know until it's too late," Kim replied. "Come on."

Within minutes, they'd slipped away and commandeered Hooper's SUV. Gravel crunched beneath the tires as Smithers accelerated down the dirt road. The air inside the SUV smelled of sunbaked leather and the unmistakable scent of gun oil.

They were five miles down the road when Kim's satellite phone buzzed. She was tempted to ignore the summons, but he'd simply keep calling if she tried.

"Otto," she said when she picked up the call.

"Agent Otto, this is a direct order," Knox's voice crackled through the speaker. The static didn't mask the cold anger in his tone. "Return to the extraction point immediately."

"Bad connection," she replied. "Can't hear you."

"Dammit, Otto. Cooper will have your badge for this."

"Not likely." She switched off the phone and tossed it onto the dashboard, where it clattered against the vinyl. "Sinclair knows something that's made her willing to risk Cooper's wrath. I want to know what it is."

"And if Cooper's waiting for us in Buenos Aires?" Smithers asked, his knuckles white against the steering wheel.

"Then we'll have a nice reunion."

The four-hour drive seemed to take forever. Heat shimmered off the asphalt, distorting the horizon. By the time they reached Buenos Aires, Sinclair had had a significant head start.

Kim had slept exactly forty-three minutes, her neck stiff from the awkward angle against the passenger window, while Smithers handled communications with Gaspar, who kept them updated on Sinclair's movements.

"Sinclair's been inside thirty minutes," Smithers said, ending another call with Gaspar. Sweat beaded his forehead despite the SUV's struggling air conditioner. "Two guards at the main entrance, one at the side door."

Kim drained the last of her bitter coffee they'd picked up at a convenience store a few miles back. The liquid was cold against her tongue. She crushed the empty paper cup in her fist. "Private security or bank personnel?"

"Bank security would be my guess," Smithers replied. "No sign of Cooper's people yet."

"They'll be here." Kim raised the binoculars again, the weight familiar in her hands. "They always are."

Through the lenses, the bank's glass facade gleamed like a knife in the sun. She scanned the building's upper floors, tension coiling between her shoulder blades.

Parked across from the bank, she fought the exhaustion. Her eyes burned. The taste of dust and coffee lingered in her mouth. While somewhere inside those walls soaring above the city, Sinclair was accessing secrets apparently worth killing for.

Kim peered through binoculars at the entrance of First National Bank. The morning crowd moved with predictable patterns, business suits and casual tourists flowing through the revolving doors like migration patterns she could track and predict.

Her focus remained locked on the glass entrance while the weight of the binoculars left imprints on her cheekbones.

"Movement at the side entrance," Smithers said, his voice cutting through the traffic noise.

Kim pivoted and the leather seat creaked beneath her. The side door swung open. Bright sunlight glinted off the polished brass handle.

Two women emerged, stepping from shadow into the harsh morning glare.

Neagley first, fluid and precise, head turning for a calculated sweep of the street.

Sinclair followed. She was carrying an oversized shoulder bag that hadn't been with her at the ranch. The leather bag hung heavy against her side, swinging with unnatural weight.

"Got them." Kim felt the adrenaline rush all at once. "Sinclair's carrying something."

Smithers eased the rental into traffic. He maintained three vehicles between them and the targets. "Cooper's going to want whatever she found."

"Cooper's got his own issues. Unless she found something that leads us to Reacher, it's not our concern." Kim kept her gaze fixed on the two women as they navigated the crowded sidewalk. Sweat trickled down her spine while the air-conditioning fought its losing battle against the summer heat. "But I do want to know what Sinclair believes was worth killing for."

Sinclair and Neagley moved easily along, showing no signs they suspected a tail. Their reflections rippled across storefront windows as they turned down a side street lined with cafés and upscale storefronts.

The scent of fresh pastries and coffee drifted through the SUV's vents. The Grand Plaza Hotel stood at the corner, its façade gleaming white against the blue sky.

"They're going inside," Kim said.

Smithers pulled to the curb half a block away. The brakes squealed softly as he slowed to park. "You think it's a trap?"

"Possibly." Kim scanned the rooftops and adjacent buildings, eyes narrowed against the glare.

Nothing obvious. No snipers. No tactical teams waiting to pounce.

The street sounds continued their normal urban rhythm.

"We'll know for sure when we get inside."

The hotel lobby sparkled with polished marble and brass fixtures. The air was cool and dry, scented with floral arrangements that stood taller than Kim. They made great cover.

Footsteps echoed slightly against the hard floors. Tourists clutched shopping bags and travel guides. Business executives huddled near leather armchairs, speaking in hushed tones that created a low, constant murmur.

Kim scanned the lobby of the hotel until she spotted Sinclair and Neagley standing near the elevators.

Neagley's back was to the wall, her posture relaxed but alert, one foot slightly ahead of the other.

Sinclair faced the doors, one hand resting on the handbag, fingers tapping an impatient rhythm against the leather.

Kim moved directly toward them. No point in subtlety now. Her shoes clicked against the marble, telegraphing her approach.

Sinclair noticed her first. Her expression remained neutral, but her fingers tightened around the bag's strap to a white-knuckled grip.

"You're late, Agent Otto," Sinclair said as Kim approached. Her voice carried a hint of amusement. "I expected you thirty minutes ago."

"Traffic was heavy." Kim stopped five feet away, Smithers at her right flank. "What did you find at the bank?"

"Bank?" Sinclair's lips curved into a thin smile. A small muscle twitched at her jaw. "I've been touring the city. Beautiful architecture."

"The safe deposit box," Kim pressed. "What was inside?"

Sinclair's gaze flicked to her watch, a quick, calculated gesture. "You're wasting your time. Knox already secured everything worth taking."

"You came here to get Wiley's money," Kim said.

Something shifted in Sinclair's expression, a flicker of genuine surprise before her mask slipped back into place. Her pupils dilated slightly.

"Cooper told you very little and only what he wanted you to know," Sinclair replied. "Just like he always does. I've worked with the man for decades. He's always been a lying snake. Watch your back, Otto."

A cold sensation crawled up Kim's spine. Somewhere in her peripheral vision, a shape moved. Just beyond the glass, a shadow where no shadow should be. The hairs on the back of her neck stiffened.

Neagley stepped forward. Her shoes made no sound against the marble. When the elevator landed on the first floor with a chime, she said, "Sinclair, take the elevator."

Sinclair moved toward the open elevator without argument. No hesitation. Like it was rehearsed. The handbag swung at her side.

The elevator doors closed behind her with a soft metallic whisper.

Before Kim had a chance to move, the big plate glass lobby window exploded.

Glass sprayed across marble, glittering like deadly diamonds in the sunlight. The concussive force knocked Kim sideways, her ears ringing with sudden pressure.

Smithers tackled her behind a marble column as gunfire erupted, sharp cracks echoed against stone and tile while marble dust filled her nostrils, chalky, acrid, and chaotic.

Hotel guests screamed.

Bodies dropped to the floor.

Security guards reached for weapons but were killed before they completed the draw. Blood spattered across polished surfaces.

"Smithers!" Kim shouted over the chaotic scene, as loudly as she could through the dust that settled into her throat. "The elevator!"

Through the settling dust and smoke, Kim saw the elevator car with Sinclair inside was stuck between floors. The lobby elevator doors were half-open, revealing an empty interior elevator shaft.

A box of empty space where Sinclair's elevator car should have been.

Neagley had taken cover behind the reception desk, shielding a fallen employee with her body. Her movements seemed automatic and unaffected by the panic around them.

More gunfire. Tactical. Controlled bursts. Professional.

The bullets punched into wood and plaster, sending splinters flying. Kim felt two sharp bits sting her cheek.

She returned fire, aiming at muzzle flashes through the shattered windows. The recoil traveled up her arms, familiar and grounding.

Smithers also returned fire.

The acrid smell of gunpowder mixed with the dust.

And then, as suddenly as it began, the shooting stopped.

Silence fell, interrupted only by whimpers from bystanders and the crunch of glass underfoot.

"Police response in ninety seconds," Smithers said, checking his watch. Blood trickled from a small cut above his eyebrow, and he swiped it aside.

Kim rose cautiously, gun still ready, muscles tense. "The elevator."

They moved together across the debris-strewn lobby. Glass crunched beneath their shoes. Neagley joined, expression unreadable. A thin scratch across her cheekbone was the only sign she'd been attacked.

The elevator remained jammed between floors. Kim pulled the doors wider, metal scraping against metal. The car returned to the lobby, but it was now unoccupied and silent.

A maintenance panel hung open on the rear wall. Darkness gaped beyond the open panel.

"She's gone," Kim said. The words felt hollow in her chest.

No blood. No body. No sign of a struggle. Nothing.

"We just got played," Smithers muttered, holstering his weapon. His breath came in controlled, measured exhales.

Neagley surveyed the destruction, her gaze lingering on the shattered glass. "See that pattern in the break points? The shots through the glass were deliberately placed. Not random."

"Sinclair set this up?" Kim stared into the empty elevator, jaw tight, anger building beneath her ribs like a physical thing. The taste of Sinclair's betrayal was metallic on her tongue.

Smithers said, "She had a head start, but she knew she was being followed. She needed more time to vanish."

Kim glanced at the damage. No bodies. Attackers gone. No evidence left behind. "The attack was a distraction. Sinclair had used it to cover her escape."

"You knew about this, Neagley, didn't you?" Smithers demanded.

"Sinclair didn't confide in me as much as you think," Neagley replied.

Which was neither a denial nor an admission.

Sirens wailed in the distance, growing louder. The screaming wail bounced off tall buildings, coming closer with each echo.

Smithers looked toward the street. Flashing lights reflected in the remaining glass as the vehicles approached.

"Police are almost here. We get stuck here, we won't get out for hours. Maybe days. We need to move."

"Let's go," Kim agreed. A moment later, she spied a comm device on the elevator car's floor. She scooped it up. "Private tech. Not one of ours."

"Lone Wolf?" Smithers asked.

"Possibly," Kim replied.

"Could be Knox or Cooper or just about anyone else," Neagley said. "It's not US military. Not one of yours, either."

"You can tell by looking at it?" Smithers asked pointedly, both eyebrows arched all the way to his hairline to convey that he didn't believe even Neagley's magic powers extended that far.

Neagley shrugged. "We need to split up before we get hauled in together. I'm not interested in spending even one minute inside an Argentine jail."

"You're in contact with Reacher now, aren't you?" Kim gave her a knowing look, but Neagley didn't offer a reply or wait for permission.

"See you when I see you, Otto," she said. "You want to talk, you know where to find me."

Half a moment later she was gone.

"She's right about Argentinian jails. Let's get out while we still can." Smithers urged as he gestured toward a side exit.

Kim nodded and turned to follow him.

At that moment, she caught another movement through the remaining window glass behind her. The same shadow she'd seen before.

Broad-shouldered. Narrow waisted. Big and tall and lumbering.

She knew that shape.

That silhouette.

The distinctive way it moved.

Reacher.

Kim rushed outside, but she was too late. Reacher, if he'd been there at all, had vanished. But Sinclair's oversized handbag had been left on the sidewalk.

She picked it up and quickly looked inside. A titanium cylinder rested easily in the bottom like a harmless water bottle. She hustled to the SUV and settled into the passenger seat.

Smithers rolled into traffic and punched the accelerator. The SUV was blocks away before the Argentine police arrived.

Kim gloved up and prepared to open the cylinder.

Before she could open it, Cooper's satellite phone rang.

CHAPTER 49

Friday, July 15
Washington, DC

COOPER'S SAFE HOUSE SAT on a quiet street in Georgetown. Red brick exterior. Black shutters. Unmarked. Unremarkable.

Smithers pulled the rental car to the curb and cut the engine. Rain pounded the windshield, distorting the streetlights into blurry amber smears. Water drummed against the roof in an uneven staccato.

"Feels like a setup." Smithers said. "Are you sure about this?"

"Not even close to sure." Kim checked her weapon which was cool and familiar against her fingertips. The leather creaked. "And it's a good bet this is a setup, although not what you might think. With Cooper, you need to be like a Boy Scout, always prepared for anything."

They'd been back in the States for less than six hours. No time to decompress. No official debriefing. Just a terse text message from Cooper with a time and an address for the meeting.

The front door opened before they reached the porch steps. A man in a dark suit nodded once, stepped aside. The bulk under his jacket said he was armed.

No words.

No ID check.

No need.

A petite Asian-American woman and an oversized African-American man were expected.

How many pairs fitting that description were wandering around Georgetown right now? Only one, probably.

When there's only one choice, it's the right choice, as Kim's mother often said.

Inside, the house smelled of furniture polish and emptiness. It looked like a realtor's staging portfolio. Generic furniture. Abstract art. No photographs. No mail. Nothing personal.

Their escort led them across hardwood floors to the back of the house.

Cooper waited in a wood-paneled study. He sat behind a heavy oak desk, reading glasses low on his nose, reviewing documents with indifference. A single desk lamp cast sharp shadows across his face.

"Otto. Smithers. Sit." He didn't look up as he waved the security detail out the door.

Kim heard the door close, but she remained standing. Her legs ached, along with most of her body, but she wouldn't give Cooper the advantage.

Smithers followed her lead and remained standing as well.

Cooper removed his glasses and placed them deliberately on the desk. A soft click against the polished wood punctuated the silence.

After allowing a few moments of her willful belligerence, Cooper said, "I understand we've had casualties."

"I filed a complete report, as usual," Kim said before she stated the bare facts. "Hooper is dead, along with several of his operatives. We believe they were all Lone Wolf mercenaries."

"So I understand," Cooper affirmed. "And Dr. Sinclair?"

"In the wind," Smithers replied.

Cooper's expression didn't change. No surprise. No concern. Nothing. Just cold, calculating assessment.

"The old nukes have been secured," Smithers said. "Knox's team has them."

Cooper nodded. The smallest gesture. "And Wiley's operation?"

"The financial network was still running when Sinclair disappeared," Kim said. The words tasted bitter on her tongue. "I imagine she's found a way to divert the funds to her own accounts somewhere by now."

"And Reacher?" Cooper leaned forward slightly. The first sign of actual interest. The leather chair creaked beneath him.

Kim caught the change immediately. "No confirmed sighting."

Cooper's eyes narrowed. "But?"

"I saw someone matching his description more than once," Kim relented.

It was a calculated admission. If she never reported any progress, Cooper had made it clear that he could easily replace her.

Not that she'd give up, even if he tried to shove her out of the way.

She didn't believe he'd actually kill her to make her stop.

Because she didn't want to believe it, even when Gaspar told her she was a fool.

Cooper stood abruptly. Wood scraped against wood as his chair pushed back. He crossed to a sideboard with a crystal decanter and glasses. "That's it? A possible sighting?"

"That's it," she lied. Cooper had to know about Neagley working with Reacher already. Kim would eat her hat if he didn't.

Cooper poured amber liquid into a tumbler with a steady hand. The smell of expensive whiskey filled the air.

"You were sent to find Reacher, Agent Otto." He didn't offer them whiskey or any alternatives, either. "Everything else was secondary."

Kim felt heat rising in her chest. Blood pounded in her ears. "We found nuclear weapons being trafficked by a private military contractor. We uncovered a financial operation worth billions. We stopped—"

"You were sent to find Reacher," Cooper repeated, cutting her off. His voice remained calm. Controlled. Dangerous.

"With respect, sir," Kim said, "those nukes were the real issue. You'd agree we don't want them detonated on American soil, I assume."

Cooper took a slow sip. Ice clinked against crystal. "The nuclear situation has been successfully managed for years. You know the tech has improved to the point where countries around the globe monitor nuclear explosions on a constant basis. We weren't worried. Those old nukes were never a primary concern."

The admission hung in the air between them, heavy as smoke.

Kim said, "You used the nukes to draw Reacher out of hiding."

Cooper met her gaze evenly. "I knew they were secure and guarded, yes."

"And you knew Reacher wouldn't ignore them," Kim said slowly. "How did you get the word to him?"

"What makes you think I was the one who did that?" Cooper replied with his own belligerent question. "Sinclair and Neagley were both on the trail of Wiley's money. They know Reacher. Maybe they're the ones who told him about Hooper's activities since Hamburg. Did you consider that?"

"Knox reported all of this to you already," Smithers said flatly.

Cooper's attention shifted to Smithers. Cold. Calculating. "Agent Smithers, your insight is not required here."

Kim stepped sideways, drawing Cooper's focus back to her. A floorboard creaked under her foot. "You sent us to Argentina knowing exactly what we'd find."

"I sent you to find Reacher," Cooper's jaw clenched tight. "The rest was incidental and not your assignment. You can't seem to stay on task, can you, Otto?"

Kim felt her jaw tighten. "*Incidental.* Four unstable nuclear warheads were *incidental*?"

"Like I said, they were accounted for, safely stored, and being watched."

"By whom?"

"Need to know, Agent Otto." Cooper's smile resembled an alligator's beckoning grin and was just as dangerous. He shook his head slowly. "And you don't."

Kim moved closer to the desk. "With all due respect, sir, that's bullshit."

Cooper's expression hardened. "You forget yourself, Otto."

Kim placed both palms on the table, leaning forward. The wood felt cool and smooth beneath her hands. "People died. For what? So you could flush out Jack Reacher?"

"Sit down, Agent Otto. I'm getting a crick in my neck." Cooper's orders carried the weight of authority and expectation of compliance.

Kim remained standing. Her legs braced, spine straight.

"Perhaps I overestimated your ability to follow orders." Cooper sighed in response to her steady outrage. After a moment, he relented. "The operation was compartmentalized by design. You were given the information necessary to complete your portion of the assignment. Others were responsible for other aspects."

"Which were?" Kim asked.

"To stop Sinclair. Before she could do more harm."

"Which you knew Reacher would not like. What about Hooper?" Kim asked.

"What about him? He's dead now. Whatever he had in mind, it died with him," Cooper replied without concern. "If you'd wanted to get more intel from him, you shouldn't have killed him."

"He was a part of the old Hamburg operation. He was a member of Reacher's 110th Special Investigation Squad after Reacher lost that command," Kim said. "Hooper was on the right side back then. What changed?"

Cooper shook his head again and shrugged. "Time. Circumstances. Men like Hooper don't do well in peacetime. He missed the adrenaline rush. Went looking for it. Found it. Rode that rush for years until the urge caught up with him. Now he's dead. Familiar story."

"Using us as bait, you thought Reacher might what? Come to assist Hooper? Use the nukes against US interests? Why would Reacher do any of that?" Smithers asked.

"We hope he wouldn't. But we don't know for sure, do we?" Cooper shrugged. "Reacher has been a loose cannon for far too long. Hamburg was years ago, but he persists in pursuing matters best left buried. When Hooper found the extra Davy Crocketts, he took up where Wiley left off. It's not a stretch to assume that Reacher heard about that, too."

"You're suggesting Reacher would disapprove?" Smithers said.

Cooper shrugged.

Kim said, "Hamburg. That's what this is about? That operation was before my time."

"Hamburg was the beginning," Cooper said. "Wiley. The weapons. The financial system. All of it stems from those events. Reacher was there, along with Neagley and Sinclair."

"But they don't have the full story, do they?" Kim asked, eyes narrowed, head cocked.

"They've probably figured it out by now," Cooper replied. "Regardless, this conversation is over. You've failed again. Do your job, Otto. It's your one and only mission. Try sticking with it until you succeed."

Kim didn't move. "That's it?"

"Find Reacher. That's always been your mission," Cooper said. "Are you giving up?"

"You sent us out there to take us off the playing field while you cleaned up loose ends. You tied off the Wiley operation, so nothing leads back to you," Kim challenged.

Cooper's expression turned dangerous. A muscle twitched in his cheek. "Remember your place, Otto."

"My place is upholding the law," Kim said. "Even when it's inconvenient."

"Give me the titanium cylinder you recovered in Buenos Aries. Hand over those drives you pulled from the Lone Wolf box in Arizona. Then go while I'm still in a good mood." Cooper's hand moved slightly toward his desk drawer.

Kim tensed. Her hand instinctively shifted toward her holster. Smithers also shifted his weight, ready to move.

Kim held Cooper's steely gaze for three long seconds. She pulled the cylinder from her pocket and dropped it on his desk.

The cylinder had contained a small leather bankbook. She'd replaced it with a copy. She intended to study the original closely before she let it out of her possession. There was more going on here than she'd dug up so far.

As for the drives, the encryption was keeping the contents sealed and away from Gaspar's prying eyes. He'd kept copies. Kim slapped the originals down on Cooper's desk.

Cooper gave her a smirk and said softly, "Keep in touch."

Kim turned and left the safe house with Smithers close behind. Their footsteps echoed through the empty hallway.

Outside, rain fell harder. Water drummed against the pavement, filling gutters and washing over their shoes. Kim pulled her jacket collar up against the downpour as they walked to the SUV.

"He's dirty," Smithers said, voice barely audible above the rain. Water plastered his hair to his forehead. "All the way dirty."

Kim nodded. "You say that like you're surprised."

Smithers started the engine. It growled to life, vibrating beneath them.

The wipers beat a steady rhythm as they pulled away from the curb. Each sweep cleared the glass for just a moment before the deluge obscured their view again.

Kim watched the side view mirror until her view of the safe house disappeared into the gray curtain of rain.

"Now what?" Smithers asked.

"I need to make a call," Kim replied.

CHAPTER 50

Friday, July 15
Buenos Aires, Argentina

THE CAFÉ SAT TUCKED between two aging colonial buildings, its wrought-iron chairs and small round tables spilling onto the narrow sidewalk. Neagley chose the corner table with her back to the wall, her gaze never settling on any one point for too long. The early evening sunset cut long shadows across the cobblestones as locals and tourists mingled in the street.

Sinclair was late. Not an accident. A statement.

Neagley sipped bitter espresso, letting the sharp taste linger. The ceramic cup clinked against the saucer when she set it down, the sound precise, almost musical. A bird called from somewhere overhead, its wild song out of place amid the traffic sounds.

She spotted Sinclair half a block away. After fleeing Wiley's ranch and successfully retrieving everything she came to Argentina for, Sinclair moved with the controlled confidence of a woman who believed herself untouchable. Her cream linen suit remained crisply pressed despite the humidity. Her shoes clicked a sharp rhythm as she approached.

The metal chair scraped against the pavers as Sinclair took the seat across from Neagley.

"You found me," Sinclair said. Not a question.

"Wasn't difficult." Neagley kept her voice neutral. "If I can do it, others can, too. Otto might not be far behind."

Sinclair's lips curved upward. "Otto's with Cooper now. Dutiful agent reporting back while the grown ups clean up the mess."

A waiter approached. Sinclair ordered coffee with a flawless Spanish accent. Neagley waited until he retreated back inside, out of earshot.

"Cooper won't leave loose ends," Neagley said.

"I'm counting on it." Sinclair's fingers drummed once against the tabletop before falling still. The habit of someone accustomed to controlling every instinctive gesture.

"What was in the cylinder?" Neagley asked.

Sinclair studied her for a long moment. Then she reached into her handbag, movements deliberate and careful. She withdrew a small, leather-bound book, its cover unmarked except for faded gilt edges that caught the fading sunlight.

"Wiley's insurance policy." Sinclair slid it across the table.

Neagley picked up the book. The leather was practically new, as if barely handled. She opened it to find columns of numbers, account details, and transaction records dating back decades.

"Gulf Continental Bank of Dubai," Neagley read aloud. She flipped through the pages, scanning dates, amounts, deposit confirmations. The numbers were precise, methodical, stretching from Hamburg to the present day. "Lot of money in there. More than the GDP of some countries."

"And even more by now." Sinclair's coffee arrived. She waited until the waiter left before continuing. "Wiley set it up before Hamburg. Before we caught onto his operation. Private numbered accounts in a country with no extradition treaty with the United States."

"With your name on it?"

"Not originally." Sinclair's mouth twitched. "But the beauty of Wiley's system is its adaptability."

Neagley flipped to the final entry. A transfer authorization and signature change.

"You've already made arrangements." Neagley closed the book and tapped it on the tabletop.

"My flight leaves soon." Sinclair took a sip of coffee, watching Neagley over the rim. "Dubai has excellent weather this time of year."

Neagley pushed the book back across the table, her fingers lingering on the leather before pulling away. "Cooper will find you."

"Cooper is compromised. Has been for a while," Sinclair replied. "He was the one who sent Hooper to find Wiley and his nukes. Did you know that?"

Neagley didn't respond. She'd suspected as much, but the confirmation still landed with weight.

"We didn't know it back then, of course. But Cooper ran the whole operation," Sinclair continued. "Hooper worked for him. They were both in the Army then. Same as you and Reacher. Cooper wanted Wiley's Davy Crocketts off the books, untraceable. Because he figured there were more to be found. He didn't want the entire US government looking for them."

"Why?" Neagley asked.

"For sale to the highest bidder." Sinclair leaned forward slightly. "Hooper was one of Lone Wolf's first members. The operation's startup funding came through Wiley's laundering system."

"And when Reacher's team found the nukes in Hamburg, that was the start of it all," Neagley said, understanding the situation.

"Something like that," Sinclair said with a nod. "But Hooper never stopped looking for more nukes. Wiley found ten. Hooper figured there had to be more than ten out there. That's when he approached Cooper and built the bunker at Wiley's ranch in La Pampa. The ranch was unoccupied. Wiley was dead. Hooper had found another cache of Davy Crocketts and needed a place to store them. The second batch was older when they were located. Possibly more unstable than the ones Wiley discovered. But just as deadly."

Neagley watched a family pass by the café. A young father carried his daughter on his shoulders. Her laughter flowed back to them on the breeze. She let the normalcy of the moment settle before turning back to Sinclair.

"That's why Reacher came after Hooper," Neagley said. "Hooper picked up where Wiley left off. Finding Davy Crocketts. Selling them to the highest bidder, including enemies of the US. Making money off stolen war machines. Got Reacher's back up."

"Hooper figured if there were ten Davy Crocketts in Hamburg, there must be others," Sinclair nodded. "He was right. Eventually, they located a dozen more and moved them to Argentina."

"And Reacher got you out of hot water back at the ranch," Neagley said. It wasn't a question. "While we were checking the bunker."

Sinclair didn't deny it. Her fingers traced the edge of the bankbook. "He knew about the bunker and the backup tunnel system for emergency exits. Said he'd studied the ranch layout years ago."

"Where is Reacher now?"

"Gone." Sinclair's expression gave nothing away. "I asked him to come with me. He declined. We had different objectives."

Neagley's doubt must have shown on her face, because Sinclair laughed softly.

"You think I'm lying."

"I think you're selective with the truth," Neagley replied.

Sinclair held her gaze. "Reacher helped me access the deposit box. Then he left. I don't know where he went."

A lie. Not the first Sinclair had told. But Neagley let it pass.

"Cooper knows about all of this now, if he didn't before. He will never stop looking," Neagley said. "Not for the money. Not for you."

"Cooper's days are numbered," Sinclair replied. "I've made sure of it."

"How?"

"There's a false copy of this. Slightly altered." Sinclair tapped the bankbook. "With account details, signature authorizations, transfer records. All pointing to Hooper, which any competent investigator would conclude means Cooper was behind it all. I left the counterfeit in the cylinder for Otto to find."

Neagley studied her. "That could implicate you, too. You can never return to the US or any allied country. The FBI and every other agency in the US government will hunt you forever. As long as it takes."

"I've made my peace with certain sacrifices." Sinclair's smile was brittle now, edged with something sharper. "If he tries to take me on, Cooper won't survive the fallout. Too many bodies. Too many secrets. He's made too many enemies over the years. One of them will see to it that he takes the fall and will move into Cooper's position."

"All you feds would eat your own," Neagley said flatly. "Reacher hates that about you. I do, too, come to think of it."

Sinclair shrugged and checked her watch. "My car will be here soon."

"To the airport."

"Yes." Sinclair leaned back. "You could come with me, you know. Dubai is beautiful this time of year. Plenty of opportunities for someone with your skills."

Neagley replied, "No thanks."

Sinclair didn't seem surprised. "Loyalty to Reacher. After all these years. How sweet."

"Call it whatever you want."

"He'll disappear again," Sinclair warned. "That's what he does. Moves through the shadows, never staying anywhere long enough to leave footprints."

"I know who Reacher is and what he is," Neagley said simply. "I thought you did, too. But I gave you too much credit. So did he."

Sinclair studied her for a long moment. Then she reached into her pocket and slid a sealed envelope across the table.

"What's this?" Neagley asked, not touching the envelope.

"What I promised to pay you for your work. Plus a bonus for your discretion." Sinclair stood, gathering her handbag and the bankbook. "Goodbye, Neagley."

Neagley remained seated. "You're playing with fire, Sinclair."

Sinclair smirked. "Can't cook without fire."

She turned and walked away.

Neagley didn't watch her go. Instead, she scanned the rooftops, the shadows between buildings, the reflections in storefront windows.

Something prickled against the back of her neck. Instinct. Honed over decades of fieldwork.

Who was watching now?

Neagley left cash on the table for her espresso and Sinclair's coffee. The envelope remained untouched. The waitress would get a substantial tip today and Neagley was sure she needed it.

She felt the weight of watchful eyes tracking her movements when she stepped into the street.

Cooper was coming for Sinclair.

Otto was hunting Reacher.

And Reacher?

Reacher was exactly where he needed to be. Always was.

Neagley smiled faintly as she turned the corner, disappearing into the late afternoon shadows.

Her phone buzzed in her pocket. A text message from Reacher appeared on the screen.

Finished.

Neagley deleted it immediately and kept walking. Whatever happened next, she'd be ready.

She always was.

CHAPTER 51

Saturday, July 16
New York City, New York

THE PRIVATE ELEVATOR ROSE with barely a whisper, fifty floors of Manhattan falling away beneath Kim's boots. Her stomach tightened, not from the ascent but from what waited above. She flexed her fingers, feeling the lingering soreness from a week spent filing reports, making calls, and chasing ghosts through cyberspace.

The doors parted with a soft electronic chime. Cool air hit her face, carrying the scent of cedar and leather and money. Real money. Old money. The kind that didn't need to announce itself.

Travis Russell filled the corridor ahead. Coiled muscle beneath a perfectly tailored suit. He was Secret Service, although nothing about his appearance advertised the fact. His eyes tracked her approach, cataloging threats by reflex.

"Agent Otto." His voice was gravel wrapped in velvet.

"Russell." She kept her tone neutral, giving away nothing.

He didn't offer his hand, but he gave her a genuine smile followed by a quick visual sweep of her person. As always, professional rather than personal, although they'd worked together several times now.

Apparently satisfied, he allowed her to enter. "You're expected."

Kim nodded. She'd requested this meeting, and Lamont Finlay had agreed with suspicious speed. As if he'd been waiting for her call. Which he probably had.

She followed Russell down a corridor where plush carpeting swallowed each footstep. The silence felt deliberate. Manufactured. A reminder that in places like this, the world outside ceased to exist until permitted entry.

The sharp notes of expensive cologne lingered in the hallway. Russell's gold watch caught the recessed lighting as he reached for the polished mahogany door and pushed it open.

"Make yourself comfortable. There's fresh coffee on the server." Russell stepped aside. "He'll be right in."

Kim moved past him into a room designed for private conversations. No windows. A single oak table anchored the center, flanked by two leather chairs. A crystal tumbler of ice water waited on a silver tray, beads of condensation tracking down the side.

The door clicked shut behind her.

She remained standing, hands loose at her sides, taking in the details. The room was soundproofed. The air tasted different here, as if it were filtered, purified, and recycled repeatedly on a short time loop. The kind of air breathed by people who considered oxygen itself a commodity to be improved upon.

Two minutes passed. Three.

The door opened again.

Lamont Finlay joined her moments after she'd poured coffee. No wasted energy. No flourish. His tie remained knotted at his throat, but his suit jacket was gone. Shirtsleeves rolled to the elbow, revealing forearms corded with lean muscle.

"Good to see you again, Otto." His gaze locked onto hers. "How can I be of service to you?"

"I gather your time is short," Kim replied, sipping the coffee.

Finlay gestured to the chair opposite his. "Sit."

She remained standing. "I've been sitting too much lately."

A slight smile flickered across his face, as if her behavior was predictable. He settled into one of the leather chairs and waited for her to begin.

Kim took a measured breath, tasting the filtered air. "Why was Reacher in Arizona?"

Finlay steepled his fingers, the gold signet ring on his right hand catching the light. "Why do you think Cooper sent you there?"

"Because he knew or at least suspected that Reacher was there," Kim replied. She kept her voice steady, unwilling to reveal how many nights she'd spent piecing it together. "He might have used the situation to bait Reacher into showing up."

Finlay nodded. Once. Barely perceptible.

"So why was Reacher there?" Kim pressed. "What drew him to that place, that situation?"

"Reacher was looking for someone." Finlay's voice was calm, measured. He was accustomed to dispensing information in precisely calibrated doses.

Kim's fingers flexed at her sides. "Bradley Hooper."

Another fractional nod.

"Hooper was running Ted to try to find Wiley's money. Cooper knew that," Kim said, the pieces clicking together like loaded chambers in a revolver. "And Reacher was looking for Hooper."

Finlay's breathing and his gaze remained steady.

"Why?" Kim demanded.

Finlay tapped a finger against the polished oak. The sound was sharp, intrusive against the room's engineered silence. "What happens when someone you trust betrays you?"

Kim stood motionless. "Reacher isn't sentimental."

"No," Finlay agreed, the word hanging between them. "But Hooper did more than simply betray Reacher."

Kim's stomach knotted. The air felt suddenly thinner.

Finlay leaned forward, the chair protesting beneath him. "You already know what was going on there."

She did. Hamburg. The 110th Special Investigators Unit. Reacher and Hooper. Brothers in arms until Hooper chose another path. That was long after Hamburg. But Reacher could carry a grudge much longer than most.

"Hooper and Lone Wolf were using Wiley's ranch to sell illegal nuclear weapons to the highest bidder," Kim said, curling her lip. "Reacher's not the only one who wouldn't approve."

Finlay tilted his head a fraction. Not quite confirmation. Not quite denial.

"Hooper wasn't concerned about the intended use of those weapons, either," Kim said. "At least some of his customers had some sort of beef with the United States."

Finlay's expression remained unchanged, but something flickered in his eyes. The barest acknowledgment.

Kim swallowed, her throat suddenly dry. She took a gulp of coffee. "Reacher was hunting Hooper because he was selling nukes."

"And you think Cooper knew about the nukes and the money," Finlay said easily. "Which he probably did. So why bait Reacher and send you out there to capture him?"

Kim felt her pulse quicken. This part was pure speculation, but it made sense. "Cooper didn't want Reacher to kill Hooper and disappear."

"I'm not sure he cared that much about Hooper. But essentially, yes," Finlay's nod was so slight it barely disturbed the air.

"That's why Cooper sent me to Arizona," Kim said, bitter understanding burning in her chest. "He used me for bait, too."

Another nod, this one more pronounced.

"He wants me to find Reacher, even if it kills me and Smithers," Kim said. "Eliminating rogue Lone Wolf soldiers in the process was a bonus for Cooper, too."

Finlay sat back, relaxing against the buttery soft leather. "And did you find Reacher?"

"No." Kim held his gaze, unwavering, as if she were under oath in a court of law, because what she said was technically true.

She had not found Reacher.

But he had found her.

Again.

Reinforcing her sense of vulnerability.

She'd learned that Reacher was a freak of nature in many ways. He had a savant's agility with numbers. He could fight and defeat five men at once. His capacity for revenge seemed endless and without guardrails of any kind.

After nine months of hunting Reacher, she'd learned a lot. Including that Reacher understood her search was not personal. Just business.

She had a job to do, and she was doing it. Reacher probably respected her dedication.

But he didn't want to kill her.

If he had, she'd be dead already.

CHAPTER 52

Saturday, July 16
New York City, New York

FINLAY STUDIED HER FOR what felt like minutes. He took a breath for a final pause before he said, "If you didn't bring Reacher back to Cooper, you've got a problem."

Kim placed her palms on the arms of her chair, feeling the cool, polished wood against her skin. "Where is Reacher? I know you've connected with him during the fifteen years since you first crossed paths in Margrave. What I don't know is just how close you two really are."

Finlay shook his head, once, decisive. "If I knew where Reacher was, I wouldn't tell you."

Kim clenched her jaw causing a muscle to twitch in her cheek.

"But I'll tell you this," Finlay's reply was stony. "Reacher isn't done. Hooper's gone. But Lone Wolf remains. And then there's Cooper."

Kim stared at him, absorbing the implications. "You're saying Reacher is going after them?"

"Them?" Finlay reached for the untouched glass of water beside his chair. Ice clinked against the crystal as he took a measured sip. "Reacher's target this time was Hooper, but Hooper was only one tentacle of a much larger beast."

"And the head of that beast?" Kim pressed.

"Cooper would like you to believe it's Sinclair." Finlay set the glass down precisely on the silver tray. "But Reacher no doubt has a more comprehensive view."

Kim felt her pulse quicken. "Cooper knew about the nuclear weapons all along."

"More than knew." Finlay's voice dropped to just above a whisper. "Hamburg was about catching arms dealers. But it was really about controlling who had access to what weapons."

"And who was doing the controlling?" Kim asked, arching both eyebrows and leaning forward. "Back then, Cooper didn't have the power or position he holds now. He couldn't have been the one with his finger on the buttons."

Finlay didn't confirm or deny. He checked his watch, a dismissive gesture.

"I'm not finished," she said.

"I've given you more than you need to know, Agent Otto."

"Where is Reacher now?" Her voice was steel.

Finlay's eyes narrowed.

"You said you wouldn't tell me if you knew. But you do know." Kim took a step closer. "He contacted you."

The door opened abruptly. Russell stood in the threshold. "Sir, there's a situation that requires your immediate attention."

Finlay held up a hand without looking away from Kim. "Five minutes."

Russell hesitated, then stepped back, closing the door.

The interruption lingered between them. Kim could almost taste the tension as Finlay considered how much to reveal.

"You've been working this case since November," Finlay finally said. "Nine months of chasing Reacher while Cooper dangles the possibility of finding him like a carrot. Have you ever asked yourself why Cooper's so fixated on one retired MP?"

Of course Kim had asked herself the same thing countless times, especially after Argentina. "Reacher knows things. About Cooper. About Hamburg."

"Reacher knows everything about it," Finlay said flatly. "About the weapons. About the money. About how deep the corruption goes. And unlike Sinclair, Reacher can't be bought off with a Dubai bank account."

A sudden coldness spread through Kim's body raising gooseflesh on her skin.

"You're suggesting Sinclair is running on Cooper's orders?" Kim asked, thinking it through. "Sinclair's mission wasn't a personal vendetta. Instead, everything had been orchestrated to keep attention away from something else."

The room seemed to contract around her. The air grew thicker, harder to breathe as her anxiety ratcheted to suffocating levels.

"How far up the chain does this corruption go?" she asked, her voice barely audible.

Finlay scowled. "Far enough that we shouldn't be having this conversation."

He moved to a side table, opened a drawer and removed a small handheld device. He switched it on, and a soft electronic whine filled the air.

"Signal jammer," Finlay explained. "Now we can speak more freely, but only for a moment. This one supplements the others, but there are ways to circumvent all electronics."

"And if their feed goes out for too long, they'll come looking for the cause," Kim replied with an understanding nod.

He stepped close enough that Kim could smell the faint trace of scotch on his breath. "Is your loyalty to Cooper absolute?"

Kim didn't flinch. "My loyalty is to the truth."

Approval flickered across Finlay's face. "Sinclair has a flash drive containing detailed records of every transaction Cooper authorized through Wiley's system. Names. Dates. Bank accounts. She thinks it's her insurance policy."

"And Reacher?"

"Reacher could have something Cooper wants more." A ghost of a smile touched Finlay's lips. "The location of more Davy Crocketts."

The implication struck Kim like a physical blow. More nuclear weapons unaccounted for and potentially in play.

"How many?" she asked.

"Enough to level more than one major city." Finlay switched off the supplemental jammer and returned it to the drawer. "Or ensure no one ever comes looking for you again."

The atmosphere shifted again now that the extra protection of the signal jammer was gone. Finlay was done sharing.

He did not retake his seat, so Kim rose too.

"Anything else?" she asked, shoulders squared.

Finlay met her gaze, his eyes cold and flat like river stones.

"Reacher and Cooper are both using you, Otto," he said. Each word fell like a hammer strike. "But only one of them plans to let you live when it's over."

Kim felt her pulse leap, a sudden rush of adrenaline flooding her veins. She kept her expression neutral through sheer force of will.

Finlay turned toward the door. His hand closed around the polished brass handle.

Russell was waiting in the hallway, stance alert, eyes watchful.

Kim didn't move right away. Her mind raced through everything Finlay had said.

And everything he hadn't.

She walked to the elevator and rode to the lobby in silence. Her reflection stared back from the polished doors, fragmented and distorted.

Outside, New York City roared back to life around her. Car horns, voices, the constant thrum of eight million lives pressed together on a single island.

She stepped onto the sidewalk, the summer heat slamming into her like a physical wall, carrying the familiar urban perfume, a combination of exhaust, hot asphalt, and pretzels from a nearby cart.

Kim pulled out her phone, thumb hovering over Cooper's number.

She hesitated, then pocketed the device.

Facing Cooper now would be suicide.

And Kim did not intend to die today.

CHAPTER 53

One week later
Washington, DC

THE RIVER FLOWED BLACK beneath the clouded sky. Sinclair checked her watch and glanced across the Potomac to the Washington Monument, a pale needle in the distance. The park lay deserted at this hour. Not quite midnight, but late enough that tourists and joggers had abandoned it to the rats and the homeless.

She chose this spot for tactical reasons. Public enough to deter immediate violence. Private enough for the conversation she planned to have. The trees created perfect shadows along the riverbank path.

A light fog rose from the water's surface, curling around her ankles as she paced. Ten steps. Turn. Ten steps back. A habit she'd adopted years ago because it made the waiting time feel shorter.

Her breath clouded in the damp air. The temperature had dropped since sunset, leaving a chill that penetrated her light jacket.

Sinclair stopped and pulled out her secure phone. She tapped in her password and opened the files. The screen's glow illuminated her face with a ghostly blue light. Transaction records. Account numbers. Authorization codes. Cooper's digital fingerprints all over Argentina, Dubai, and a dozen other black-site operations spanning two decades.

She had him. Finally.

Five days ago, she'd made contact through encrypted channels. The demand was explicit. Ten million dollars in untraceable funds and guaranteed security for the rest of her life. Otherwise, his career, freedom, and reputation would crumble beneath the weight of evidence she'd compiled.

Cooper agreed to the meeting with suspicious speed. His response came within an hour of her message. A singular line of text: *East Potomac Park. Wednesday. Midnight.* The text included the precise location.

Sinclair had expected resistance, negotiation, maybe threats. His immediate capitulation concerned her. Cooper wasn't a man who surrendered advantage or control.

She switched off the phone and returned it to her jacket pocket. Her hand brushed against the compact pistol nestled in its usual place. The solid weight of the weapon in her shoulder holster reassured her.

Footsteps crunched on the gravel path behind her. Sinclair turned, expecting Cooper.

Larry Knox emerged from the darkness instead.

His face hardened when he saw her. His eyes narrowed with cold calculation beneath the brim of his hat.

"You should have told me you were coming back to DC," Knox said. He stopped ten feet away, hands tucked inside his jacket pockets. "We could have coordinated."

Sinclair replied coldly, "This isn't your meeting, Knox."

He laughed, a sharp sound without humor. "You contacted Cooper. What were you thinking?"

"How did you know?" Sinclair kept her voice steady.

"Cooper called me after you reached out." Knox stepped closer. "He wanted to know if I had any idea what you might have on him."

"And you told him what?"

"That you were dangerous." Knox shrugged. "Which you are. But so are we all."

Sinclair scanned the path behind him. No sign of Cooper or his security detail. The predicted fog had thickened, obscuring the distant bridge and the far shore. Sounds carried in the fog, but visuals were impaired.

"You're playing a game you can't win," she said.

"I've spent years building leverage against Cooper," Knox replied. "Records. Recordings. Contacts. You think you're the first person who tried to control him with blackmail?"

Sinclair considered this information. Knox had his own agenda and his own evidence. He believed himself valuable enough to survive Cooper. Maybe he was, but Sinclair had her doubts.

"We could work together," Knox continued. "Your evidence combined with mine would be ironclad. Cooper would have no choice but to capitulate."

"No," Sinclair cut him off. "You're a liability."

"And you're a fool if you think he'll come alone." Knox's hand moved inside his jacket. "Cooper never meets anyone without backup plans."

Sinclair tensed, ready to reach for her weapon. "Then where is he?"

"Right here."

Cooper's voice came from behind her.

Sinclair spun around to peer into the fog.

Cooper stood five yards away, having approached silently from the river path. He wore a dark overcoat against the chill, hands tucked into the pockets. His face remained in shadow beneath the brim of his hat.

He looked exactly as he had the last time she'd seen him. Composed, controlled, deadly. Like her.

"You're both early," Cooper said. His tone carried no emotion. No urgency. No concern. "Eager, I suppose."

Knox stepped forward, positioning himself to form a triangle with Cooper and Sinclair.

Knox spoke first, his tone shifting to deference. "I came to warn you about Sinclair."

"I know why you're here," Cooper interrupted. "Both of you."

Sinclair kept her eyes on Cooper. "Then you know my terms."

"I do." Cooper nodded slightly. "Ten million dollars and guaranteed security for the rest of your peaceful existence in a country without a US extradition treaty. In exchange for your silence regarding certain operational details."

"Not details," Sinclair corrected. "Evidence of illegal arms trading, financial fraud, and treason. Enough to put you away for multiple lifetimes. You'll get the death penalty."

Cooper seemed to consider this. "And you, Knox? What's your price?"

Knox straightened. "Protection. And a lifetime contract with the FBI for Lone Wolf."

Sinclair snorted. "As if."

"I've earned it," Knox snapped when she cracked his composure. "Years of loyal service. Years of cleaning up his messes. And yours, Sinclair."

Cooper remained silent, observing the exchange like a scientist examines a rat's corpse.

The fog swirled thicker around them. A distant siren wailed, then faded.

"Your evidence," Cooper said finally. "How extensive is it?"

"Everything," Sinclair replied. "From Hamburg to Argentina. Every transaction. Every code. Every operative you burned. Every asset you compromised. Even this Reacher business. I've documented it all."

"I see." Cooper's tone betrayed nothing.

Knox's patience broke. "This is ridiculous. She's bluffing. I've been tracking her for weeks. She has nothing but accusations and theories."

"I assure you," Sinclair said to Cooper, "what I have is substantial."

Knox's hand emerged from his jacket, gripping a pistol. He pointed it at Sinclair. "Enough games. I can handle this situation, Cooper."

A single gunshot cracked through the night air.

Knox's body jerked. His eyes widened in shock as he looked down at the spreading darkness on his chest. His gun slipped from his fingers and bounced on the ground.

Cooper lowered his weapon.

Knox dropped to his knees, mouth working silently. After a few moments, he toppled forward onto the damp grass.

"Disappointing," Cooper said. "He always lacked patience."

Sinclair's hand moved toward her holster.

"I wouldn't," Cooper warned. The gun now pointed at her.

She froze.

"Did you really believe it would be so simple?" Cooper asked. "That you could threaten me and walk away with my protection forever?"

"I have the evidence secured," Sinclair said. "If anything happens to me, it goes public."

"No," Cooper replied. "You don't. And it won't."

Her confidence faltered. "What?"

"Your evidence was compromised the moment you accessed it the first time," Cooper explained. "The flash drive you used for the transfers contained a tracker. The bank accounts you located have been purged. The witnesses you might have called upon are, like poor Knox here, sadly no longer available."

Sinclair's heart raced. Cooper wasn't bluffing. She could tell.

"The hotel in Buenos Aires. The safe deposit box. The backup copies you sent to secured locations from Dubai," Cooper recited each detail like a robot reading names from a phone book. "I've had teams working to neutralize every contingency. You're done, Sinclair."

Which was when Sinclair realized she'd been outmaneuvered from the beginning.

"Otto," Sinclair said, desperate for an alternative. "She knows."

"Otto knows exactly what I allow her to know," Cooper replied. "No more. No less."

He stepped closer. The barrel of his gun gleamed in the dim light.

"You had a distinguished career, Marian." His voice softened with what might have been genuine regret. "You could have retired with honor."

"Honor?" Sinclair laughed bitterly. "There's no honor in what we do."

Cooper sighed. "Perhaps not."

He raised the weapon.

Sinclair lunged to the side, reaching for her gun, too late.

Cooper fired twice.

The bullets tore through her chest, burning white-hot all the way.

The impact knocked her backward toward the river's edge.

Her legs tangled.

Her balance failed.

She fell.

The cold water shocked her system as she plunged into the Potomac. Pain blazed through her torso. Her lungs seized.

The current pulled her down, into the black depth.

She fought against it, arms flailing, legs kicking weakly.

Water filled her throat.

Her chest burned from the bullet wounds and the river's invasion.

Her body grew heavier.

Darkness closed in around the edges of her vision.

In her final moments of consciousness, Sinclair thought of Hamburg. Of Reacher. Of the weapons they'd failed to contain.

Of Cooper, who would continue unchecked.

The current swept her deeper.

Her struggles weakened.

Until finally, darkness claimed her.

CHAPTER 54

One week later
Miami, Florida

THE SETTING SUN PAINTED Biscayne Bay in shades of amber and gold. Light fractured across the water like scattered glass.

Kim sat on the hotel rooftop twelve stories above Coconut Grove, swirling ice in a tumbler of scotch she hadn't touched. Heat radiated from the concrete beneath her feet, the day's accumulation still burning off as evening slowly settled over the city.

She tracked a cruise ship navigating the channel, white hull gleaming against the darkening water. From this perspective, Miami sprawled out in a concrete jungle of high-rises and palm trees.

Intriguing but dangerous.

Just like the game she'd been playing these past nine months.

Gaspar leaned against the railing, profile sharp against the skyline. His bad right leg was propped on a footstool, a concession to the pain he never mentioned but Kim always noticed. The old injury from before she'd met him. Another scar from a mission gone sideways when the brass made promises they couldn't keep.

"Let me get this straight," Gaspar said quietly beneath the distant hum of traffic. "Cooper claims Knox and Sinclair shot each other on the banks of the Potomac. Both bodies were recovered from the river. Case closed."

"That's the official story." Kim's tone remained flat, emotionless. The facts were easier to process that way.

"You buy that?"

"Not for a second."

"What do you think actually happened?" Gaspar asked.

"Pretty obvious," she shrugged. "They were murdered and the killer escaped. Probably with help."

Gaspar nodded, unsurprised. "Someone cleaning house, then."

"Definitely." Kim shifted in her chair. The metal creaked beneath her. "Evidence was manufactured after making them both disappear. The Potomac is convenient that way. Washes away too much to leave anything that would contradict the official reports."

Kim thought about Sinclair's final moments, wondering if she had realized her fatal miscalculation before the shooter pulled the trigger.

Sinclair was smart, calculating, ruthless even. But she'd underestimated her enemies. Which was a life-altering mistake in Sinclair's line of work.

"Solid play, though. Seals off embarrassing truths he didn't want spread around." Gaspar took a sip of his drink, ice clinking against crystal. "Where's Smithers during all this? He should be watching your back."

"Family wedding in Colorado. His only sister's only kid. The father died in the line of duty. Afghanistan. Smithers is giving the bride away. Couldn't get out of it." Kim's gaze drifted to a yacht cutting through the bay, leaving a white wake that stretched back to the horizon.

"Convenient timing." Gaspar raised an eyebrow. "Cooper's always been good at that sort of thing."

"Don't start. Some things are actually outside of Cooper's control, whether he believes that or not." Kim finally lifted the tumbler and let the scotch burn down her throat. Smooth and expensive. Gaspar never skimped on the important things. "Besides, if Cooper wanted me dead, I'd be dead already. You and Smithers, too, for that matter. Hell, he could have killed Reacher long ago if that's what he wanted."

"Okay," Gaspar nodded. "What does he want, then?"

Kim had no reply, so she said nothing.

A ship's horn bellowed from the harbor. Long blasts echoing across the water, a warning to smaller vessels to clear the channel.

Kim felt the vibration in her chest. She appreciated the physical reminder she was still above ground and not below it. That situation could change in any given moment, she knew all too well.

Gaspar turned toward the sound, muscles tight across his shoulders. He'd been carrying that tension since Kim had arrived three hours ago.

They'd gone over everything about the Wiley matter. The nuclear weapons. The money. The betrayals. The murders. The encrypted drives they still hadn't been able to breach.

Kim had finished writing her reports and storing them on her private server. Paying her insurance, she called it. Should she die unexpectedly, Gaspar and Smithers knew how to retrieve the intel she'd hidden there.

Which might not be enough, but it was the most she could do.

A silence settled over them as they waited for the ship to pass.

"Something on your mind, Chico?" Kim asked, when the noise finally receded. She'd worked with Gaspar long enough to know when he was holding back.

He didn't answer immediately. Just stared at the darkening horizon as twilight crept across the sky. The first stars were appearing, though the city lights would soon drown them out.

"Chico." Her voice firmer now.

"What?" He turned to face her. His eyes were troubled beneath the careful mask he wore. Years spent in the Bureau had taught him how to hide his thoughts, but not from her.

"I've been running some fact checks while you were busy," he said. "Following breadcrumbs."

"And?"

"You won't like it."

Kim set her glass down. The hollow click against the table punctuated the silence. "Try me."

Gaspar crossed to the table where his laptop sat open. The screen bathed his face in a bluish glow when he pulled up a file. Fingers moved swiftly across the keyboard as he navigated through layers of security.

"After everything that went down in Argentina, I got curious. Started looking deeper into possible connections. Reacher. Cooper. Wiley. Knox. Hooper. Sinclair." Gaspar shifted the screen toward her. "Found something you should see."

Kim leaned forward, scanning the intel displayed on the screen.

Immigration records.

Financial transactions.

A redacted personnel file with just enough visible to make her blood run cold.

"Van Nguyen," she whispered.

Her ex-husband's name on the screen felt like an intrusion into the already complicated situation.

She hadn't seen or spoken to Nguyen in years. Not since the divorce was finalized after his sudden decision to become a politician.

A career move he'd chosen over their marriage.

A lifetime ago. Kim had been a different person back then.

"I don't understand," she said, the words tasting like ash in her mouth. "What does Van Nguyen have to do with Reacher?"

Gaspar reached over to scroll down past pages of redacted text and blacked-out photos. He stopped about halfway down the list.

"Records show Van Nguyen worked this classified operation. Looks like Reacher was involved."

Kim's pulse quickened. Her head raced through memories, searching for any hint that Nguyen had known about Reacher. Any casual mention. Any connection she might have missed.

"That's not possible," she said barely above a whisper. "Nguyen never mentioned Reacher. Not once. And I never even heard Reacher's name until nine months ago."

"You were divorced already when this operation took place." Gaspar tapped the screen where a heavily redacted paragraph sat beneath a CLASSIFIED stamp. "This was buried too deep for casual searchers to find it. The kind of deep we use when we want intel to stay secret longer than the truth about the JFK assassination."

"And you think Cooper buried it?" Kim asked. The pieces were falling into place with sickening clarity.

"He assigned you to find Reacher." Gaspar's tone was gentle but insistent, the way he spoke to victims who weren't ready to face certain unwelcome truths. "Of all the agents he could have chosen, he picked you. At the time, you were flattered. The big boss chose a lowly agent with little experience to handle a top-secret black ops hunt for what you were told was a vicious killer. A matter of national security, even. Did you ever ask him why he chose you? He definitely had lots of other options."

Kim stared at the screen at the fragments of a connection she'd never have guessed existed. The room seemed to tilt slightly beneath her feet. She gripped the edge of the table to steady herself.

"There's more," Gaspar said, scrolling to another document. "Nguyen's election to Congress? Supported and sponsored by Cooper's pets. Several of Nguyen's subsequent major projects were also touched by Cooper in some way."

A cold sensation spread through Kim's chest. "Cooper is manipulating Nguyen's career? For what purpose?"

"I don't know yet." Gaspar closed the laptop with a soft click. "But it's a very safe bet to say it's no coincidence that you're chasing Reacher now. There's an angle here we've missed."

Kim stood and paced to the railing. The heavy humidity pressed against her skin like a physical weight.

Cars crawled along the streets below, headlights cutting through the gathering darkness. The city was alive with people living ordinary lives unaware of the shadows that hid behind government credentials and classified files.

She tried to process the implications.

Cooper had chosen her specifically for the Reacher assignment.

Had known about her connection to Nguyen.

Had manipulated her from the beginning.

The Reacher mission she'd devoted nearly a year of her life to suddenly felt hollow. A construct built on more lies and hidden agendas than she'd believed.

And, she was now certain, a mission she was not expected to complete during her lifetime.

"You need to quit, Sunshine." Gaspar's voice reached her through the chaos of her thoughts. "As I've said before, Cooper's playing a game where all the people and pieces are expendable. Including you."

She turned, facing him squarely. "I can't just walk away."

"You can." Gaspar cut her off, rising from his chair with a slight wince as he put weight on his bad leg. "Scarlett Investigations needs qualified investigators and Flint asked about you specifically. You've worked with him before. He values your skill set. It's been a great move for me. We could work together again."

"You want me to quit the Bureau? Just like that?" A humorless laugh escaped her lips. "Throw away years of my work? Give up the biggest goal I've devoted my life to?"

"Being Director of the FBI isn't much of a goal, Kim. Trust me, the job isn't what you think it is anyway." Gaspar spoke from experience, from years of watching the politics and compromises that came with advancement up the ladder at the Bureau. "They don't let good people reach the top without changing them first. And if they can't change you, they make sure you never get where you're going. You must have figured that out by now."

Kim considered his suggestion. For half a second. Maybe less.

The Bureau had been her life for so long. Her ambition to achieve the Director's position had driven every career decision since her divorce, every sacrifice. But now Cooper had tainted even that.

"I appreciate the concern and Flint's offer," she said finally. "But I can't walk away. Not yet."

"You don't want to end up like Marian Sinclair, do you? Betrayed. Passed over. Replaced. Forgotten." He paused a moment. "Dead."

"No." She cut him off as her entire body shivered despite the heat. "Especially not now. I'm close to finding Reacher. Neagley keeps in touch with him and she's not difficult to find. I actually know where she lives. Along the way, we've seen illegal weapons trades, financial fraud, and multiple counts of murder, just from what I've personally witnessed in the past few days."

"All the more reason to quit while you still have the option."

"If he's behind all of this, we can't allow Cooper to remain at the helm. I'm a lawyer and an FBI agent. I took an oath to uphold the law. An oath I believe in," Kim said. "I can't just leave while things are what they are."

The Miami skyline glittered behind her, a thousand lights against the deepening blue of twilight. Evidence that civilization continued while agents like Cooper operated in the background.

Gaspar stood beside her at the railing. "And you think you can take down corruption in the FBI single-handedly?"

"No. Not alone. I'm not that good." Kim was already working through angles, possibilities, people she could trust, those she definitely could not. "Finlay can help. He hinted that he might be willing. And now I have leverage of my own."

"The Van Nguyen connection."

"Yes," she replied. "And maybe whatever's on those Lone Wolf drives. If we can get to the data."

Gaspar sighed. He knew she was as stubborn as any mule he'd ever seen. "Your funeral, Sunshine."

"Maybe." Kim offered a weak smile, trying to lighten the moment. "But not tonight. And isn't your family expecting us for dinner? We'd better get going. I'm sure Marie has made my favorite Tres Leches. Which is not something I want to miss."

They stood in silence for a moment, the weight of all that remained unsaid hanging between them.

Gaspar respected her enough not to argue, but his concern was valid. They'd been partners and now they were friends. He'd saved her life and she his. He'd earned the right to worry.

The breeze shifted, carrying the scent of salt and distant rain. A storm gathering somewhere out over the Atlantic. A fitting backdrop for the revelation that had just upended her world.

Kim's phone buzzed in her pocket. She slipped it out to read the text message from an unknown number.

She read it once. Twice. The words refused to make sense for several long seconds.

"Kim?" Gaspar stepped toward her. "What is it?"

She handed him the phone, her fingers suddenly numb, unable to hold onto the device properly.

The message was brief:

Van Nguyen isn't collateral damage. Neither are you.
—R

Gaspar looked up, meeting her gaze. "Collateral damage? What the hell does that mean?"

"I don't know." Kim was strangely calm despite the phantom earthquake rumbling beneath her feet. "But I intend to find out."

She took the phone back, staring at the end of the message. Reacher. He'd contacted her directly before. She knew it was him.

She'd been told he didn't own a cell phone, another thing that was not always true.

The message felt like the final piece of a puzzle.

Cooper had manipulated her from the beginning. Used her connection to Van Nguyen as some sort of weapon she didn't understand. But Cooper did. He knew Van Nguyen had almost destroyed her.

And Reacher knew.

Had always known.

Or maybe found out later, as Gaspar had.

"What are you going to do?" Gaspar asked, watching her closely.

"I need to go," she said, already moving toward the door.

"Where?" Gaspar called after her.

Kim paused, hand on the doorframe. "I'll contact you when I can," she said, ignoring his question. "But if Cooper asks—"

"I haven't seen you. You're in the wind. No longer my partner nor my problem," Gaspar finished with a shrug. "I know the drill."

Kim nodded once, grateful for his understanding. "Be careful, Chico. Cooper has a long reach."

"You too, Sunshine."

She stepped toward the exit, leaving Gaspar's curiosity hanging in the air behind her.

Reacher was out there.

And he had answers she suddenly needed more than her next breath.

FROM LEE CHILD
THE REACHER REPORT:
March 2nd, 2012

The other big news is Diane Capri—a friend of mine—wrote a book revisiting the events of KILLING FLOOR in Margrave, Georgia. She imagines an FBI team tasked to trace Reacher's current-day whereabouts. They begin by interviewing people who knew him—starting out with Roscoe and Finlay. Check out this review: "Oh heck yes! I am in love with this book. I'm a huge Jack Reacher fan. If you don't know Jack (pun intended!) then get thee to the bookstore/wherever you buy your fix and pick up one of the many Jack Reacher books by Lee Child. Heck, pick up all of them. In particular, read Killing Floor. Then come back and read Don't Know Jack. This story picks up the other from the point of view of Kim and Gaspar, FBI agents assigned to build a file on Jack Reacher. The problem is, as anyone who knows Reacher can attest, he lives completely off the grid. No cell phone, no house, no car…he's not tied down. A pretty daunting task, then, wouldn't you say?

First lines: "Just the facts. And not many of them, either. Jack Reacher's file was too stale and too thin to be credible. No human could be as invisible as Reacher appeared to be, whether he was currently above the ground or under it. Either the file had been sanitized, or Reacher was the most off-the-grid paranoid Kim Otto had ever heard of." Right away, I'm sensing who Kim Otto is and I'm delighted that I know something she doesn't. You see, I DO know Jack. And I know he's not paranoid. Not really. I know why he lives as he does, and I know what kind of man he is. I loved having that over Kim and Gaspar. If you haven't read any Reacher novels, then this will feel like a good, solid story in its own right. If you have…oh if you have, then you, too, will feel like you have a one-up on the FBI. It's a fun feeling!

"Kim and Gaspar are sent to Margrave by a mysterious boss who reminds me of Charlie, in Charlie's Angels. You never see him…you hear him. He never gives them all the facts. So they are left with a big pile of nothing. They end up embroiled in a murder case that seems connected to Reacher somehow, but they can't see how. Suffice to say the efforts to find the murderer and Reacher, and not lose their own heads in the process, makes for an entertaining read.

"I love the way the author handled the entire story. The pacing is dead on (okay another pun intended), the story is full of twists and turns like a Reacher novel would be, but it's another viewpoint of a Reacher story. It's an outside-in approach to Reacher.

"You might be asking, do they find him? Do they finally meet the infamous Jack Reacher?

"Go…read…now…find out!"

Sounds great, right? Check out "Don't Know Jack," and let me know what you think.

So that's it for now…again, thanks for reading THE AFFAIR, and I hope you'll like A WANTED MAN just as much in September.

Lee Child

ABOUT THE AUTHOR

Diane Capri is an award-winning *New York Times*, *USA Today*, and worldwide bestselling author. She's a recovering lawyer and snowbird who divides her time between Florida and Michigan. An active member of Mystery Writers of America, Author's Guild, International Thriller Writers, Alliance of Independent Authors, Novelists, Inc., and Sisters in Crime, she loves to hear from readers. She is hard at work on her next novel.

Please connect with her online:
http://www.DianeCapri.com
Twitter: http://twitter.com/@DianeCapri
Facebook: http://www.facebook.com/Diane.Capri1
http://www.facebook.com/DianeCapriBooks

Made in the USA
Monee, IL
03 June 2025